"CHOOSE YOUR FATE"

The stunningly lovely girl looked at me somberly. "You saw the victim before the red-hot grill?"

"Yes," I replied.

"You saw those who were being bent and broken for the dance of the cripples?"

"I did."

"And now you see this luxurious room—and me. Which would you choose?"

"The conditions?" I asked.

"That you serve the Jed's every whim . . . and administer tortures such as those you have witnessed in the pits of the palace."

I drew myself to my full height. *"I choose the fire."*

Edgar Rice Burroughs
MARS NOVELS
Now available from Ballantine Books:

A PRINCESS OF MARS (#1)

THE GODS OF MARS (#2)

THE WARLORD OF MARS (#3)

THUVIA, MAID OF MARS (#4)

THE CHESSMEN OF MARS (#5)

THE MASTER MIND OF MARS (#6)

A FIGHTING MAN OF MARS (#7)

SWORDS OF MARS (#8)

SYNTHETIC MEN OF MARS (#9)

LLANA OF GATHOL (#10)

JOHN CARTER OF MARS (#11)

A FIGHTING MAN
OF MARS

Edgar Rice Burroughs

BALLANTINE BOOKS • NEW YORK

A FIGHTING MAN OF MARS
Originally published in *The Blue Book Magazine* in six
installments, April to September 1930.

First, Second and Third Installments:
Copyright © 1930 EDGAR RICE BURROUGHS

Fourth, Fifth and Sixth Installments:
Copyright © 1930 EDGAR RICE BURROUGHS, INC.

ISBN 0-345-27840-2

This authorized edition published by arrangement
with Edgar Rice Burroughs, Inc.

Manufactured in the United States of America

First U.S. Printing: January 1964
Sixth U.S. Printing: September 1975

First Revised U.S. Printing: November 1976
Third Revised U.S. Printing: April 1979

First Canadian Printing: March 1964
Second Canadian Printing: April 1979

Cover art by Michael Whelan, Copyright © 1979
Edgar Rice Burroughs, Inc.

CONTENTS

FOREWORD

TO JASON GRIDLEY of Tarzana, discoverer of the Gridley Wave, belonged the credit of establishing radio communication between Pellucidar and the outer world.

It was my good fortune to be much in his laboratory while he was carrying on his experiments and to be, also, the recipient of his confidences, so that I was fully aware that while he hoped to establish communication with Pellucidar he was also reaching out towards even more stupendous accomplishment—he was groping through space for contact with another planet; nor did he attempt to deny that the present goal of his ambition was radio communication with Mars.

Gridley had constructed a simple, automatic device for broadcasting signals intermittently and for recording whatever might be received during his absence.

For a period of five minutes the Gridley Wave carried a simple code signal consisting of two letters, "J. G.," out into the ether, following which there was a pause of ten minutes. Hour after hour, day after day, week after week, these silent, invisible messengers sped out to the uttermost reaches of infinite space, and after Jason Gridley left Tarzana to embark upon his expedition to Pellucidar, I found myself drawn to his laboratory by the lure of the tantalizing possibilities of his dream, as well as by the promise I had made him that I would look in occasionally to see that the device was functioning properly and to examine the recording instruments for any indication that the signals had been received and answered.

My considerable association with Gridley had given me a fair working knowledge of his devices and sufficient knowledge of the Morse Code to enable me to receive with moderate accuracy and speed.

Months passed; dust accumulated thickly upon everything except the working parts of Gridley's device, and the white ribbon of ticker tape that was to receive an answering signal retaining its virgin purity; then I went away for a short trip into Arizona.

I was absent for about ten days, and upon my return one of the first things with which I concerned myself was an inspection of Gridley's laboratory and the instruments he had left in my care. As I entered the familiar room and switched on the lights it was with the expectation of meeting with the same blank unresponsiveness to which I was by now quite accustomed.

As a matter of fact, hope of success had never been raised to any considerable degree in my breast, nor had Gridley been over sanguine—his was merely an experiment. He considered it well worth while to make it, and I considered it equally worth while to lend him what small assistance I might.

It was therefore with feelings of astonishment that assumed the magnitude of a distinct shock that I saw upon the ticker tape the familiar tracings which stand for the dots and dashes of code.

Of course I realized that some other researcher might have duplicated Jason's discovery of the Gridley Wave and that the message might have originated upon earth, or, again, it might be a message from Jason himself in Pellucidar, but when I had deciphered it, all doubts were quickly put to rest. It was from Ulysses Paxton, one time captain, —th U.S. Infantry, who, miraculously transported from a battle-field in France to the bosom of the great Red Planet, had become the right-hand man of Ras Thavas, the master mind of Mars, and later the husband of Valla Dia, daughter of Kor San, Jeddak of Duhor.

In brief, the message explained that for months mysterious signals had been received at Helium, and while they were unable to interpret them, they felt that

they came from Jasoom, the name by which the planet
Earth is known upon Mars.

John Carter being absent from Helium, a fast flier
had been dispatched to Duhor bearing an urgent re-
quest to Paxton to come at once to the twin cities and
endeavour to determine if in truth the signals they were
receiving actually originated upon the planet of his
birth.

Upon his arrival at Helium, Paxton immediately
recognized the Morse Code signals, and no doubt was
left in the minds of the Martian scientists that at last
something tangible had been accomplished towards
the solution of inter-communication between Jasoom
and Barsoom.

Repeated attempts to transmit answering signals to
Earth proved fruitless and then the best minds of
Helium settled down to the task of analyzing and re-
producing the Gridley Wave.

They felt that at last they had succeeded. Paxton
had sent his message and they were eagerly awaiting
an acknowledgment.

I have since been in almost constant communication with Mars, but out of loyalty to Jason Gridley,
to whom all the credit and honour are due, I have
made no official announcement, nor shall I give out
any important information, leaving all that for his
return to the outer world; but I believe that I am be-
traying no confidence if I narrate to you the interesting story of Hadron of Hastor, which Paxton told me
one evening not long since.

I hope that you will enjoy it as much as I did.

But before I go on with the story a brief description
of the principal races of Mars, their political and
military organization and some of their customs may
prove of interest to many of my readers. The domi-
nant race in whose hands rest the progress and civilization—yes, the very life of Mars—differ but little in
physical appearance from ourselves. The facts that
their skins are a light reddish-copper colour and that
they are oviparous constitute the two most marked

divergences from Anglo-Saxon standards. No, there is another—their longevity. A thousand years is the natural span of life of a Martian, although, because of their warlike activities and the prevalence of assassination among them, few live their allotted span.

Their general political organization has changed little in countless ages, the unit still being the tribe, at the head of which is a chief or jed, corresponding in modern times to our king. The princes are known as lesser jeds, while the chief of chiefs, or the head of consolidated tribes, is the jeddak, or emperor, whose consort is a jeddara.

The majority of red Martians live in walled cities, though there are many who reside in isolated, though well walled and defended, farm homes along those rich irrigated ribbons of land that we of earth know as the Canals of Mars.

In the far south, that is in the south polar region, dwells a race of very handsome and highly intelligent black men. There, also, is the remnant of a white race; while the north polar regions are dominated by a race of yellow men.

In between the two poles and scattered over all the arid waste lands of the dead sea bottoms, often inhabiting the ruined cities of another age, are the feared green hordes of Mars.

The terrible green warriors of Barsoom are the hereditary enemies of all the other races of this martial planet. They are of heroic size, and in addition to being equipped with two legs and two arms apiece, they have an intermediary pair of limbs, which may be used at will either as arms or legs. Their eyes are set at the extreme sides of their heads, a trifle above the centre, and protrude in such a manner that they may be directed either forward or back and also independently of each other, thus permitting these remarkable creatures to look in any direction, or in two directions at once without the necessity of turning their heads.

Their ears, which are slightly above the eyes and

closer together, are small cup-shaped antennæ, protruding several inches from the head, while their noses are but longitudinal slits in the centre of their faces, midway between their mouths and ears.

They have no hair on their bodies, which are of a very light yellowish-green color in infancy, deepening to an olive green towards maturity, the adult males being darker in colour than the females.

The iris of the eyes is blood red, as an albino's, while the pupil is dark. The eyeball itself is very white, as are the teeth, and it is these latter which add a most ferocious appearance to an otherwise fearsome and terrible countenance, as the lower tusks curve upward to sharp points which end about where the eyes of earthly human beings are located. The whiteness of the teeth is not that of ivory, but of the snowiest and most gleaming of china. Against the dark background of their olive skins their tusks stand out in a most striking manner, causing these weapons to present a singularly formidable appearance.

They are a cruel and taciturn race, entirely devoid of love, sympathy or pity.

They are an equestrian race, never walking other than to move about their camps.

Their mounts, called thoats, are great savage beasts, whose proportions harmonize with those of their giant masters. They have eight legs and broad flat tails larger at the tips than at the roots. They hold these tails straight out while running. Their mouths are enormous, splitting their heads from their snouts to their long, massive necks. Like their masters, they are entirely devoid of hair, their skins being a dark slate colour and exceedingly smooth and glossy, with the exception of the belly, which is white, and the legs, which shade from the slate of the shoulders and hips to a vivid yellow at the feet. The feet are heavily padded and nailless.

Like the red men, the green hordes are ruled by jeds and jeddaks, but their military organization is not carried to the same detail of perfection as is that of the red men.

The military forces of the red men are highly organized, the principal arm of the service being the navy, an enormous air force of battleships, cruisers and an infinite variety of lesser craft down to one-man scout fliers. Next in size and importance is the infantry branch of the service, while the cavalry, mounted on a breed of small thoats, similar to those used by the green Martian giants, is utilized principally in patrolling the avenues of the cities and the rural districts that border the irrigating systems.

The principal basic unit, although not the smallest one of the military organization, is a utan, consisting of one hundred men, which is commanded by a dwar with several padwars of lieutenants junior to him. An odwar commands a umak of ten thousand men, while next above him is a jedwar, who is junior only to the jed or king.

Science, literature, art and architecture are in some of their departments further advanced upon Mars than upon earth, a remarkable thing when one considers the constant battle for survival which is the most marked characteristic of life upon Barsoom.

Not only are they waging a continual battle against Nature, which is slowly diminishing their already scant atmosphere, but from birth to death they are constantly faced by the stern necessity of defending themselves against enemy nations of their own race and the great hordes of roving green warriors of the dead sea bottom; while within the walls of their own cities are countless professional assassins, whose calling is so well recognized that in some localities they are organized into guilds.

But notwithstanding all the grim realities with which they have to contend, the red Martians are a happy, social people. They have their games, their dances and their songs, and the social life of a great capital of Barsoom is as gay and magnificent as any that may be found in the rich capitals of earth.

That they are a brave, noble and generous people is indicated by the fact that neither John Carter nor Ulysses Paxton would return to earth if they might.

And now to return to the tale that I had from Paxton across forty-three million miles of space.

—Edgar Rice Burroughs

CHAPTER I

SANOMA TORA

THIS IS THE story of Hadron of Hastor, Fighting Man of Mars, as narrated by him to Ulysses Paxton:

I am Tan Hadron of Hastor, my father is *Had Urtur,* Odwar of the 1st Umak of the Troops of Hastor. He commands the largest ship of war that Hastor has ever contributed to the navy of Helium, accommodating as it does the entire ten thousand men of the 1st Umak, together with five hundred lesser fighting ships and all the paraphernalia of war. My mother is a princess of Gathol.

As a family we are not rich except in honour, and, valuing this above all mundane possessions, I chose the profession of my father rather than a more profitable career. The better to further my ambition I came to the capital of the empire of Helium and took service in the troops of Tardos Mors, Jeddak of Helium, that I might be nearer the great John Carter, Warlord of Mars.

My life in Helium and my career in the army were similar to those of hundreds of other young men. I passed through my training days without notable accomplishment, neither heading nor trailing my fellows, and in due course I was made a Padwar in the 91st Umak, being assigned to the 5th Utan of the 11th Dar.

What with being of noble lineage by my father and inheriting royal blood from my mother, the palaces of the twin cities of Helium were always open to me and I entered much into the gay life of the capital. It was thus that I met Sanoma Tora, daughter of Tor Hatan, Odwar of the 91st Umak.

Tor Hatan is only of the lower nobility, but he is

1

fabulously rich from the loot of many cities well invested in farm land and mines; and because here in the capital of Helium riches count for more than they do in Hastor. Tor Hatan is a powerful man, whose influence reaches even to the throne of the Jeddak.

Never shall I forget the occasion upon which I first set eyes upon Sanoma Tora. It was upon the occasion of a great feast at the marble palace of the Warlord. There were gathered under one roof the most beautiful women of Barsoom, where, notwithstanding the gorgeous and radiant beauty of Dejah Thoris, Tara of Helium and Thuvia of Ptarth, the pulchritude of Sanoma Tora was such as to arrest attention. I shall not say that it was greater than that of those acknowledged queens of Barsoomian loveliness, for I know that my adoration of Sanoma Tora might easily influence my judgment, but there were others there who remarked that her gorgeous beauty, which differs from that of Dejah Thoris as the chaste beauty of a polar landscape differs from the beauty of the tropics, as the beauty of a white palace in the moonlight differs from the beauty of its garden at midday.

When at my solicitation I was presented to her, she glanced first at the insignia upon my armour, and noting therefrom that I was but a Padwar, she vouchsafed me but a condescending word and turned her attention again to the Dwar with whom she had been conversing.

I must admit that I was piqued, and yet it was, indeed, the contumelious treatment she accorded me that fixed my determination to win her, for the goal most difficult of attainment has always seemed to me the most desirable.

And so it was that I fell in love with Sanoma Tora, the daughter of the commander of the Umak to which I was attached.

For a long time I found it difficult to further my suit in the slightest degree; in fact I did not even see Sanoma Tora for several months after our first meeting, since when she found that I was poor as well as low in rank I found it impossible to gain an invitation to her home, and it chanced that I did not meet her elsewhere for a long time; but the more inaccessible she became the more I loved her, until every waking moment of my time that was not actually occupied by the performance of my military-duties was devoted to the devising of new and ever-increasingly rash plans to possess her. I even had the madness to consider abducting her, and I believe that I should eventually have gone this far had there been no other way in which I could see her, but about this time a fellow-officer of the 91st, in fact the Dwar of the Utan to which I was attached, took pity on me and obtained for me an invitation to a feast in the palace of Tor Hatan.

My host, who was also my commanding officer, had never noticed me before this evening, and I was surprised to note the warmth and cordiality of his greetings.

"We must see more of you here, Hadron of Hastor," he said. "I have been watching you and I prophesy that you will go far in the military service of the Jeddak."

Now I knew he was lying when he said that he had been watching me, for Tor Hatan was notoriously lax in his duties as a commanding officer, all of which were performed by the senior Teedwar of the Umak. While I could not fathom the cause of this sudden interest in me, it was nevertheless very pleasing, since through it I might in some degree further my pursuit of the heart and hand of Sanoma Tora.

Sanoma Tora herself was slightly more cordial than upon the occasion of our first meeting, though she noticeably paid more attention to Sil Vagis than she did to me.

Now if there is any man in Helium whom I particularly detest more than another it is Sil Vagis, a nasty little snob who holds the title of Teedwar, though so far as I was ever able to ascertain he commands no troops, but is merely on the staff of Tor

Hatan, principally, I presume, because of the great wealth of his father.

Such creatures we have to put up with in times of peace, but when war comes and the great Warlord takes command it is the fighting men who rank, and riches do not count.

But be that as it may, while Sil Vagis spoiled this evening for me as he would spoil many others in the future, nevertheless I left the palace of Tor Hatan that night with a feeling bordering upon elation, for I had Sanoma Tora's permission to see her again in her father's home when my duties would permit me to pay my respects to her.

Returning to my quarters I was accompanied by my friend, the Dwar, and when I commented on the warmth of Tor Hatan's reception of me he laughed.

"You find it amusing," I said. "Why?"

"Tor Hatan, as you know," he said, "is very rich and powerful, and yet it is seldom, as you may have noticed, that he is invited to any one of the four places of Helium in which ambitious men most crave to be seen."

"You mean the palaces of the Warlords, the Jeddak, the Jed and Carthoris?" I asked.

"Of course," he replied. "What other four in Helium count for so much as these? Tor Hatan," he contined, "is supposed to come from the lower nobility, but there is a question in my mind as to whether there is a drop of noble blood in his veins, and one of the facts upon which I base my conjecture is his cringing and fawning reverence for anything pertaining to royalty—he would give his fat soul to be considered an intimate of any one of the four."

"But what has that to do with me?" I demanded.

"A great deal," he replied; "in fact, because of it you were invited to his palace to-night."

"I do not understand," I said.

"I chanced to be talking with Tor Hatan the morning of the day you received your invitation, and in the course of our conversation I mentioned you. He had never heard of you, and as a Padwar in the 5th Utan you aroused his interest not a particle, but when I told him that your mother was a princess of Gathol, he pricked up his ears, and when he learned that you were received as a friend and equal in the palaces of the four demigods of Helium, he became almost enthusiastic about you. Now do you understand?" he concluded with a short laugh.

"Perfectly," I replied, "but none the less I thank you. All that I wanted was the opportunity, and inasmuch as I was prepared to achieve it criminally if necessary, I cannot quibble over any means that were employed to obtain it, however unflattering they may be to me."

For months I haunted the palace of Tor Hatan, and being naturally a good conversationalist and well schooled in the stately dances and joyous games of Barsoom, I was by no means an unwelcome visitor. Also I made it a point often to take Sanoma Tora to one or another of the four great palaces of Helium. I was always welcome because of the blood relationship which existed between my mother and Gahan of Gathol, who had married Tara of Helium.

Naturally I felt that I was progressing well with my suit, but my progress was not fast enough to keep pace with the racing desires of my passion. Never had I known love before, and I felt that I should die if I did not soon possess Sanoma Tora, and so it was that upon a certain night I visited the palace of her father definitely determined to lay my heart and sword at her feet before I left, and, although the natural complexes of a lover convinced me that I was an unworthy worm that she would be wholly justified in spurning, I was yet determined to declare myself so that I might openly be accounted a suitor, which, after all, gives one greater freedom even though he be not entirely a favoured suitor.

It was one of those lovely nights that transform old Barsoom into a world of enchantment. Thuria and Cluros were racing through the heavens, casting their soft light upon the garden of Tor Hatan, empurpling the vivid, scarlet sward and lending strange hues to the gorgeous blooms of pimalia and sorapus, while the winding walks, gravelled with semi-precious stones, shot back a thousand scintillant rays that, clothed in ever-changing colours, danced at the feet of the marble statuary that lent an added artistic charm to the ensemble.

In one of the spacious halls that overlooked the garden of the palace, a youth and a maiden sat upon a massive bench of rich sorapus wood, such a bench as might have graced the halls of the great Jeddak himself, so intricate its rich design, so perfect the carving of the master craftsman who produced it.

Upon the leathern harness of the youth were the insignia of his rank and service—a Padwar in the 91st Umak. The youth was I, Hadron of Hastor, and with me was Sanoma Tora, daughter of Tor Hatan. I had come filled with the determination boldly to plead my cause, but suddenly I had become aware of my unworthiness. What had I to offer this beautiful daughter of the rich Tor Hatan? I was only a Padwar, and a poor one at that. Of course, there was the royal blood of Gathol in my veins, and that, I knew, would have weight with Tor Hatan, but I am not given to boasting, and I could not have reminded Sanoma Tora of the advantages to be derived because of it even had I known positively that it would influence her. I had, therefore, nothing to offer but my great love, which is perhaps, after all, the greatest gift that man or woman can bring to another, and I had thought of late that Sanoma Tora might love me. Upon several occasions she had sent for me, and although in each instance she had suggested going to the palace of Tara of Helium, I had been vain enough to hope that this was not her sole reason for wishing to be with me.

"You are uninteresting to-night, Hadron of Hastor," she said after a particularly long silence, during which I had been endeavouring to formulate my proposal in some convincing and graceful phrases.

"Perhaps," I replied, "it is because I am trying to find the words in which to clothe the most interesting thought I have ever entertained."

"And what is that?" she asked politely, though with no great show of interest.

"I love you, Sanoma Tora," I blurted awkwardly.

She laughed. It was like the tinkling of silver upon crystal—beautiful but cold. "That has been apparent for a long while," she said; "but why speak of it?"

"And why not?" I asked.

"Because even if I returned your love, I am not for you, Hadron of Hastor," she replied coldly.

"You cannot love me then, Sanoma Tora?" I asked.

"I did not say that," she replied.

"You could love me?"

"I could love you if I permitted myself the weakness," she said; "but what is love?"

"Love is everything," I told her.

Sanoma Tora laughed. "If you think that I would link myself for life to a threadbare Padwar even if I loved him, you are mistaken," she said haughtily. "I am the daughter of Tor Hatan, whose wealth and power are but little less than those of the royal families of Helium. I have suitors whose wealth is so great that they could buy you a thousand times over. Within the year an emissary of the Jeddak Tul Axtar of Jahar waited upon my father; he had seen me and said that he would return, and merely for love you would ask me, who may some day be Jeddara of Jahar, to become the wife of a poor Padwar."

I arose. "Perhaps you are right," I said. "You are so beautiful that it does not seem possible that you could be wrong, but deep in my heart I cannot but feel that happiness is the greatest treasure that one may possess, and love the greatest power. Without these, Sanoma Tora, even a Jeddara is poor indeed."

"I shall take my chance," she said.

"I hope that the Jeddak of Jahar is not as greasy as his emissary," I remarked, rather peevishly, I am afraid.

"He may be an animated grease-pot for all I care if he will make me his Jeddara," said Sanoma Tora.

"Then there is no hope for me?" I asked.

"Not while you have so little to offer, Padwar," she replied.

It was then that a slave announced Sil Vagis, and I took my leave. I had never before plumbed such depths of despondency as that which engulfed me as I made my unhappy way back to my quarters, but even though hope seemed dead I had not relinquished my determination to win her. If wealth and power were her price, then I would achieve wealth and power. Just how I was going to accomplish it was not entirely clear, but I was young, and to youth all things are possible.

I had tossed in wakefulness upon my sleeping silks and furs for some time when an officer of the guard burst suddenly into my quarters.

"Hadron!" he shouted," are you here?"

"Yes," I replied.

"Praised be the ashes of my ancestors!" he exclaimed. "I feared that you were not."

"Why should I not be?" I demanded. "What is this all about?"

"Tor Hatan, the fat old treasure-bag, is gone mad," he exclaimed.

"Tor Hatan gone mad? What do you mean? What has that got to do with me?"

"He swears that you have abducted his daughter."

In an instant I was upon my feet. "Abducted Sanoma Tora!" I cried. "Has something happened to her? Tell me, quickly."

"Yes, she is gone all right," said my informant, "and there is something mighty mysterious about it."

But I did not wait to hear more. Seizing my harness, I adjusted it as I ran up the spiral runway towards the hangars on the roof of the barracks. I had no authority nor permit to take out a flier, but what did that mean to me if Sanoma Tora was in danger?

The hangar guards sought to detain and question

me. I do not recall what I told them; I know that I must have lied to them, for they let me run out a swift one-man flier, and an instant later I was racing through the night towards the palace of Tor Hatan.

As it stands but little more than two haads from the barracks, I was there in but a few moments, and as I landed in the garden, which was now brilliantly lighted, I saw a number of people congregated there, among whom were Tor Hatan and Sil Vagis.

As I leaped from the deck of the flier, the former came angrily towards me. "So it is you!" he cried. "What have you to say for yourself? Where is my daughter?"

"That is what I have come to ask, Tor Hatan," I replied.

"You are at the bottom of this," he cried. "You abducted her. She told Sil Vagis that this very night you had demanded her hand in marriage and that she had refused you."

"I did ask for her hand," I said, "and she refused me. That part is true; but if she has been abducted, in the name of your first ancestors, do not waste time trying to connect me with the diabolical plot. I had nothing to do with it. How did it happen? Who was with her?"

"Sil Vagis was with her. They were walking in the garden," replied Tor Hatan.

"You saw her abducted," I asked, turning to Sil Vagis, "and you are here unwounded and alive?"

He started to stammer. "There were many of them," he said. "They overpowered me."

"You saw them?" I asked

"Yes."

"Was I among them?" I demanded.

"It was dark. I could not recognize any of them; perhaps they were disguised."

"They overpowered you?" I asked him.

"Yes," he said.

"You lie!" I exclaimed. "Had they laid hands upon

you they would have killed you. You ran away and hid, never drawing a weapon to defend the girl."

"That is a lie," cried Sil Vagis. "I fought with them, but they overpowered me."

I turned to Tor Hatan. "We are wasting time," I said. "Is there no one who can give us a clue as to the identity of these men and the direction they took in their flight? How and whence came they? How and whence did they depart?"

"He is trying to throw you off the track, Tor Hatan," said Sil Vagis. "Who else could it have been but a disgruntled suitor? What would you say if I should tell you that the metal of the men who stole Sanoma Tora was the metal of the warriors of Hastor?"

"I would say that you are a liar," I replied. "If it was so dark that you could not recognize faces, how could you decipher the insignia upon their harness?"

At this juncture another officer of the 91st Umak joined us. "We have found one who may, perhaps, shed some light upon the subject," he said, "if he lives long enough to speak."

Men had been searching the grounds of Tor Hatan and that portion of the city adjacent to his palace, and now several approached bearing a man, whom they laid upon the sward at our feet. His broken and mangled body was entirely naked, and as he lay there gasping feebly for breath, he was a pitiful spectacle.

A slave dispatched into the palace returned with stimulants, and when some of these had been forced between his lips, the man revived slightly.

"Who are you?" asked Tor Hatan.

"I am a warrior of the city guard," replied the man feebly.

An officer approached Tor Hatan excitedly. "My men have just found six more bodies close to the point at which we discovered this man," he said. "They are all naked and similarly broken and mangled."

"Perhaps we shall get to the bottom of this yet," said Tor Hatan, and, turning again to the poor, broken thing upon the scarlet sward, he directed him to proceed.

"We were on night patrol over the city when we saw a craft running without lights. As we approached it and turned our searchlights upon it, I caught a single, brief glimpse of it. It bore no colours or insignia to denote its origin, and its design was unlike that of any ship I have ever seen. It had a long, low, enclosed cabin, upon either side of which were mounted two peculiar-looking guns. This was all I had time to note, except that I saw a man directing one of the guns in our direction. The padwar in command of our ship immediately gave orders to fire upon the stranger, and at the same time he hailed him. At that instant our ship dissolved in mid-air; even my harness fell from me. I remember falling, that is all," and with these words he gasped once and died.

Tor Hatan called his people around him. "There must have been someone about the palace or the grounds who saw something of this occurrence," he said. "I command that no matter who may be involved, whoever has any knowledge whatsoever of this affair shall speak."

A slave stepped forward, and as he approached, Tor Hatan eyed him with haughty arrogance.

"Well," demanded the Odwar, "what have you to say? Speak!"

"You have commanded it, Tor Hatan," said the slave, "otherwise I should not speak, for when I have told what I saw I shall have incurred the enmity of a powerful noble," and he glanced quickly towards Sil Vagis.

"And if you speak the truth, man, you will have won the friendship of a padwar whose sword is not so mean but that it may protect you even from a powerful noble," I said quickly, and I, too, glanced at Sil Vagis, for it was in my mind that what the fellow had to tell might be none too flattering to the soft fop who masqueraded beneath the title of a warrior.

"Speak!" commanded Tor Hatan impatiently. "And see to it that thou dost not lie."

"For fourteen years I have served faithfully in your palace, Tor Hatan," replied the man, "ever since I was brought to Helium a prisoner of war after the fall and sack of Kobol, where I served in the bodyguard of the Jed of Kobol, and in all that time you have had no reason to question my truthfulness. Sanoma Tora trusted me, and had I had a sword this night she might still be with us."

"Come! Come!" cried Tor Hatan. "Get to the point. What saw you?"

"The fellow saw nothing," snapped Sil Vagis. "Why waste time upon him? He seeks but to glory in a little brief notoriety."

"Let him speak," I exclaimed.

"I had just ascended the first ramp to the second level of the palace," explained the slave, "on my way to the sleeping quarters of Tor Hatan to arrange his sleeping silks and furs for the night as is my custom, and, pausing for a moment to look out into the garden, I saw Sanoma Tora and Sil Vagis walking in the moonlight. Conscious that I should not thus observe them, I was about to continue on my way about my duties when I saw a flier dropping silently out of the night towards the garden. Its motors were noiseless, it showed no light. It seemed a spectral ship, and of such strange design that even if for no other reason it would have arrested my attention, but there were other reasons. Unlighted ships move through the night for no good purpose, and so I paused to watch it.

"It landed silently and quickly behind Sanoma Tora and Sil Vagis; nor did they seem aware of its presence until their attention was attracted by the slight clanking of the accoutrements of one of the several warriors who sprang from its low cabin as it grounded. Then Sil Vagis wheeled about. For just an instant he stood as though petrified and then as the strange warriors leaped towards him, he turned and fled into the concealing shrubbery of the garden."

"It is a lie," cried Sil Vagis.

"Silence, coward" I commanded.

"Continue, slave!" directed Tor Hatan.

"Sanoma Tora was not aware of the presence of the strange warriors until she was seized roughly from behind. It all happened so quickly that I scarce had time to realize the purpose of the sinister visitation before they laid hands upon her. When I comprehended that my mistress was the object of this night attack, I rushed hurriedly down the ramp, but ere I reached the garden they had dragged her aboard the flier. Even then, however, had I had a sword I might at least have died in the service of Sanoma Tora, for I reached the ship of mystery as the last warrior was clambering aboard. I seized him by the harness and attempted to drag him to the ground, at the same time shouting loudly to attract the palace guard, but ere I did so one of his fellows on the deck above me drew his long sword and struck viciously at my head. The blade caught me but a glancing blow, which, however, sufficed to stun me for a moment, so that I relaxed my hold upon the strange warrior and fell to the sward. When I regained consciousness the ship had gone and the tardy palace guard was pouring from the guardroom. I have spoken—and spoken truthfully."

Tor Hatan's cold gaze sought out the lowered eyes of Sil Vagis. "What have you to say to this?" he demanded.

"The fellow is in the employ of Hadron of Hastor," shouted Sil Vagis. "He speaks nothing but lies. I attacked them when they came, but there were many and they overpowered me. This fellow was not present."

"Let me see thy head," I said to the slave, and when he had come and knelt before me I saw a great red welt the length of one side of his head above the ear, just such a welt as a glancing blow from the flat side of a long sword might have made. "Here," I said to Tor Hatan, pointing to the great welt, "is the proof of a slave's loyalty and courage. Let us see the wounds received by a noble of Helium who by his own testimony engaged in single-handed combat against great odds. Surely in such an encounter he must have received at least a single scratch."

"Unless he is as marvellous a swordsman as the great John Carter himself," said the dwar of the palace guard with a thinly veiled sneer.

"It is all a plot," cried Sil Vagis. "Do you take the word of a slave, Tor Hatan, against that of a noble of Helium?"

"I rely on the testimony of my eyes and my senses," replied the Odwar, and he turned his back upon Sil Vagis and again addressed the slave. "Didst thou recognize any of those who abducted Sanoma Tora," he demanded, "or note their harness or their metal?"

"I got no good look at the face of any of them, but I did see the harness and the metal of him whom I tried to drag from the flier."

"Was it the metal of Hastor?" asked Tor Hatan.

"By my first ancestor it was not," replied the slave emphatically; "nor was it the metal of any other city of the Empire of Helium. The design and the insignia were unknown to me, and yet there was a certain familiarity about them that tantalizes me. I feel that I have seen them before, but when and where I cannot recall. In the service of my Jed I fought invaders from many lands and it may be that upon some of these I saw similar metal many years ago."

"Are you satisfied, Tor Hatan," I demanded, "that the aspersions cast upon me by Sil Vagis are without foundation?"

"Yes, Hadron of Hastor," replied the Odwar.

"Then with your leave I shall depart," I said.

"Where are you going?" he asked.

"To find Sanoma Tora," I replied.

"And if you find her," he said, "and return her safely to me, she is yours."

I made no other acknowledgment of his generous offer than to bow deeply, for I had it in my mind that Sanoma Tora might have something to say about that, and whether she had or not, I wished no mate who came not to me willingly.

Leaping to the deck of the flier that brought me, I rose into the night and sped in the direction of the marble palace of the Warlord of Barsoom, for even though the hour was late, I was determined to see him without an instant's unnecessary loss of time.

·

CHAPTER II

BROUGHT DOWN

As I APPROACHED the Warlord's palace I saw signs of activity unusual for that hour of the night. Fliers were arriving and departing, and when I alighted upon that portion of the roof reserved for military ships, I saw the fliers of a number of high officers of the Warlord's staff.

Being a frequent visitor at the palace and being well known by all the officers of the Warlord's bodyguard, I had no difficulty in gaining admission to the palace, and presently I was waiting in the hall, just off the small compartment in which the Warlord is accustomed to give small, private audiences, while a slave announced me to his master.

I do not know how long I waited. It could not have been a long while, yet it seemed to me a veritable eternity, because my mind was harassed by the conviction that the woman I loved was in dire danger. I was possessed by a conviction, ridiculous perhaps, but none the less real, that I alone could save her and that every instant I was delayed reduced her chances for succour before it was too late.

But at last I was invited to enter, and when I stood

in the presence of the great Warlord I found him surrounded by men high in the councils of Helium.

"I assume," said John Carter, coming directly to the point, "that what brings you here to-night, Hadron of Hastor, pertains to the matter of the abduction of the daughter of Tor Hatan. Have you any knowledge or any theory that might cast any light upon the subject?"

"No," I replied. "I have come merely to obtain your authority to depart at once in an attempt to pick up the trail of the abductors of Sanoma Tora."

"Where do you intend to search?" he demanded.

"I do not yet know, sir," I replied, "but I shall find her."

He smiled. "Such assurance is at least an asset," he said, "and knowing as I do what prompts it, I shall grant you the permission you desire. While the abduction of a daughter of Helium is in itself of sufficient gravity to warrant the use of every resource to apprehend her abductors and return her to her home, there is also involved in this occurrence an element that may portend high danger to the empire. As you doubtless know, the mysterious ship that bore her away mounted a gun from which emanated some force that entirely disintegrated all the metal parts of the patrol flier that sought to intercept and question it. Even the weapons and the metal portions of the harness of the crew were dissipated into nothing, a fact that was easily discernible from an examination of the wreck of the patrol flier and the bodies of its crew. Wood, leather, flesh, everything of the animal and vegetable kingdom that was aboard the flier, has been found scattered about the ground where it fell, but no trace of any metallic substance remains.

"I am impressing this upon you because it suggests to my mind a possible clue to the general location of the city of these new enemies of Helium. I am convinced that this is but the first blow, since any navy armed with such guns could easily hold Helium at its mercy, and few indeed are the cities of Barsoom outside the empire that would not seize with avidity upon any instrument that would give them the sack of the Twin Cities.

"For some time now we have been deeply concerned by the increasing number of missing ships of the navy. In nearly all instances these were ships engaged in charting air currents and recording atmospheric pressures in different parts of Barsoom far from the empire, and recently it has become apparent that the vast majority of these ships which never return were those cruising in the southern part of the western hemisphere, an unhospitable portion of our planet concerning which we have unfortunately but little knowledge owing to the fact that we have developed no trade with the unfriendly people inhabiting this vast domain.

"This, Hadron of Hastor, is only a suggestion, only the vaguest of clues, but I offer it to you for what it is worth. A thousand one-man scout fliers will be dispatched between now and noon tomorrow in search of the abductors of Sanoma Tora; nor will these be all. Cruisers and battleships will take the air as well, for Helium must know what city or what nation has developed a weapon of destruction such as that used above Helium this night.

"It is my belief that the weapon is of very recent invention and that whatever power possesses it must be bending every effort to perfect it and produce it in such quantities as to make them masters of the world. I have spoken. Go, and may fortune be with you."

You may believe that I lost no time in setting out upon my mission now that I had authority from John Carter. Going to my quarters I hastened my preparation for departure, which consisted principally of making a careful selection of weapons and of exchanging a rather ornate harness I had been wearing for one of simpler design and of heavier and more durable leather. My fighting harness is always the best and plainest that I can procure and is made for me by a famous harness-maker of Lesser Helium. My equipment of weapons was standard, consisting of a long sword, a short sword, a dagger and a pistol. I also provided myself with extra ammunition and a supply of the concentrated ration used by all Martian fighting men.

As I gathered together these simple necessities which, with a single sleeping-fur, would constitute my equipment, my mind was given over to consideration of various explanations for the disappearance of Sanoma Tora. I searched my brain for any slightest memory that might suggest an explanation, or point towards the possible identity of her abductors. It was while thus engaged that I recalled her reference to the Jeddak, Tul Axtar of Jahar; nor was there within the scope of my recollection any other incident that might point a clue. I distinctly recalled the emissary of Tul Axtar who had visited the court of Helium not long since. I had heard him boast of the riches and power of his Jeddak and the beauty of his women. Perhaps, then, it might be as well to search in the direction of Jahar as elsewhere, but before departing I determined once again to visit the palace of Tor Hatan and question the slave who had been the last to see Sanoma Tora.

As I was about to set out, another thought occurred to me. I knew that in the Temple of Knowledge might be found either illustrations or replicas of the metal and harness of every nation of Barsoom concerning which aught was known in Helium. I therefore repaired immediately to the temple, and with the assistance of a clerk I presently found a drawing of the harness and metal of a warrior of Jahar. By an ingenious photostatic process a copy of this illustration was made for me in a few seconds, and with this I hastened to the palace of Tor Hatan.

The Odwar was absent, having gone to the palace of the Warlord, but his major-domo summoned the slave, Kal Tavan, who had witnessed the abduction of Sanoma Tora and grappled with one of her abductors.

As the man approached I noticed him more particularly than I had previously. He was well built, with clear-cut features and that air which definitely bespeaks the fighting man.

"You said, I believe, that you were from Kobol?" I asked.

"I was born in Tjanath," he replied. "I had a wife and a daughter there. My wife fell before the hand of an assassin and my daughter disappeared when she was very young. I never knew what became of her. The familiar scenes of Tjanath reminded me of happier days and so increased my grief that I could not remain. I turned panthan then and sought service in other cities; thus I served in Kobol."

"And there you became familiar with the harness and the metal of many cities and nations?" I asked.

"Yes," he replied.

"What harness and metal are these?" I demanded, handing him the copy of the illustration I had brought from the Temple of Knowledge.

He examined it briefly and then his eyes lighted with recognition. "It is the same," he said. "It is identical."

"Identical with what?" I asked.

"With the harness worn by the warrior with whom I grappled at the time that Sanoma Tora was stolen," he replied.

"The identity of the abductors of Sanoma Tora is established," I said, and then I turned to the major-domo. "Send a messenger at once to the Warlord informing him that the daughter of Tor Hatan was stolen by men from Jahar and that it is my belief that they are the emissaries of Tul Axtar, Jeddak of Jahar," and without more words I turned and left the palace, going directly to my flier.

As I rose above the towers and domes and lofty landing-stages of Greater Helium, I turned the prow of my flier towards the west and opening wide the throttle sped swiftly through the thin air of dying Barsoom towards that great unknown expanse of her remote south-western hemisphere, somewhere within the vast reaches of which lay Jahar, towards which, I was now

convinced, Sanoma Tora was being borne to become
not the Jeddara of Tul Axtar, but his slave, for jeddaks take not their jeddaras by force upon Barsoom.

I believed that I understood the explanation of
Sanoma Tora's abduction, an explanation that would
have caused her intense chagrin, since it was far from
flattery. I believed that Tul Axtar's emissary had reported to his master the charm and beauty of the
daughter of Tor Hatan, but that she was not of sufficiently noble birth to become his jeddara, and so he
had adopted the only expedient by which he might
possess her. My blood boiled at the suggestion, but
my judgment told me that it was doubtless right.

During the past few years—I should say the last
ten or twenty—greater strides have been taken in the
advancement of aeronautics than had been previously
achieved in the preceding five hundred years.

The perfection of the destination control compass
by Carthoris of Helium is considered by many authori-
ties to have marked the beginning of a new era of invention. For centuries we seemed to have stagnated in
a quiet pond of self-sufficiency, as though we had
reached the acme of perfection beyond which it was
useless to seek for improvement upon what we considered the highest possible achievements of science.

Carthoris of Helium, inheriting the restless, inquir-
ing mind of his earth-born sire, awoke us. Our best
minds took up the challenge, and the result was rapid
improvement in design and construction of airships of
all classes, leading to a revolution in motor building.

We had thought that our light, compact, powerful
radium motors never could be improved upon and
that man never would travel, either safely or eco-
nomically, at a speed greater than that attained by our
swift one-man scout fliers—about eleven hundred
haads per zode (*Note: approximately one hundred
and sixty-six earth miles per hour*), when a virtually
unknown padwar in the navy of Helium announced
that he had perfected a motor that, with one-half the

weight of our present motors, would develop twice the speed.

It was this type of motor with which my scout flier was equipped—a seemingly fuelless motor, since it derived its invisible and imponderable energy from the inexhaustible and illimitable magnetic field of the planet.

There are certain basic features of the new motor that only the inventor and the government of Helium are fully conversant with, and these are most jealously guarded. The propeller shaft, which extends well within the hull of the flier, is constructed of numerous lateral segments insulated from one another. Around this shaft and supporting it is a series of armature-like bearings, through the centre of which it passes.

These are connected in series with a device called an accumulator through which the planet's magnetic energy is directed to the peculiar armatures which encircle the propeller shaft.

Speed is controlled by increasing or diminishing the number of armature bearings in series with the accumulator—all of which is simply accomplished by a lever which the pilot moves from his position on deck, where he ordinarily lies upon his stomach, his safety belt snapped to heavy rings in the deck.

The limit of speed, the inventor claims, is dependent solely upon the ratio of strength to weight in the construction of the hull. My one-man scout flier easily attains a speed of two thousand haads per zode (*Note: approximately three hundred miles per hour*), nor could it have withstood the tremendous strain of a more powerful motor, though it would have been easy to have increased both the power of the one and the speed of the other by the simple expedient of a longer propeller shaft carrying an additional number of armature bearings.

In experimenting with the new motor at Hastor last year, an attempt was made to drive a scout flier at the exceptional speed of thirty-three hundred haads per zode (*Note: approximately five hundred miles per hour; being* 1949.0592 *earth feet and a zode* 2.462 *earth hours*), but before the ship had attained a speed of three thousand haads per zode it was torn to pieces by its own motor. Now we are trying to attain the greatest strength with the minimum of weight, and as our engineers succeed we shall see speed increased until, I am sure, we shall easily attain to seven thousand haads per zode (*Note: over one thousand miles per hour*), for there seems to be no limit to the power of these marvelous motors.

Little less marvellous is the destination control compass of Carthoris of Helium. Set your pointer upon any spot on either hemisphere; open your throttle and then lie down and go to sleep if you will. Your ship will carry you to your destination, drop within a hundred yards or so of the ground and stop, while an alarm awakens you. It is really a very simple device, but I believe that John Carter has fully described it in one of his numerous manuscripts.

In the adventure upon which I had embarked the destination control compass was of little value to me, since I did not know the exact location of Jahar. However, I set it roughly at a point about thirty degrees south latitude, thirty-five degrees east longitude, as I believed that Jahar lay somewhere to the south-west of that point.

Flying at high speed I had long since left behind the cultivated areas near Helium and was crossing above a desolate and deserted waste of ochre moss that clothed the dead sea bottoms where once rolled a mighty ocean bearing upon its bosom the shipping of a happy and prosperous people, now but a half-forgotten memory in the legends of Barsoom.

Upon the edges of plateaus that once had marked the shore-line of a noble continent I passed above the lonely monuments of that ancient prosperity, the sad, deserted cities of old Barsoom. Even in their ruins there is a grandeur and magnificence that still have power to awe a modern man. Down towards the lowest sea bottoms other ruins mark the tragic trail that

that ancient civilization had followed in pursuit of the receding waters of its ocean to where the last city finally succumbed, bereft of commerce, shorn of power, to fall at last an easy victim to the marauding hordes of fierce, green tribesmen, whose descendants now are the sole rulers of many of these deserted sea bottoms. Hating and hated, ignorant of love, laughter or happiness, they lead their long, fierce lives, quarrelling among themselves and their neighbors and preying upon any chance adventurers who happen within the confines of their bitter and desolate domain.

Fierce and terrible as are all green men, there are few whose cruel natures and bloody exploits have horrified the minds of red men to such an extent as have the green hordes of Torquas.

The city of Torquas, from which they derive their name, was once of the most magnificent and powerful of ancient Barsoom. Though it has been deserted for ages by all but roaming tribes of green men, it is still marked upon every map, and as it lay directly in the path of my search for Jahar, and as I had never seen it, I had purposely laid my course to pass over it, and when, far ahead, I saw its lofty towers and battlements I felt the thrill of excitement and the lure of adventure which these dead cities of Barsoom proverbially exert upon us red men.

As I approached the city I reduced my speed and dropped lower that I might obtain a better view of it. What a beautiful city it must have been in its time! Even to-day, after all the ages that have passed since its broad avenues surged with the life of happy, prosperous throngs, its great palaces still stand in all their glorious splendour, that time and the elements have softened and mellowed but not yet destroyed.

As I circled low above the city I saw miles of avenues that have not known the foot of man for countless ages. The stone flagging of their pavement was overgrown with ochre moss, with here and there a stunted tree or a grotesque shrub of one of those varieties that somehow find sustenance in the arid waste-land. Silent, deserted courtyards looked up at me, gorgeous gardens of another happier day. Here and there the roof of a building had fallen in, but for the most part they remained intact, dreaming, doubtless, of the wealth and beauty that they had known in days of yore, and in imagination I could see the gorgeous sleeping-silks and furs spread out in the sunlight, while the women idled beneath gay canopies of silks, their jewelled harnesses scintillating with each move of their bodies. I saw the pennons waving from countless thousands of staffs, and the great ships at anchor in the harbour rose and fell to the undulations of the restless sea. There were swaggering sailors upon the avenues, and burly fighting men before the doors of every palace. Ah, what a picture imagination conjured from the death-like silence of that deserted city, and then, as a long, swinging circle brought me above the courtyard of a splendid palace that faced upon the city's great central square, my eyes beheld that which shattered my beautiful dream of the past. Directly below me I saw a score of great thoats penned in what once may have been the royal garden of a jeddak.

The presence of these huge beasts meant but one thing, and that was that their green masters were to be found near by.

As I passed above the courtyard one of the restless, vicious beasts looked up and saw me and instantly he commenced to squeal angrily. Immediately the other thoats, their short tempers aroused by the squealing of their fellow and their attention directed by his upward gaze, discovered me and set up a perfect pandemonium of grunts and squeals, which brought the result that I had immediately foreseen. A green warrior leaped into the courtyard from the interior of the palace and looked up just in time to see me before I passed from his line of vision above the roof of the building.

Realizing immediately that this was no place for me to loiter, I opened my throttle and at the same time rose swiftly towards a greater altitude. As I passed over the building and out across the avenue in front of it, I saw some twenty green warriors pour out of the building, their upward gaze searching the skies. The warrior on guard had apprised them of my presence.

I cursed myself for a stupid fool in having taken this unnecessary chance merely to satisfy my idle curiosity. Instantly I took a zigzag, upward course, rising as swiftly as I could, while from below a savage war-cry rose plainly to my ears. I saw long, wicked-looking rifles aimed at me. I heard the hiss of projectiles hurtling by me, but, though the first volley passed close to us, not a bullet struck the ship. In a moment more I would be out of range and safe, and I prayed to a thousand ancestors to protect me for the few brief minutes that would be necessary to place me entirely out of harm's way. I thought that I had made it and was just about to congratulate myself upon my good luck when I heard the thud of a bullet against the metal of my ship and almost simultaneously the explosion of the projectile, and then I was out of range.

Angry cries of disappointment came faintly to my ears as I sped swiftly towards the south-west, relieved that I had been so fortunate as to be able to get away without suffering any damage.

I had already flown about seventy karads (*Note: a karad is equivalent to a degree of longitude*) from Helium, but I was aware that Jahar might still be fifty to seventy-five karads distant, and I made up my mind that I would take no more chances such as those from which I had just so fortunately escaped.

I was now moving at great speed again, and I had scarcely finished congratulating myself upon my good fortune when it suddenly became apparent to me that I was having difficulty in maintaining my altitude. My flier was losing buoyancy, and almost immediately I guessed, what investigation later revealed, that one of my buoyancy tanks had been punctured by the explosive bullet of the green warriors.

To reproach myself for my carelessness seemed a useless waste of mental energy, though I can assure you that I was keenly aware of my fault and of its possible bearing upon the fate of Sanoma Tora, from the active prosecution of whose rescue I might now be entirely eliminated. The results as they affected me did not appeal to me half so much as did the contemplation of the unquestioned danger in which Sanoma Tora must be, from which my determination to rescue her had so obsessed me that there had not entered into my thoughts any slightest consideration of failure.

The mishap was a severe blow to my hopes and yet it did not shatter them entirely, for I am so constituted that I know I shall never give up hope of success in any issue as long as life remains to me.

How much longer my ship would remain afloat it was difficult to say, and, having no means of making such repairs as would be necessary to conserve the remaining contents of the punctured buoyancy tank, the best that I could do was to increase my speed so that I might cover as much distance as possible before I was forced down. The construction of my ship was such that at high speed it tended to maintain itself in the air with a minimum of the Eighth Ray in its buoyancy tanks; yet I knew that the time was not far distant when I should have to make a landing in this dreary, desolate waste-land.

I had covered something in the neighbourhood of two thousand haads since I had been fired upon above Torquas, crossing what had been a large gulf when the waters of the ocean rolled over the vast plains that now lay moss-covered and arid beneath me. Far ahead I could see the outlines of low hills that must have marked the southwestern shoreline of the gulf. Towards the north-west the dead sea bottom extended as far as the eye could reach, but this was not the direction I wished to take, and so I sped on towards the hills, hoping that I might maintain sufficient altitude to cross them, but as they swiftly loomed closer this hope died in my breast and I realized that the

end of my flight was now but a matter of moments.
At the same time I discerned the ruins of a deserted
city nestling at the foot of the hills; nor was this an
unwelcome sight, since water is almost always to be
found in the wells of these ancient cities, which have
been kept in repair by the green nomads of the waste-
land.

By now I was skimming but a few ads above the
surface of the ground. (*Note: an ad is about* 9.75
earth feet.) I had greatly diminished my speed to
avoid a serious accident in landing, and because of
this the end was hastened, so that presently I came
gently to rest upon the ochre vegetation scarcely a
haad from the water-front of the deserted city.

CHAPTER III

CORNERED

MY LANDING WAS most unfortunate in that it left me
in plain sight of the city without any place of concealment in the event that the ruins happened to be occupied by one of the numerous tribes of green men who
infest the dead sea bottoms of Barsoom, often making
their headquarters in one or another of the deserted
cities that line the ancient shore.

The fact that they usually choose to inhabit the
largest and most magnificent of the ancient palaces
and that these ordinarily stand back some little distance from the water-front rendered it quite possible
that even in the event that there were green men in the
city I might reach the concealing safety of one of the
nearer buildings before I was discovered by them.

My flier being now useless, there was nothing to do
but abandon it, and so, with only my weapons, am-

munition and a little concentrated rations, I walked quickly in the direction of the age-old waterfront. Whether or not I reached the buildings unobserved I was unable to determine, but at any rate I did reach them without seeing any sign of a living creature about.

Portions of many of these ancient deserted cities are inhabited by the great white apes of Barsoom, which are in many respects more to be feared than the green warriors themselves, for not only are these man-like creatures endowed with enormous strength and characterized by intense ferocity, but they are also voracious man-eaters. So terrible are they that it is said that they are the only living creatures that can instil fear within the breasts of the green men of Barsoom.

Knowing the possible dangers that might lurk within the precincts of this ruin, it may be wondered that I approached it at all, but as a matter of fact there was no safe alternative. Out upon the dead monotony of the ochre moss of the sea bottom, I should have been discovered by the first white ape or green Martian that approached the city from that direction, or that chanced to come from the interior of the ruins to the water-front. It was, therefore, necessary for me to seek concealment until night had fallen, since only by night might I travel in safety across the sea bottom, and as the city offered the only concealment near by, I had no choice but to enter it. I can assure you that it was not without feelings of extreme concern that I clambered to the surface of the broad avenue that once skirted the shore of a busy harbour. Across its wide expanse rose the ruins of what once had been shops and warehouses, but whose eyeless windows now looked down upon a scene of arid desolation. Gone were the great ships! Gone the busy, hurrying throngs! Gone the ocean!

Crossing the avenue I entered one of the taller buildings, which I noticed was surmounted by a high tower. The entire structure, including the tower, seemed to be in an excellent state of preservation, and it occurred to me that if I could ascend into the latter, I should be able to obtain an excellent view of the city and of the country that lay beyond it to the southwest, which was the direction in which I intended to pursue my search for Jahar. I reached the building apparently unobserved, and, entering, found myself in a large chamber, the nature and purpose of which it was no longer possible to determine, since such decorations as may possibly have adorned its walls in the past were no longer discernible and whatever furniture it may have contained to give a clue to its identity had long since been removed. There was an enormous fireplace in the far end of the room, and at one side of this fireplace a ramp led downward, and upon the other a similar ramp led upward.

Listening intently for a moment, I heard no sound, either within or without the building, so that it was with considerable confidence that I started to ascend the ramp.

Upward I continued from floor to floor, each of which consisted of a single large chamber, a fact which finally convinced me that the building had been a warehouse for the storing of goods passing through this ancient port.

From the upper floor a wooden ladder extended upward through the centre of the tower above. It was of solid skeel, which is practically indestructible, so that though I knew it might be anywhere from five hundred thousand to a million years old, I did not hesitate to trust myself to it.

The circular interior core of the tower, upward through which the ladder extended, was rather dark. At each landing there was an opening into the tower chamber at that point, but as many of these openings were closed, only a subdued light penetrated to the central core.

I had ascended to the second level of the tower when I thought that I heard a strange noise beneath me.

Just the suggestion of a noise it was, but such utter silence had reigned over the deserted city that the faintest sound must have been appreciable to me.

Pausing in my ascent, I looked down, listening; but the sound which I had been unable to translate was not repeated, and I continued my way on upward.

Having it in mind to climb as high up in the tower as possible, I did not stop to examine any of the levels that I passed.

Continuing upward for a considerable distance my progress was finally blocked by heavy planking that appeared to form the ceiling of the shaft. Some eight or ten feet below me was a small door that probably led to one of the upper levels of the tower, and I could not but wonder why the ladder had been continued on upward above this doorway, since it could serve no practical purpose if it merely ended at the ceiling. Feeling above me with my fingers I traced the outlines of what appeared to be a trap-door. Obtaining a firm footing upon the ladder as high up as I could climb, I placed a shoulder against the barrier. In this position I was able to exert considerable pressure upward, with the result that presently I felt the planking rise above me, and a moment later, to the accompaniment of subdued groans, the trap-door swung upward upon ancient wooden hinges long unused. Clambering into the apartment above I found myself upon the top level of the tower, which rose to a height of some two hundred feet above the avenue below. Before me were the corroded remains of an ancient and long obsolete beacon-light, such as was used by the ancients long before the discovery of radium and its practical and scientific application to the lighting requirements of modern civilization upon Barsoom. These ancient lamps were operated by expensive machines which generated electricity, and this one was doubtless used as a beacon for the safe guidance of ancient mariners into the harbour, whose waters once rolled almost to the foot of the tower.

This upper level of the tower afforded an excellent

view in all directions. To the north and north-east stretched a vast expanse of dead sea bottom as far as the eye could reach. To the south was a range of low hills that curved gently in a north-easterly direction, forming in bygone days the southern shore-line of what is still known as the Gulf of Torquas. Towards the west I looked out over the ruins of a great city, which extended far back into low hills, the flanks of which it had mounted as it expanded from the seashore. There in the distance I could still discern the ancient villas of the wealthy, while in the nearer foreground were enormous public buildings, the most pretentious of which were built upon the four sides of a large quadrangle that I could easily discern a short distance from the water-front. Here, doubtless, stood the official palace of the jeddak who once ruled the rich country of which this city was the capital and the principal port. There, now, only silence reigns. It was indeed a depressing sight and one fraught with poignant prophecy for us of present-day Barsoom.

Where they battled valiantly but futilely against the menace of a constantly diminishing water supply, we are faced with a problem that far transcends theirs in the importance of its bearing upon the maintenance of life upon our planet. During the past several thousand years only the courage, resourcefulness and wealth of the red men of Barsoom have made it possible for life to exist upon our dying planet, for were it not for the great atmosphere plants conceived and built and maintained by the red race of Barsoom, all forms of air-breathing creatures would have become extinct thousands of years ago.

As I gazed out over the city, my mind occupied with these dismal thoughts, I again became aware of a sound coming from the interior of the tower beneath me, and, stepping to the open trap, I looked down into the shaft and there, directly below me, I saw that which might well make the stoutest Barsoomian heart quail—the hideous, snarling face of a great white ape of Barsoom.

As our eyes met, the creature voiced an angry growl and, abandoning its former stealthy approach, rushed swiftly up the ladder. Acting almost mechanically I did the one and only thing that might even temporarily stay its rush upon me—I slammed down the heavy trap-door above its head, and as I did so I saw for the first time that the door was equipped with a heavy wooden bar, and you may well believe that I lost no time in securing this, thus effectually barring the creature's ascent by this route into the veritable *cul de sac* in which I had placed myself.

Now, indeed, was I in a pretty predicament—two hundred feet above the city, with my only avenue of escape cut off by one of the most feared of all the savage beasts of Barsoom.

I had hunted these creatures in Thark as a guest of the great green Jeddak, Tars Tarkas, and I knew something of their cunning and resourcefulness as well as of their ferocity. Extremely man-like in conformation, they also approach man more closely than any other of the lower orders in the size and development of their brain. Occasionally these creatures are captured when young and trained to perform, and so intelligent are they that they can be taught to do almost anything that man can do that lies within the range of their limited reasoning capacity. Man has, however, never been able to subdue their ferocious nature, and they are always the most dangerous of animals to handle, which probably accounts more even than their intelligence for the interest displayed by the large audiences which they unfailingly attract.

In Hastor I have paid a good price to see one of these creatures, and now I found myself in a position where I should very gladly pay a good deal more not to see one, but from the noise he was making in the shaft beneath me it appeared to me that he was determined that I should have a free show and he a free meal. He was hurling himself as best he could against the trap-door, above which I stood with some misgivings, which were presently allayed when I realized that not even the vast strength of the white ape could avail against the still staunch and sturdy skeel of the ancient door.

Finally convinced that he could not come at me by this avenue, I set about taking stock of my situation. Circling the tower I examined its outward architecture by the simple expedient of leaning far outward above each of the four sides. Three sides terminated at the roof of the building a hundred and fifty feet below me, while the fourth extended to the pavement of the courtyard two hundred feet below. Like much of the architecture of ancient Barsoom, the surface of the tower was elaborately carved from top to bottom and at each level there were window embrasures, some of which were equipped with small stone balconies. As a rule there was but a single window to a level, and as the window for the level directly beneath never opened upon the same side of the tower as the window for the level above, there was always a distance of from thirty to forty feet between windows upon the same side, and, as I was examining the outside of the tower with a view to its offering me an avenue of escape, this point was of great importance to me, since a series of window ledges, one below another, would have proved a most welcome sight to a man in my position.

By the time I had completed my survey of the exterior of the tower the ape had evidently come to the conclusion that he could not demolish the barrier that kept him from me, and I hoped that he would abandon the idea entirely and depart. But when I lay down on the floor and placed an ear close to the door I could plainly hear him just below as he occasionally changed from one uncomfortable position to another upon the small ladder beneath me. I did not know to what extent these creatures might have developed pertinacity of purpose, but I hoped that he might soon tire of his vigil and his thoughts be diverted into some other channel. However, as the day wore to a close this possibility seemed to grow more and more remote, until at last I became almost convinced that the creature had determined to lay siege until hunger or desperation forced me from my retreat.

How longingly I gazed at the beckoning hills beyond the city where lay my route towards the southwest—towards fabled Jahar.

The sun was low in the west. Soon would come the sudden transition from daylight to darkness, and then what? Perhaps the creature would abandon its vigil; hunger or thirst might attract it elsewhere, but how was I to know? How easily it might descend to the bottom of the tower and await me there, confident that sooner or later I must come down.

One unfamiliar with the traits of these savage creatures might wonder why, armed as I was with sword and pistol, I did not raise the trap-door and give battle to my jailer. Had I known positively that he was the only white ape in the vicinity I should not have hesitated to do so, but experience assured me that there was doubtless an entire herd of them quartered in the ruined city. So scarce is the flesh they crave that it is their ordinary custom to hunt alone, so that in the event that they make a kill they may be more certain of retaining the prize for themselves, but if I should attack him he would most certainly raise such a row as to attract his fellows, in which event my chance for escape would have been reduced to the ultimate zero.

A single shot from my pistol might have dispatched him, but it was equally possible that it would not, for these great white apes of Barsoom are tremendous creatures, endowed with almost unbelievable vitality. Many of them stand fully fifteen feet in height and are endowed by nature with tremendous strength. Their very appearance is demoralizing to an enemy; their white, hairless bodies are in themselves repulsive to the eye of a red man; the great shock of white hair bristling erect upon their pates accentuates the brutality of their countenances, while their intermediary set of limbs, which they use either as arms or legs as necessity or whim suggests, render them most formidable antagonists. Quite generally they carry a club, in the use of which they are terribly proficient. One of them, therefore, seemed sufficiently a menace in itself, so that I had no desire to attract others of its kind, though I was fully aware that eventually I might be forced to carry the battle to him.

Just as the sun was setting my attention was attracted towards the water-front, where the long shadows of the city were stretching far out across the dead sea bottom. Riding up the gentle acclivity towards the city was a party of green warriors, mounted upon their great savage thoats. There were perhaps twenty of them, moving silently over the soft moss that carpeted the bottom of the ancient harbour, the padded feet of their mounts giving forth no sound. Like spectres, they moved in the shadows of the dying day, giving me further proof that Fate had led me to a most unfriendly shore, and then, as though to complete the trilogy of fearsome Barsoomian menaces, the roar of a banth rolled down out of the hills behind the city.

Safe from observation in the high tower above them, I watched the party as it emerged from the hollow of the harbour and rode out upon the avenue below me, and then for the first time I noted a small figure seated in front of one of the warriors. Darkness was coming swiftly now, but before the little cavalcade passed out of sight momentarily behind the corner of the building, as it entered another avenue leading towards the heart of the city, I thought that I recognized the little figure as that of a woman of my own race. That she was a captive was a foregone conclusion, and I could not but shudder as I contemplated the fate that lay in store for her. Perhaps my own Sanoma Tora was in equal jeopardy. Perhaps—but no, that could not be possible —how could Sanoma Tora have fallen into the clutches of warriors of the fierce horde of Torquas?

It could not be she. No, that was impossible. But the fact remained that the captive was a red woman, and whether she were Sanoma Tora or another, whether she were from Helium or Jahar, my heart went out in sympathy to her, and I forgot my own predicament as something within me urged me to pursue her captors and seek to snatch her from them; but, alas, how futile seemed my fancy. How might I, who might not even save himself, aspire to the rescue of another?

The thought galled me, it hurt my pride, and forthwith I determined that if I could not chance dying to save myself, I might at least chance it for a woman of my own race, and always in the back of my head was the thought that perhaps the object of my solicitude might, indeed, be the woman I loved.

Darkness had fallen as I pressed my ear again to the trapdoor. All was silent below, so that presently I became assured that the creature had departed. Perhaps he was lying in wait for me further down; but what of that? I must face him eventually if he elected to remain. I loosened my pistol in its holster and was upon the point of slipping the bar that secured the door when I distinctly heard the beast directly beneath me.

For an instant I paused. What was the use? It meant certain death to raise that door, and in what way might I be profiting either myself or the poor captive if I gave my life thus uselessly? But there was an alternative—one that I had been planning to adopt in case of necessity from the moment that I had first examined the exterior construction of the tower. It offered a slender chance of escape from my predicament, and even a very slender chance was better than what would confront me should I raise the trap-door.

I stepped to one of the windows of the tower and looked down upon the city. Neither moon was in the sky; I could see nothing. Towards the interior of the city I heard the squealing of thoats. There would the camp of the green men be located. Thus by the squealing of their vicious mounts would I be guided to it. Again a hunting banth roared in the hills. I sat upon the sill and swung both legs across, and then turning on my belly slipped silently over the edge until I hung only by my hands. Groping with my sandalled toes, I felt for a foothold upon the deep-cut carvings of the tower's face. Above me was a blue-black void shot with stars; below me a blank and empty void. It might have been a thousand sofads to the roof below me, or it might have been one; but though I could see nothing I knew that it was one hundred and fifty and that at the bottom lay death if a foot or a hand slipped.

In daylight the sculpturing had seemed large and deep and bold, but by night how different! My toes seemed to find but hollow scratches in a smooth surface of polished stone. My arms and fingers were tiring. I must find a foothold or fall, and then, when hope seemed gone, the toe of my right sandal slipped into a horizontal groove and an instant later my left found a hold.

Flattened against the sheer wall of the tower I lay there resting my tired fingers and arms for a moment, and when I felt that they would bear my weight again I sought for hand holds. Thus painfully, perilously, monotonously, I descended inch by inch. I avoided the windows, which naturally greatly increased the difficulty and danger of my descent; yet I did not care to pass directly in front of them for fear that by chance the ape might have descended from the summit of the ladder and would see me.

I cannot recall that ever in my life I felt more alone than I did that night as I was descending the ancient beacon-tower of that deserted city, for not even hope was with me. So precarious were my holds upon the rough stone that my fingers were soon numb and exhausted. How they clung at all to those shallow cuts I do not know. The only redeeming feature of the descent was the darkness, and a hundred times I blessed my first ancestors that I could not see the dizzy depths below me; but on the other hand it was so dark that I could not tell how far I had descended; nor did I dare to look up where the summit of the tower must have been silhouetted against the starlit sky for fear that in doing so I should lose my balance and be precipitated to the courtyard or the roof below. The air of Barsoom is thin; it does not greatly diffuse the starlight, and so, while the heavens above were shot with brilliant points of light, the ground beneath was obliterated in darkness.

Yet I must have been nearer the roof than I thought when that happened which I had been assiduously endeavouring to prevent—the scabbard of my long sword pattered noisily against the face of the tower. In the darkness and the silence it seemed a veritable din, but, however exaggerated it might appear to me, I knew that it was sufficient to reach the ears of the great ape in the tower. Whether a suggestion of its import would occur to him I could not guess—I could only hope that he would be too dull to connect it with me or my escape.

But I was not to be left long in doubt, for almost immediately afterwards a sound came from the interior of the tower that sounded to my overwrought nerves like a heavy body rapidly descending a ladder. I realize now that imagination might easily have construed utter silence into such a sound, since I had been listening so intently for that very thing that I might easily have worked myself into such a state of nervous apprehension that almost any sort of an hallucination was possible.

With redoubled speed and with a measure of recklessness that was almost suicidal, I hastened my descent and an instant later I felt the solid roof beneath my feet.

I breathed a sigh of relief, but it was destined to be but a short sigh and but brief relief, for almost instantly I was made aware that the sound from the interior of the tower had been no hallucination as the huge bulk of a great white ape loomed suddenly from a doorway not a dozen paces from me.

As he charged me he gave forth no sound. Evidently he had not held his solitary vigil this long with any intention of sharing his feast with another. He would dispatch me in silence, and with similar intent I drew my long sword, rather than my pistol, to meet his savage charge.

What a puny, futile thing I must have appeared confronting that towering mountain of bestial ferocity!

Thanks be to a thousand fighting ancestors that I wielded a long sword with swiftness and with strength: otherwise I must have been gathered into that savage embrace in the brute's first charge. Four powerful hands were reached out to seize me, but I swung my long sword in a terrific cut that severed one of them cleanly at the wrist, and at the same instant I leaped quickly to one side, and as the beast rushed past me, carried onward by its momentum, I ran my blade deep into its body. With a savage scream of rage and pain it sought to turn upon me, but its foot slipped upon its own dismembered hand and it stumbled awkwardly on, trying to regain its equilibrium, but that it never accomplished, and still stumbling grotesquely, it lunged over the edge of the roof to the courtyard below.

Fearing that the beast's scream might attract others of its kind to the roof, I ran swiftly to the north edge of the building, where I had noted from the tower earlier in the afternoon a series of lower buildings adjoining, over the roofs of which I might possibly accomplish my descent to the street level.

Cold Cluros was rising above the distant horizon, shedding his pale light upon the city so that I could plainly see the roofs below me as I came to the north edge of the building. It was a long drop, but there was no safe alternative, since it was quite probable that should I attempt to descend through the building, I would meet other members of the ape's herd who had been attracted by the scream of their fellow.

Slipping over the edge of the roof I hung an instant by my hands and then dropped. The distance was about two ads, but I alighted safely and without injury. Upon your own planet, with its larger bulk and greater gravity, I presume that a fall of that distance might be serious, but not so, necessarily, upon Barsoom. From this roof I had a short drop to the next, and from that I leaped to a low wall and thence to the ground below.

Had it not been for the fleeting glimpse of the girl captive that I had caught just at sunset, I should have set out directly for the hills west of the town, banth or no banth, but now I felt strongly upon me a certain moral obligation to make the best efforts that I could for succouring the poor unfortunate that had fallen into the clutches of these cruellest of creatures.

Keeping well within the shadows of the buildings I moved stealthily towards the central plaza of the city, from which direction I had heard the squealing of the thoats.

The plaza was a full haad from the water-front and I was compelled to cross several intersecting avenues as I cautiously made my way towards it, guided by an occasional squeal from the thoats quartered in some deserted palace courtyard.

I reached the plaza in safety, confident that I had not been observed.

Upon the opposite side I saw light within one of the great buildings that faced it, but I dared not cross the open space in the moonlight, and so, still clinging to the shadows, I moved to the far end of the quadrangle where Cluros cast his densest shadows, and thus at last I won to the building in which the green men were quartered. Directly before me was a low window that must have opened into a room adjoining the one in which the warriors were congregated. Listening intently I heard nothing within the chamber, and slipping a leg over the sill I entered the dark interior with the utmost stealth.

Tiptoeing across the room to find a door through which I might look into the adjoining chamber, I was suddenly arrested as my foot touched a soft body, and I froze into rigidity, my hand upon my long sword, as the body moved.

CHAPTER IV

TAVIA

THERE ARE OCCASIONS in the life of every man when he becomes impressed by the evidence of the existence of an extraneous power which guides his acts, which is sometimes described as the hand of providence, or is again explained on the hypothesis of a sixth sense which transports to the part of our brain that controls our actions, perceptions of which we are not objectively aware; but, account for it as one may, the fact remains that as I stood there that night in the dark chamber of the ancient palace of the deserted city I hesitated to thrust my sword into the soft body moving at my feet. This might after all have been the most reasonable and logical course for me to pursue. Instead I pressed my swordpoint firmly against yielding flesh and whispered a single word: "Silence!"

A thousand times since then have I given thanks to my first ancestors that I did not follow my natural impulse, for, in response to my admonition, a voice whispered: "Do not thrust, red man; I am of your own race and a prisoner," and the voice was that of a girl.

Instantly I withdrew my blade and knelt beside her. "If you have come to help me, cut my bonds," she said, "and be quick, for they will soon return for me."

Feeling rapidly over her body I found that her wrists and ankles were secured with leather thongs, and drawing my dagger I quickly severed these.

"Are you alone?" I asked as I helped her to her feet.

"Yes," she replied. "In the next room they are playing for me to decide to which one I shall belong." At that moment there came the clank of side-arms from

41

the adjoining room. "They are coming," she said. "They must not find us here."

Taking her by the hand I moved to the window through which I had entered the apartment, but fortunately I reconnoitred before stepping out into the avenue, and it was well for us that I did so, for as I looked to the right along the face of the building, I saw a green Martian warrior emerging from the main entrance. Evidently it had been the rattling of his side-arms that we had heard as he moved across the adjoining apartment to the doorway.

"Is there another exit from this room?" I asked in a low whisper.

"Yes," she replied. "Opposite this window there is a doorway leading into a corridor. It was open when they brought me in, but they closed it."

"We shall be better off inside the building than out for a while at least," I said. "Come!" And together we crossed the apartment, groping along the wall for the door, which I soon located. With the utmost care I drew it ajar, fearing that its ancient hinges might betray us by their complaining. Beyond the doorway lay a corridor dark as the depths of Omean, and into this I drew the girl, closing the door silently behind us. Groping our way to the right away from the apartment occupied by the green warriors, we moved slowly through a black void until presently we saw just ahead a faint light, which investigation revealed as coming through the open doorway of an apartment that faced upon the central courtyard of the edifice. I was about to pass this doorway and seek a hiding-place further within the remote interior of the building when my attention was attracted by the squealing of a thoat in the courtyard beyond the apartment we were passing.

From earliest boyhood I have had a great deal of experience with the small breed of thoats used as saddle animals by the men of my race, and while I was visiting Tars Tarkas of Thark I became quite familiar with the methods employed by the green men in controlling their own huge vicious beasts.

For travel over the surface of the ground the thoat compares to other methods of land transportation as the one-man scout flier does to all other ships of the air in aerial navigation. He is at once the swiftest and the most dangerous, so that, faced as I was with a problem of land transportation, it was only natural that the squeal of the thoat should suggest a plan to my mind.

"Why do you hesitate?" asked the girl. "We cannot escape in that direction since we cannot cross the courtyard."

"On the contrary," I replied, "I believe that in this direction may lie our surest avenue of escape."

"But their thoats are penned in the courtyard," she remonstrated, "and green warriors are never far from their thoats."

"It is because the thoats are there that I wish to investigate the courtyard," I replied.

"The moment they catch our scent," she said, "they will raise a disturbance that will attract the attention of their masters and we shall immediately be discovered and captured."

"Perhaps," I said; "but if my plan succeeds it will be well worth the risk, but if you are very much afraid I will abandon it."

"No," she said, "it is not for me to choose or direct. You have been generous enough to help me and I may only follow where you lead, but if I knew your plan perhaps I might follow more intelligently."

"Certainly," I said; "it is very simple. There are thoats. We shall take one of them and ride away. It will be much easier than walking and our chances of escape will be considerably greater; at the same time we shall leave the courtyard gates open, hoping that the other thoats will follow us out, leaving their masters unable to pursue us."

"It is a mad plan," said the girl, "but it is a brave one. If we are discovered, there will be fighting, and I am unarmed. Give me your short sword, warrior, that we may at least make the best account of ourselves that is possible."

I unsnapped the scabbard of my short sword from my harness and attached it to hers at her left hip, and, as I touched her body in doing so, I could not but note that there was no sign of trembling such as there would have been had she been affected by fright or excitement. She seemed perfectly cool and collected and her tone of voice was most reassuring to me. That she was not Sanoma Tora I had known when she had first spoken in the darkness of the room in which I had stumbled upon her, and while I had been keenly disappointed, I was still determined to do the best that I could to assist in the escape of the stranger, although I was confident that her presence might greatly delay and embarrass me, while it subjected me to far greater danger than would have fallen to the lot of a warrior travelling alone. It was, therefore, reassuring to find that my unwelcome companion would not prove entirely helpless.

"I trust you will not have to use it," I said as I finished hooking my short sword to her harness.

"You will find," she said, "that if necessity arises I can use it."

"Good," I said. "Now follow me and keep close to me."

A careful survey of the courtyard from the window of the huge chamber overlooking it revealed about twenty huge thoats, but no green warriors, evidence that they felt perfectly secure against enemies.

The thoats were congregated in the far end of the courtyard; a few of them had lain down for the night, but the balance were moving restlessly about as is their habit. Across the courtyard from us and at the same end stood a pair of massive gates. As far as I could determine they barred the only opening into the courtyard large enough to admit a thoat, and I assumed that beyond them lay an alley leading to one of the avenues near by.

To reach the gates unobserved by the thoats was the

first step in my plan, and the better to do this I decided to seek an apartment near the gate, on either side of which I saw windows similar to that from which we were looking. Therefore, motioning my companion to follow me, I returned to the corridor, and again groping through the darkness we made our way along it. In the third apartment which I explored I found a window letting into the courtyard close beside the gate. And in the wall which ran at angles to that in which the window was set I found a doorway that opened into a large vaulted corridor upon the opposite side of the gate. This discovery greatly encouraged me, since it harmonized perfectly with the plan I had in mind, at the same time reducing the risk which my companion must run in the attempted adventure of escape.

"Remain here," I said to her, placing her just behind the gate. "If my plan is successful I shall ride into this corridor upon one of the thoats, and as I do so you must be ready to seize my hand and mount behind me. If I am discovered and fail I shall cry out 'For Helium!' and that must be your signal to escape as best you may."

She laid her hand upon my arm. "Let me go into the courtyard with you," she begged. "Two swords are better than one."

"No," I said. "Alone I have a better chance of handling the thoats than if their attention is distracted by another."

"Very well," she said, and with that I left her, and, reentering the chamber, went directly to the window. For a moment I reconnoitred the interior of the courtyard, and finding conditions unchanged, I slipped stealthily through the window and edged slowly towards the gate. Cautiously I examined the latch, and discovering it easy to manipulate, I was soon silently pushing one of the gates back upon its hinges. When it was opened sufficiently wide to permit the passage of a thoat, I turned my attention to the beasts within the enclosure. Practically untamed, these savage creatures are as wild as their uncaptured fellows of the remote sea bottoms, and, being controlled solely by telepathic means, they are amenable only to the suggestion of the more powerful minds of their masters, and even so it requires considerable skill to dominate them.

I had learned the method from Tars Tarkas himself and had come to feel considerable proficiency, so that I approached this crucial test of my power with the confidence that was absolutely requisite to success.

Placing myself close beside the gate, I concentrated every faculty of my mind to the direction of my will, telepathically, upon the brain of the thoat I had selected for my purpose, the selection being determined solely by the fact that he stood nearest to me. The effect of my effort was immediately apparent. The creature, which had been searching for the occasional tufts of moss that grew between the stone flags of the courtyard, raised his head and looked about him. At once he became restless, but he gave forth no sound, since I was willing him to silence. Presently his eyes moved in my direction and halted upon me. Then, slowly, I drew him towards me. It was slow work, for he evidently sensed that I was not his master, but on he came. Once, when he was quite near me, he stopped and snorted angrily. He must have caught my scent then and realized that I was not even of the same race as that to which he was accustomed. Then it was that I exterted to their fullest extent every power of my mind. He stood there shaking his ugly head to and fro, his snarling lips baring his great fangs. Beyond him I could see that the other thoats had been attracted by his actions. They were looking towards us and moving about restlessly, always drawing closer. Should they discover me and start to squeal, which is the first and always ready sign of their easily aroused anger, I knew that I should have their riders upon me in no time, since because of his nervous and irritable nature the thoat is the watchdog as well as the beast of burden of the green Barsoomians.

For a moment the beast I had selected hesitated before me as though undecided whether to retreat or to charge, but he did neither; instead he came slowly up to me, and as I backed through the gate into the vaulted corridor beyond, he followed me. This was better than I had expected, for it permitted me to compel him to lie down, so that the girl and I were able to mount with ease.

Before us lay a long vaulted corridor, at the far end of which I could discern a moonlit archway, through which we presently passed on to a broad avenue.

To the left lay the hills, and, turning this way, I urged the fleet animal along the ancient deserted thoroughfare between rows of stately ruins towards the west and—what?

Where the avenue turned to wind upward into the hills, I glanced back; nor could I restrain a feeling of exultation as I saw strung out behind us in the moonlight a file of great thoats, which I was confident would well know what to do with their new-found liberty.

"Your captors will not pursue us far," I said to the girl, indicating the thoats with a nod of my head.

"Our ancestors are with us to-night," she said. "Let us pray that they may never desert us."

Now, for the first time, I had a fairly good look at my companion, for both Cluros and Thuria were in the heavens and it was quite light. If I revealed my surprise it is not to be wondered at, for, in the darkness, having only my companion's voice for a guide, I had been perfectly confident that I had given aid to a female, but now as I looked at that short hair and boyish face I did not know what to think; nor did the harness that my companion wore aid me in justifying my first conclusion, since it was quite evidently the harness of a man.

"I thought you were a girl," I blurted out.

A fine mouth spread into a smile that revealed strong, white teeth. "I am," she said.

"But your hair—your harness—even your figure belies your claim."

She laughed gaily. That, as I was to find later, was one of her chief charms—that she could laugh so easily, yet never to wound.

"My voice betrayed me," she said. "It is too bad."

"Why is it too bad?" I asked.

"Because you would have felt better with a fighting man as a companion, whereas now you feel that you have only a burden."

"A light one," I replied, recalling how easily I had lifted her to the thoat's back. "But tell me who you are and why you are masquerading as a boy."

"I am a slave girl," she said; "just a slave girl who has run away from her master. Perhaps that will make a difference," she added a little sadly. "Perhaps you will be sorry that you have defended just a slave girl."

"No," I said, "that makes no difference. I, myself, am only a poor padwar, not rich enough to afford a slave. Perhaps you are the one to be sorry that you were not rescued by a rich man."

She laughed. "I ran away from the richest man in the world," she said. "At least I guess he must have been the richest man in the world, for who could be richer than Tul Axtar, Jeddak of Jahar?"

"You belong to Tul Axtar, Jeddak of Jahar?" I exclaimed.

"Yes," she said. "I was stolen when I was very young from a city called Tjanath, and ever since I have lived in the palace of Tul Axtar. He has many women—thousands of them. Sometimes they live all their lives in his palace and never see him. I have seen him," she shuddered; "he is terrible. I was not unhappy there, for I had never known my mother; she died when I was young, and my father was only a memory. You see I was very, very young indeed when the emissaries of Tul Axtar stole me from my home in Tjanath. I made friends with everyone about the palace of Tul Axtar. They all liked me, the slaves and the warriors and the chiefs, and because I was always boyish it amused them to train me in the use of arms and even to navigate the smaller fliers; but then came a day when my happiness was ended for ever—Tul Axtar saw me. He saw me and he sent for me. I pretended that I was ill and did not go, and when night came I went to the quarters of a soldier whom I knew to be on guard and stole harness, and I cut off my long hair and painted my face that I might look more like a man, and then I went to the hangars on the palace roof and by a ruse deceived the guard there and stole a one-man flier.

"I thought," she continued, "that if they searched for me at all they would search in the direction of Tjanath, and so I flew in the opposite direction, towards the north-east, intending to make a great circle to the north, turning back towards Tjanath. After I passed over Xanator I discovered a large grave of mantalia growing out upon the dead sea bottom, and I immediately descended to obtain some of the milk from these plants, as I had left the palace so hurriedly that I had had no opportunity to supply myself with provisions. The mantalia grove was an unusually large one, and as the plants grew to a height of from eight to twelve sofads, the grove offered excellent protection from observation. I had no difficulty in finding a landing-place well within its confines. In order to prevent detection from above, I ran my plane in among the concealing foliage of two over-arching mantalias and then set about obtaining a supply of milk.

"As near objects never appear as attractive as those more distant, I wandered some little distance from my flier before I found the plants that seemed to offer a sufficiently copious supply of rich milk.

"A band of green warriors had also entered the grove to procure milk, and, as I was tapping the tree I had selected, one of them discovered me and a moment later I was captured. From their questions I became assured that they had not seen me enter the grove and that they knew nothing of the presence of my flier. They must have been in a portion of the grove very thickly overhung by foliage while I was approaching from above and making my landing; but be that as it may, they were ignorant of the presence of my flier, and I determined to keep them in ignorance of it.

"When they had obtained as much milk as they required they returned to Xanator, bringing me with them. The rest you know."

"This is Xanator?" I asked.

"Yes," she replied.

"And what is your name?" I asked.

"Tavia," she replied. "And what is yours?"

"Tan Hadron of Hastor," I replied.

"It is a nice name," she said. There was a certain boyish frankness about the way she said it that convinced me that she would have been just as quick to tell me had she not liked my name. There was no suggestion of brainless flattery in her tone, and I was to learn, as I became better acquainted with her, that honesty and candour were two of her marked characteristics, but at the moment I was giving such matters little thought, since my mind was occupied with a portion of her narrative that had suggested to me an easy and swift method of escape from our predicament.

"Do you believe," I asked, "that you can find the mantalia grove where you hid your flier?"

"I am positive of it," she replied.

"Will the craft carry two?" I asked.

"It is a one-man flier," she replied, "but it will carry both of us, though both its speed and altitude will be reduced."

She told me that the grove lay to the south-east of Xanator, and accordingly I turned the thoat's head towards the east. After we had passed well beyond the limits of the city we moved in a southerly direction down out of the hills on to the dead sea bottom.

Thuria was winging her swift flight through the heavens, casting strange and ever-moving shadows upon the ochre moss that covered the ground, while far above cold Cluros took his slow and stately way. The light of the two moons clearly illuminated the landscape and I was sure that keen eyes could easily have detected us from the ruins of Xanator, although the swiftly moving shadows cast by Thuria were helpful to us, since the shadows of every shrub and stunted tree produced a riot of movement upon the surface of the sea bottom in which our own moving shadow was less conspicuous, but the hope that I entertained most fondly was that all of the thoats had followed our beast from the courtyard and that the green Martian warriors were left dismounted, in which event no pursuit could overtake us.

The great beast that was carrying us moved swiftly and silently, so that it was not long before we saw in the distance the shadowy foliage of the mantalia grove, and shortly afterwards we entered its gloomy confines. It was not without considerable difficulty, however, that we located Tavia's flier, and mighty glad was I, too, when we found it in good condition, for we had seen more than a single shadowy form slinking through the forest, and I knew that the fierce animals of the barren hills and the great white apes of the ruined cities were equally fond of the milk of the mantalia and that we should be fortunate indeed if we escaped an encounter.

I rode as close to the flier as possible, and, leaving Tavia on the thoat, slipped quickly to the ground and dragged the small craft out into the open. An examination of the controls showed that they had not been tampered with, which was a great relief to me, as I had feared that the flier might have been damaged by the great apes, which are inclined to be both inquisitive and destructive.

Assured that all was well I assisted Tavia to the ground, and a moment later we were upon the deck of the flier. The craft responded satisfactorily, though a little sluggishly, to the controls, and immediately we were floating gently upward into the temporary safety of a Barsoomian night.

The flier, which was of a design now almost obsolete in Helium, was not equipped with a destination

control compass, which rendered it necessary for the
pilot to be constantly at the controls. Our quarters on
the narrow deck were exceedingly cramped and I fore-
saw a most uncomfortable journey ahead of us. Our
safety-belts were snapped to the same deck ring as we
lay almost touching one another upon the hard skeel.
The cowl which protected our faces from the rush of
the wind that was generated even by our relatively
slow speed was not sufficiently high to permit us to
change our positions to any considerable degree,
though occasionally we found it a relief to sit up with
our backs towards the bow and thus relieve the tedium
of remaining constantly prone in one position. When
I thus rested my cramped muscles, Tavia guided the
flier, but the cold wind of the Barsoomian night always brought me down behind the cowl in a very few
moments.

By mutual consent we were heading in a south-
westerly direction while we discussed our eventual destination.

I had told Tavia that I wished to go to Jahar and
why. She appeared much interested in the story of the
abduction of Sanoma Tora, and, from her knowledge
of Tul Axtar and the customs of Jahar, she thought it
most probable that the missing girl might be found
there, but as to the possibility of rescuing her, that
was another matter over which she shook her head
dubiously.

It was obvious to me that Tavia did not desire to
return to Jahar, yet she put no obstacles in the path of
my search for this my great objective; in fact, she gave
me Jahar's position, and herself set the nose of the
flier upon the right course.

"Will there be any great danger to you in returning
to Jahar?" I asked her.

The danger will be very great," she said, "but where
the master goes, the slave must follow."

"I am not your master," I said, "and you are not
my slave. Let us consider ourselves as comrades in
arms."

"That will be nice," she said simply, and then after a pause, "and if we are to be comrades, then let me warn you against going directly to Jahar. This flier would be recognized immediately. Your harness would mark you as an alien, and you would accomplish nothing more towards rescuing your Sanoma Tora than to achieve the pits of Tul Axtar and sooner or later the games in the great arena, where eventually you must be slain."

"What would you suggest then?" I asked.

"Beyond Jahar, to the south-west, lies Tjanath, the city of my birth. Of all the cities upon Barsoom that is the only one where I may hope to be received in a friendly manner, and as they receive me, so will they receive you. There you may better prepare to enter Jahar, which you may only accomplish by disguising yourself as a Jaharian, for Tul Axtar permits no alien within the confines of his empire other than those who are brought as prisoners of war and as slaves. In Tjanath you can obtain the harness and metal of Jahar, and there I can coach you in the customs and manners of the empire of Tul Axtar so that in a short time you may enter it with some reasonably slight assurance that you may deceive them as to your identity. To enter without proper preparation would be fatal."

I saw the wisdom of her counsel, and accordingly we altered our course so as to pass south of Jahar, as we headed straight towards Tjanath, six thousand haads away.

All the balance of the night we travelled steadily at the rate of about six hundred haads per zode—a slow speed when compared with that of the good one-man flier that I had brought out of Helium.

As the sun rose, the first thing that attracted my particular attention was the ghastly blue colour of the flier.

"What a colour for a flier!" I exclaimed.

Tavia looked up at me. "There is an excellent reason for it though," she said; "a reason that you must fully understand before you enter Jahar."

CHAPTER V

TO THE PITS

BELOW US, IN the ever-changing light of the two moons, stretched the weird landscape of a Barsoomian night as our little craft, sorely overloaded, winged slowly away from Xanator above the low hills that mark the south-western boundary of the fierce green hordes of Torquas. With the coming of the new day we discussed the advisability of making a landing and waiting until night before proceeding upon our journey, since we realized that should we be sighted by an enemy craft we could not possibly hope to escape.

"Few fliers pass this way," said Tavia, "and if we keep a sharp look-out I believe that we shall be as safe in the air as on the ground, for although we have passed beyond the limits of Torquas, there would still be danger from their raiding parties, which often go far afield."

And so we proceeded slowly in the direction of Tjanath, our eyes constantly scanning the heavens in all directions.

The monotony of the landscape, combined with our slow rate of progress, would ordinarily have rendered such a journey unendurable to me, but to my surprise the time passed quickly, a fact which I attributed solely to the wit and intelligence of my companion, for there was no gainsaying the fact that Tavia was excellent company. I think that we must have talked about everything upon Barsoom, and naturally a great deal of the conversation revolved about our own experiences and personalities, so that long before we reached Tjanath I felt that I knew Tavia better than I had ever known any other woman, and I was quite sure that I had never confided so completely in any other person.

Tavia had a way with her that seemed to compel confidences, so that, to my own surprise, I found myself discussing the most intimate details of my past life, my hopes, ambitions and aspirations, as well as the fears and doubts which, I presume, assail the minds of all young men.

When I realized how fully I had unbosomed myself to this little slave girl, I experienced a distinct shock of embarrassment, but the sincerity of Tavia's interest dispelled this feeling, as did the realization that she had been almost equally as free with her confidences as had I.

We were two nights and a day covering the distance between Xanator and Tjanath, and as the towers and landing stages of our destination appeared upon the distant horizon towards the end of the first zode of the second day, I realized that the hours that stretched away behind us to Xanator were, for some unaccountable reason, as happy a period as I had ever experienced.

Now it was over. Tjanath lay before us, and with the realization I experienced a distinct regret that Tjanath did not lie upon the opposite side of Barsoom.

With the exception of Sanoma Tora, I had never been particularly keen to be much in the company of women. I do not mean to convey the impression that I did not like them, for that would not be true. Their occasional company offered a diversion, which I enjoyed and of which I took advantage, but that I could be for so many hours in the exclusive company of a woman I did not love and thoroughly enjoy every minute of it would have seemed to me quite impossible; yet such had been the fact, and I found myself wondering if Tavia had shared my enjoyment of the adventure.

"That must be Tjanath," I said, nodding in the direction of the distant city.

"Yes," she replied.

"You must be glad that the journey is over," I ventured.

She looked up at me quickly, her brows contracting suddenly in conjecture. "Perhaps I should be," she replied enigmatically.

"It is your home," I reminded her.

"I have no home," she replied.

"But your friends are here," I insisted.

"I have no friends," she said.

"You forget Hadron of Hastor," I reminded her.

"No," she said, "I do not forget that you have been kind to me, but I remember that I am only an incident in your search for Sanoma Tora. Tomorrow, perhaps, you will be gone and we shall never see each other again."

I had not thought of that and I found that I did not like to think about it, and yet I knew that it was true. "You will soon make friends here," I said.

"I hope so," she replied; "but I have been gone a very long time and I was so young when I was taken away that I have but the faintest of memories of my life in Tjanath. Tjanath really means nothing to me. I could be so happy anywhere else in Barsoom with—with a friend."

We were now close above the outer wall of the city, and our conversation was interrupted by the appearance of a flier, evidently a patrol, bearing down upon us. She was sounding an alarm—the shrill screaming of her horn shattering the silence of the early morning. Almost immediately the warning was taken up by gongs and shrieking sirens throughout the city. The patrol boat changed her course and rose swiftly above us, while from landing-stages all about rose scores of fighting planes until we were entirely surrounded.

I tried to hail the nearer of them, but the infernal din of the warning signals drowned my voice. Hundreds of guns covered us, their crews standing ready to hurl destruction upon us.

"Does Tjanath always receive visitors in this hostile manner?" I inquired of Tavia.

She shook her head. "I do not know," she replied.
"Had we approached in a strange ship of war, I might
understand it; but why this little scout flier would attract half the navy of Tjanath is——Wait!" she exclaimed suddenly. "The design and colour of our flier
mark its origin as Jahar. The people of Tjanath have
seen this colour before and they fear it; yet if that is
true, why it it that they have not fired upon us?"

"I do not know why they did not fire upon us at
first," I replied, "but it is obvious why they do not
now. Their ships are so thick about us that they could
not fire without endangering their own craft and men."

"Can't you make them understand that we are
friends?"

Immediately I made the sign of friendship and of
surrender, but the ships seemed afraid to approach.
The alarms had ceased and the ships were circling
silently about us.

Again I hailed a near-by ship. "Do not fire," I
shouted; "we are friends."

"Friends do not come to Tjanath in the blue death
ships of Jahar," replied an officer upon the deck of
the ship I had hailed.

"Let us come alongside," I insisted, "and at least I
can prove to you that we are harmless."

"You will not come alongside my ship," he replied.
"If you are friends you can prove it by doing as I in-
struct you."

"What are your wishes?" I asked.

"Come about and take your flier beyond the city
walls. Ground her at least a haad beyond the east gate
and then, with your companion, walk towards the
city."

"Can you promise that we will be well received?" I
asked.

"You will be questioned," he replied, "and if you
are all right, you have nothing to fear."

"Very well," I replied, " we will do as you say. Signal your other ships to make way for us," and then,
through the lane that they opened, we passed slowly

back above the walls of Tjanath and came to the ground about a haad beyond the east gate.

As we approached the city the gates swung open and a detachment of warriors marched out to meet us. It was evident that they were very suspicious and fearful of us. The padwar in charge of them ordered us to halt while those were yet fully a hundred sofads between us.

"Throw down your weapons," he commanded, "and then come forward."

"But we are not enemies," I replied. "Do not the people of Tjanath know how to receive friends?"

"Do as you are told or we will destroy you both," was his only reply.

I could not refrain a shrug of disgust as I divested myself of my weapons, while Tavia threw down the short sword that I had loaned her. Unarmed we advanced towards the warriors, but even then the padwar was not entirely satisfied, for he searched our harness carefully before he finally conducted us into the city, keeping us well surrounded by warriors.

As the east gate of Tjanath closed behind us I realized that we were prisoners rather than the guests that we had hoped to be, but Tavia tried to reassure me by insisting that when they had heard our story we would be set at liberty and accorded the hospitality that she insisted was our due.

Our guards conducted us to a building that stood upon the opposite side of the avenue, facing the east gate, and presently we found ourselves upon a broad landing-stage upon the roof of the building. Here a patrol flier awaited us and our padwar turned us over to the officer in charge, whose attitude towards us was marked by ill-concealed hatred and distrust.

As soon as we had been received on board the patrol flier rose and proceeded towards the centre of the city.

Below us lay Tjanath, giving the impression of a city that had not kept abreast of modern improvements. It was marked by signs of antiquity; the buildings reflected the architecture of the ancients and many of them were in a state of disrepair, though much of the city's ugliness was hidden or softened by the foliage of great trees and climbing vines, so that on the whole the aspect was more pleasing than otherwise. Towards the centre of the city was a large plaza, entirely surrounded by imposing public buildings, including the palace of the Jed. It was upon the roof of one of these buildings that the flier landed.

Under a strong guard we were conducted into the interior of the building, and after a brief wait were ushered into the presence of some high official. Evidently he had already been advised of the circumstances surrounding our arrival at Tjanath, for he seemed to be expecting us and was familiar with all that had transpired up to the present moment.

"What do you at Tjanath, Jaharian?" he demanded.

"I am not from Jahar," I replied. "Look at my metal."

"A warrior may change his metal," he replied, gruffly.

"This man has not changed his metal," said Tavia. "He is not from Jahar; he is from Hastor, one of the cities of Helium. I am from Jahar."

The official looked at her in surprise. "So you admit it!" he cried.

"But first I was from Tjanath," said the girl.

"What do you mean?" he demanded.

"As a little child I was stolen from Tjanath," replied Tavia. "All my life since I have been a slave in the palace of Tul Axtar, Jeddak of Jahar. Only recently I escaped in the same flier upon which we arrived at Tjanath. Near the dead city of Xanator I landed and was captured by the green men of Torquas. This warrior, who is Hadron of Hastor, rescued me from them. Together we came to Tjanath, expecting a friendly reception."

"Who are your people in Tjanath?" demanded the official.

"I do not know," replied Tavia; "I was very young.

I remember practically nothing about my life in Tjanath."

"What is your name?"

"Tavia."

The man's interest in her story, which had seemed wholly perfunctory, seemed suddenly altered and galvanized.

"You know nothing about your parents or your family?" he demanded.

"Nothing," replied Tavia.

He turned to the padwar who was in charge of our escort. "Hold them here until I return," he said, and, rising from his desk, he left the apartment.

"He seemed to recognize your name," I said to Tavia.

"How could he?" she asked.

"Possibly he knew your family," I suggested; "at least his manner suggested that we are going to be given some consideration."

"I hope so," she said.

"I feel that our troubles are about over, Tavia," I assured her, "and for your sake I shall be very happy."

"And you, I suppose," she said, "will endeavour to enlist aid in continuing your search for Sanoma Tora?"

"Naturally," I replied. "Could anything less be expected of me,"

"No," she admitted in a very low voice.

Notwithstanding the fact that something in the demeanour of the official who had interrogated us had raised my hope for our future, I was still conscious of a feeling of depression as our conversation emphasized the near approach of our separation. It seemed as though I had always known Tavia, for the few days that we had been thrown together had brought us very close indeed. I knew that I should miss her sparkling wit, her ready sympathy and the quiet companionship of her silences, and then the beautiful features of Sanoma Tora were projected upon memory's screen and, knowing where my duty lay, I cast vain regrets aside, for love, I knew, was greater than friendship, and I loved Sanoma Tora.

After a considerable lapse of time the official re-entered the apartment. I searched his face to read the first tidings of good news there, but his expression was inscrutable; however, his first words, addressed to the padwar, were entirely understandable.

"Confine the woman in the East Tower," he said, "and send the man to the pits."

That was all. It was like a blow in the face. I looked at Tavia and saw her wide eyes upon the official. "You mean that we are to be held as prisoners?" she demanded; "I, a daughter of Tjanath, and this warrior who came here from a friendly nation seeking your aid and protection?"

"You will each have a hearing later before the Jed," snapped the official. "I have spoken. Take them away."

Several of the warriors seized me rather roughly by the arms. Tavia had turned away from the official and was looking at me. "Good-bye, Hadron of Hastor!" she said. "It is my fault that you are here. May my ancestors forgive me!"

"Do not reproach yourself, Tavia," I begged her, "for who might have foreseen such a stupid reception?"

We were taken from the apartment by different doorways, and there we turned, each for a last look at the other, and in Tavia's eyes there were tears, and in my heart.

The pits of Tjanath, to which I was immediately conducted, are gloomy, but they are not enveloped in impenetrable darkness as are the pits beneath most Barsoomian cities. Into the dungeon dim light filtered through the iron grating from the corridors, where ancient radium bulbs glowed faintly. Yet it was light, and I gave thanks for that, for I have always believed that I should go mad imprisoned in utter darkness.

I was heavily fettered, and unnecessarily so, it seemed to me, as they chained me to a massive iron ring set deep in the masonry wall of my dungeon, and then, leaving me, locked also the ponderous iron grating before the doorway.

As the footfalls of the warriors diminished to nothingness in the distance I heard the faint sound of something moving near by me in my dungeon. What could it be? I strained my eyes into the gloomy darkness.

Presently, as my eyes became more accustomed to the dim light in my cell, I saw the figure of what appered to be a man crouching against the wall near me. Again I heard a sound as he moved, and this time it was accompanied by the rattle of a chain, and then I saw a face turn towards me, but I could not distinguish the features.

"Another guest to share the hospitality of Tjanath," said a voice that came from the blurred figure beside me. It was a clear voice—the voice of a man—and there was a quality to its timbre that I liked.

"Do our hosts entertain many such as we?" I asked.

"In this cell there was but one," he replied; "now there are two. Are you from Tjanath or elsewhere?"

"I am from Hastor, city of the Empire of Tardos Mors, Jeddak of Helium."

"You are a long way from home," he said.

"Yes," I replied; "and you?"

"I am from Jahar," he answered. "My name is Nur An."

"And mine is Hadron," I said. "Why are you here?"

"I am a prisoner because I am from Jahar," he replied. "What is your crime?"

"It is that they think I am from Jahar," I told him.

"What made them think that? Do you wear the metal of Jahar?

"No, I wear the metal of Helium, but I chanced to come to Tjanath in a Jaharian flier."

He whistled. "That would be hard to explain," he said.

"I found it so," I admitted. "They would not believe a word of my story, nor of that of my companion."

"You had a companion, then?" he asked. "Where is he?"

"It was a woman. She was born in Tjanath, but for long years had been a slave in Jahar. Perhaps later they will believe her story, but for the present we are in prison. I heard them order her to the East Tower, while they sent me here to the prison."

"And here you will stay until you rot, unless you are lucky enough to be called for the games, or unlucky enough to be sentenced to The Death."

"What is The Death?" I asked, my curiosity piqued by his emphasis of the words.

"I do not know," he replied. "The warriors who come here often speak of it as though it was something quite horrible. Perhaps they do it to frighten me, but if that is true, then they have had very little satisfaction, for, whether or not I have been frightened, I have not let them see it."

"Let us hope for the games, then," I said.

"They are dull and stupid people here in Tjanath," said my companion. "The warriors have told me that sometimes many years elapse between games in the arena, but we may hope at least, for surely it would be better to die there with a good long sword in one's hand rather than to rot here in the darkness, or die The Death, whatever it may be."

"You are right," I said. "Let us beseech our ancestors that the Jed of Tjanath decrees games in the near future."

"So you are from Hastor," he said, musingly, after a moment's silence. "That is a long way from Tjanath. Pressing must have been the service that brought you so far afield!"

"I was searching for Jahar," I replied.

"Perhaps you are as well off that you found Tjanath first," he said, "for, though I am a Jaharian, I cannot boast the hospitality of Jahar."

"You think I would not have been accorded a cordial welcome there, then?" I asked.

"By my first ancestor, no," he exclaimed most emphatically. "Tul Axtar would have had you in the pits before he asked your name, and the pits of Jahar are not as light nor as pleasant as these."

"I did not intend that Tul Axtar should know that I was visiting him," I said.

"You are a spy?" he asked.

"No," I replied. "The daughter of the commander of the umak to which I was attached was abducted by Jaharians, and, I have reason to believe, by the orders of Tul Axtar himself. To effect her rescue was the object of my journey."

"You tell this to a Jaharian?" he asked lightly.

"With perfect impunity," I replied. "In the first place, I have read in your words and your tone that you are no friend to Tul Axtar, Jeddak of Jahar, and, secondly, there is evidently little chance that you ever will return to Jahar."

"You are right in both conjectures," he said. "I most assuredly have no love for Tul Axtar. He is a beast, hated by all decent men. The cause of my hatred for him so closely parallels your own reason to hate Tul Axtar that we are indeed bound by a common tie."

"How is that?" I demanded.

"All my life I have never felt aught but contempt for Tul Axtar, Jeddak of Johar, but this contempt was not transmuted into hatred until he stole a woman, and it was the stealing of a woman, also, that directed your venom against him."

"A woman of your family?" I asked.

"My sweetheart, the woman I was to marry," replied Nur An. "I am a noble. My family is of ancient lineage and great wealth. For these reasons Tul Axtar knew that he had good cause to fear me, and, urged on by this fear, he confiscated my property and sentenced me to death, but I have many friends in Jahar and one of these, a common warrior of the guard, connived at my escape after I had been imprisoned in the pits.

"I made my way to Tjanath and told my story to Haj Osis, the Jed, and, laying my sword at his feet, I offered him my services, but Haj Osis is a suspicious old fool and saw in me only a spy from Jahar. He ordered me to the pits, and here I have lain for a long time."

"Jahar must be, indeed, an unhappy country," I said, "ruled over, as she is, by such a man as Tul Axtar. Recently I have heard much of him, but as yet I have not heard him credited with a single virtue."

"He has none," said Nur An. "He is a cruel tyrant, rotten with corruption and vice. If any of the great powers of Barsoom could have guessed what was in his mind, Jahar would have been reduced long ago and Tul Axtar destroyed."

"What do you mean?" I asked.

"For at least two hundred years Tul Axtar has fostered a magnificent dream, the conquest of all Barsoom. During all this time he has made manpower his fetish; no eggs might be destroyed, each woman being compelled to preserve all that she laid. (*Note: Martians are oviparous.*) An army of officials and inspectors took a record of the production of each female. Those that had the greatest number of males were rewarded; the unproductive were destroyed. When it was discovered that marriage tended to reduce the productivity of the females of Jahar, marriage among any classes beneath the nobility was proscribed by imperial edict.

"The result has been an appalling increase in population, until many of the provinces of Jahar cannot support the incalculable numbers that swarm like ants in a hill. The richest agricultural land upon Barsoom could not support such numbers; every natural resource has been exhausted; millions are starving, and in large districts cannibalism is prevalent.

"During all this time Tul Axtar's officers have been training the males for war. From earliest consciousness the thought of war has been implanted within their minds. To war and to war alone do they look for relief from the hideous conditions which oppress them, until to-day countless millions are clamouring for war, realizing that victory means loot, and that loot means food and riches. Already Tul Axtar commands an army of such vast proportions that the fate of Barsoom might readily lie in the palm of his hand were it not for but a single obstacle."

"And what is that?" I asked.

"Tul Axtar is a coward," replied Nur An. "Having fulfilled his dream of man-power, he is afraid to use it lest by some accident of fate his military plans should fail and his troops meet defeat. Therefore he has waited while he urged on the scientists of Jahar to produce some weapon that would be so far superior in its destructive power to anything possessed by any other nation of Barsoom that his armies would be invincible.

"For years the best minds of Jahar laboured with the problem until at last one of our most eminent scientists, an old man named Phor Tak, developed a rifle of amazing properties. The success of Phor Tak aroused the jealousies of other scientists, and though the old man had given Tul Axtar what he sought, yet the tyrant showed no gratitude, and Phor Tak was subjected to such indignities and oppressions that eventually he fled from Jahar.

"That, however, is of no import; all that Phor Tak could do for Tul Axtar he had done, and with the new rifle in his possession, the Jeddak was glad to be rid of the old scientist."

Naturally I was much interested in the rifle which Nur An had mentioned, and I hoped that he would go into a further and more detailed description of it, but I dared not suggest that for fear that the natural loyalty which every man feels for the country of his birth might restrain him from divulging her military secrets to a stranger. I was to learn, however, that those lofty sentiments of patriotism, which are a part of every man of Helium, were induced as much by the love and respect in which we held our great jeddaks as by our natural attachment to the land of our birth; while, upon the other hand, the Jaharians looked only

with contempt and loathing upon the head of their
state, and feeling no loyalty for him, who was in
effect the state, they looked upon patriotism as nothing more than an empty catchword, which an unworthy master had used to his own end until it had
become meaningless, and so, while at the moment I
was surprised, I later came to understand why it was
that Nur An voluntarily explained in detail to me all
that he knew about the strange new weapon of Jahar
and the means of defence against it.

"This new rifle," he continued after a moment's
silence, "would render all the other armies and navies
of Barsoom impotent before us. It projects an invisible
ray, the vibrations of which effect such a change in the
constitution of metals as to cause them to disintegrate.
I am not a scientist; I do not fully understand the
exact explanation of the phenomenon, but from what
I was able to gather while the new weapon was being
discussed in Jahar, I am under the impression that
these rays change the polarity of the protons in metallic substances, releasing the whole mass as free
electrons. I have also heard the theory expounded that
Phor Tak, in his investigation, discovered that the
fundamental principles underlying time, matter and
space are identical, and that what the rays projected
from his rifle really accomplish is to translate any
mass of metal upon which it is directed into the most
elementary constituents of space.

"But be that as it may, Tul Axtar had the man-
power and the weapon, yet still he hesitated. He was
afraid, and he sought for some excuse further to delay
the war of conquest and loot which his millions of
subjects now demanded, and to this end he hit upon
the plan of insisting upon some medium of defence
against this new rifle, basing his demands upon the
possibility that some other power might also have
discovered a similar weapon or would eventually, by
the use of spies or informers, learn the secret from
Jahar. Probably greatly to his surprise, and unquestionably to his embarrassment, a man who had been

an assistant in Phor Tak's laboratory presently developed a substance which dissipated the rays of the new weapon, rendering them harmless. With this substance, which is of a bluish colour, the metal portions of the ships, weapons and harness of Jahar are now painted.

"But yet again Tul Axtar postponed his war, insisting upon the production of an enormous quantity of the new rifles and a mighty fleet of warships upon which to mount them. Then, he says, he will sail forth and conquer all Barsoom."

The destruction of the patrol boat above Helium the night of the abduction of Sanoma Tora was now quite clear to me, and when Nur An told me later that Tul Axtar had sent experimental fliers to attack Tjanath, I understood why it was that the blue flier in which Tavia and I had arrived had caused such consternation, but the thought that upset my mind now almost to the exclusion of the plight of Sanoma Tora was that somewhere in the thin air of dying Barsoom a great Heliumetic fleet was moving to attack Jahar, or at least that was what I supposed, since I had no reason to doubt that the message that I had given to the major-domo of Tor Hatan's palace had not been delivered to the Warlord. To lie here enchained in the pits of Tjanath while the great fleet of Helium sped to its destruction, filled me with horror. With my own eyes had I seen the effects of this terrible new weapon, and I knew that it was no idle dream upon the part of Nur An when he had stated that with it Tul Atar could conquer a world; but there was a defence against it. If I could but regain my freedom, I might not only warn the ships of Helium and save them from inevitable doom, but also, in connection with my quest for Sanoma Tora in the city of Jahar, I might discover the secret of the defence against the weapon which the Jaharians had evolved.

Freedom! Before it had only seemed the most desirable thing in the world; now it had become imperative.

CHAPTER VI

SENTENCED TO DIE

I WAS NOT LONG in the pits of Tjanath before warriors came and, removing my fetters, led me from my dungeon. There were only two of them, and I could not but note their carelessness and the laxness of their discipline as they escorted me to an upper level of the palace, but at the time I thought it meant only that the attitude of the officials had altered and that I was to be free.

There was nothing remarkable about the palace of the Jed of Tjanath. It was a poor place by comparison with the palaces of some of the great nobles of Helium, yet never before, I imagined, had I challenged with greater interest every detail of architecture, every corridor and doorway, or the manners, harness and decorations of the people that passed us, for, though in my heart was the hope that I was about to be free, yet I considered this place my prison and these people my jailers, and, as my one object in life was to escape, I was determined to let no detail elude my eye that might possibly in any way aid me if the time should come when I must make a break for liberty.

It was such thoughts that were uppermost in my mind as I was ushered through wide portals into the presence of a bejewelled warrior. As my eyes first alighted upon him I knew at once that I was in the presence of Haj Osis, Jed of Tjanath.

As my guard halted me before him, the Jed scrutinized me intently with that air of suspicion which is his most marked characteristic.

"Your name and country?" he demanded.

"I am Hadron of Hastor, padwar in the navy of Helium," I replied.

"You are from Jahar," he accused. "You came here from Jahar with a woman of Jahar in a flier of Jahar. Can you deny it?"

I told Haj Osis in detail everything that had led up to my arrival at Tjanath. I told him Tavia's story as well, and I must at least credit him with listening to me with patience, though I was constantly impressed by a feeling that my appeal was being directed at a mind already so prejudiced against me that nothing that I might say could alter its convictions.

The chiefs and courtiers that surrounded the Jed evinced open scepticism in their manner, until I became convinced that fear of Tul Axtar so obsessed them that they were unable to consider intelligently any matter connected with the activities of the Jeddak of Jahar. Terror made them suspicious, and suspicion sees everything through distorted lenses.

When I had finished my story, Haj Osis ordered me to be removed from the room, and I was held in a small antechamber for some time while, I imagined, he discussed my case with his advisers.

When I was again ushered into his presence I felt that the whole atmosphere of the chamber was charged with antagonism, as for the second time I was halted before the dais upon which the Jed sat in his carved throne-chair.

"The laws of Tjanath are just," proclaimed Haj Osis, glaring at me, "and the Jed of Tjanath is merciful. The enemies of Tjanath shall receive justice, but they may not expect mercy. You, who call yourself Hadron of Hastor, have been adjudged a spy of our most malignant enemy, Tul Axtar of Jahar, and as such I, Haj Osis, Jed of Tjanath, sentence you to die The Death. I have spoken." With an imperious gesture he signalled the guards to remove me.

There was no appeal. My doom was sealed, and in silence I turned and left the chamber, escorted by a guard of warriors, but for the honour of Helium I may say that my step was firm and my chin high.

On my return to the pits I questioned the padwar in charge of my escort relative to Tavia, but if the fellow knew aught of her, he refused to divulge it to me, and presently I found myself again fettered in the gloomy dungeon by the side of Nur An of Jahar.

"Well?" he asked.

"The Death," I replied.

He extended a manacled hand through the darkness and placed it upon one of mine. "I am sorry, my friend," he said.

"Man has but one life," I replied; "if he is permitted to give it in a good cause, he should not complain."

"You die for a woman," he said.

"I die for a woman of Helium," I corrected.

"Perhaps we shall die together," he said.

"What do you mean?"

"While you were gone a messenger came from the major-domo of the palace advising me to make peace with my ancestors as I should die The Death in a short time."

"I wonder what The Death is like," I said.

"I do not know," replied Nur An, "but from the awe-hushed tones in which they mention it, I imagine that it must be very terrible."

"Torture, do you imagine?" I asked.

"Perhaps," he replied.

"They will find that the men of Helium, who know so well how to live, know also how to die," I said.

"I shall hope to render a good account of myself also," said Nur An. "I shall not give them the satisfaction of knowing that I suffer. Still, I wish I might know beforehand what it is like that I might better be prepared to meet it."

"Let us not depress our thoughts by dwelling upon it," I suggested. "Let us rather take the part of men and consider only plans for thwarting our enemies and effecting our escape."

"I am afraid that is hopeless," he said.

"I may answer that," I said, "in the famous words of John Carter: 'I still live!'"

"The blind philosophy of absolute courage," he said admiringly, "but yet futile."

"It served him well many a time," I insisted, "for it gave him the will to attempt the impossible and to succeed. We still live, Nur An; do not forget that—we still live!"

"Make the best of it while you can," said a gruff voice from the corridor, "for it will not long be true."

The speaker entered our dungeon—a warrier of the guard—and with him was a single companion. I wondered how much of our conversation they had overheard, but I was soon reassured, for the very next words of the warrior who had first spoken revealed the fact that they had heard nothing but my assertion that we still lived.

"What did you mean by that," he asked; "'remember, Nur An, we still live'?"

I pretended not to hear his question and he did not repeat it, but came directly to me and unlocked my fetters. As he turned to unlock those which held Nur An, he turned his back to me and I could not but note his inexcusable carelessness. His companion lolled at the doorway while the first warrior bent over the padlock that held the fetters of Nur An.

My ancestors were kind to me; little had I expected such an opportunity as this, yet I waited—like a great banth ready to spring I waited until he should have released Nur An, and then, as the fetters fell away from my companion, I flung myself upon the back of the warrior. He sprawled forward upon his face on the stone flagging, falling heavily beneath my weight, and as he did so I snatched his dagger from its sheath and plunged it between his shoulder-blades. With a single cry he died, but I had no fear that the echo of that cry would carry upward out of the gloomy pits of Tjanath to warn his fellows upon the level above.

But the fellow's companion had seen and heard and

with a bound he was across the dungeon, his long sword ready in his hand, and now I was to see the mettle of which Nur An was made.

The affair had occurred so quickly, like a bolt of lightning out of a clear sky, that any man might have been excused had he been momentarily stunned into inactivity by the momentousness of my act, but Nur An was guilty of no fatal delay. As though we had planned the thing together, it seemed that he leaped forward the instant that I sprang for the warrior and ran to meet his companion. Barehanded he faced the long sword of his antagonist.

The gloom of the dungeon reduced the advantage of the armed man. He saw a figure leaping to meet his attack, and in the excitement of the moment and in the dark of the cell he did not know that Nur An was unarmed. He hesitated, paused and stepped back to receive the impetuous attack coming out of the darkness, and in that instant I had whipped the long sword of the fallen warrier from its scabbard and was charging the fellow at a slightly different angle from Nur An.

An instant later we were engaged, and I found the fellow no mean swordsman; yet from the instant that our blades crossed I knew that I was his master, and he must soon have realized it too, for he fell back, fully on the defensive, evidently bent upon escaping to the corridor. This, however, I was determined not to permit, and so I pressed him so closely that he dared not turn to run; nor did he call for help, and this, I guess, was because he realized the futility of so doing.

With the desperation of caged animals Nur An and I were fighting for our lives. There could be no question here of the scrupulous observance of the niceties of combat. It was his life or ours. Realizing this, Nur An snatched the short sword from the corpse of the fallen warrior and an instant later the second man was lying in a pool of his own blood.

"And now what?" asked Nur An.

"Are you familiar with the palace?" I asked.

"No," he replied.

"Then we must depend upon what little I was able to glean from my observation of it," I said. "Let us get into the harnesses of these two men at once. Perhaps they will offer a sufficient disguise to permit us to reach one of the upper levels at least, for without an intimate knowledge of the pits it is useless for us to try to seek escape below ground."

"You are right," he said, and a few moments later we emerged into the corridors, to all intents and purposes two warriors of the guard of Haj Osis, Jed of Tjanath. Believing that up to a certain point boldness of demeanour would be our best safeguard against detection, I led the way towards the ground level of the palace without attempting in any way to resort to stealth or secrecy.

"There are many warriors at the main entrance of the palace," I told Nur An, "and without knowing something of the regulations governing the coming and going of the inmates of the building it would be suicidal to attempt to reach the avenue beyond the palace by that route."

"What do you suggest then?" he asked.

"The ground level of the palace is a busy place, people are coming and going constantly through the corridors. Doubtless some of the upper levels are less frequented. Let us therefore seek a hiding-place higher up, and from the vantage point of some balcony we may be able to work out a feasible plan of escape."

"Good!" he said. "Lead on!"

Ascending the winding ramp from the lower pits, we passed two levels before we reached the ground level of the palace, without meeting a single person, but the instant that we emerged upon the ground level we saw people everywhere: officers, courtiers, warriors, slaves and merchants moved to and fro upon their various duties or in pursuit of the business that had brought them to the palace, but their very numbers proved a safeguard for us.

Upon the side of the corridor opposite from the

point at which we entered it lay an arched entrance to another ramp running upward. Without an instant's hesitation I crossed through the throng of people, and, with Nur An at my side, passed beneath the arch and entered the ascending ramp.

Scarcely had we started upward when we met a young officer descending. He accorded us scarcely a glance as we passed, and I breathed more easily as I realized that our disguises did, in fact, disguise us.

There were fewer people on the second level of the palace, but yet far too many to suit me, and so we continued on upward to the third level, the corridors of which we found almost deserted.

Near the mouth of the ramp lay the intersection of two main corridors. Here we hesitated for an instant to reconnoitre. There were people approaching from both directions along the corridor into which we had emerged, but in one direction the transverse corridor seemed deserted and we quickly entered it. It was a very long corridor, apparently extending the full length of the palace. It was flanked at intervals upon both sides by doorways, the doors to some of which were open, while others were closed or ajar. Through some of the open doorways we saw people, while the apartments revealed through others appeared vacant. The location of these we noted carefully as we moved slowly along, carefully observing every detail that might later prove of value to us.

We had traversed about two-thirds of this long corridor when a man stepped into it from a doorway a couple of hundred feet ahead of us. He was an officer, apparently a padwar of the guard. He halted in the middle of the corridor as a file of warriors emerged from the same doorway, and, forming in a column of twos, marched in our direction, the officer bringing up the rear.

Here was a test for our disguises that I did not care to risk. There was an open doorway at our left; beyond it I could see no one. "Come!" I said to Nur An, and without accelerating our speed we walked nonchalantly into the chamber, and as Nur An crossed the threshold, I closed the door behind him, and as I did so I saw a young woman standing at the opposite side of the apartment looking squarely at us.

"What do you here, warriors?" she demanded.

Here, indeed, was an embarrassing situation. In the corridor without I could hear the clank of the accoutrements of the approaching warriors, and I knew that the girl must hear it too. If I did aught to arouse her suspicion, she had but to call for help. And how might I allay her suspicion when I had not the faintest conception of what might pass for a valid excuse for the presence of two warriors in this particular apartment, which for all I knew might be the apartment of a princess of the royal house, to enter which without permission might easily mean death to a common warrior? I thought quickly, or perhaps I did not think at all; often we act rightly upon impulse and then credit the result to superintelligence.

"We have come for the girl," I stated brusquely. "Where is she?"

"What girl?" demanded the young woman in surprise.

"The prisoner, of course," I replied.

"The prisoner?" She looked more puzzled than before.

"Of course," said Nur An, "the prisoner. Where is she?" and I almost smiled, for I knew that Nur An had not the faintest idea of what was in my mind.

"There is no prisoner here," said the young woman. "These are the apartments of the infant son of Haj Osis."

"The fool misdirected us," I said. "We are sorry that we intruded. We were sent to fetch the girl Tavia, who is a prisoner in the palace."

It was only a guess. I did not know that Tavia was a prisoner, but after the treatment that had been accorded me I surmised as much.

"She is not here," said the young woman, "and as for you, you had better leave these apartments at once, for if you are discovered here it will go ill with you."

Nur An, who was standing beside me, had been looking at the young woman intently. He stepped forward now, closer to her.

"By my first ancestor," he exclaimed in a low voice, "it is Phao!"

The girl stepped back, her eyes wide with surprise, and then slowly recognition dawned within them. "Nur An!" she exclaimed.

Nur An came close to the girl and took her hand in his. "All these years, Phao, I have thought that you were dead," he said. "When the ship returned the captain reported that you and a number of others were killed."

"He lied," said the girl. "He sold us into slavery here in Tjanath; but you, Nur An, what are you doing here in the harness of Tjanath?"

"I am a prisoner," replied my companion, "as is this warrior also. We have been confined in the pits beneath the palace and to-day we were to have died The Death, but we killed the two warriors who were sent to fetch us and now we are trying to find our way out of the palace."

"Then you are not looking for the girl Tavia?" she asked.

"Yes," I said, "we are looking for her too. She was made a prisoner at the same time that I was."

"Perhaps I can help you," said Phao; "perhaps," she added wistfully, "we may all escape together."

"I shall not escape without you, Phao," said Nur An.

"My ancestors have been good to me at last," said the girl.

"Where is Tavia?" I asked.

"She is in the East Tower," replied Phao.

"Can you lead us there, or tell us how we may reach it?" I asked.

"It would do no good to lead you to it," she replied, "as the door is locked and guards stand before it. But there is another way."

"And that?" I asked.

"I know where the keys are," she said, "and I know other things that will prove helpful."

"May our ancestors protect and reward you, Phao," I said. "And now tell me where I may find the keys."

"I shall have to lead you to the place myself," she replied, "but we shall stand a better chance to succeed if there are not too many of us. I therefore suggest that Nur An remain here. I shall place him in hiding where he will not be found. I will then lead you to the prisoner, and, if possible, we will make our way back to this apartment. I am in charge here. Only at regular hours, twice a day, night and morning, does any other visit the apartment of the little prince. Here I can hide you and feed you for a long time, and perhaps eventually we shall be able to evolve some feasible plan for escape."

"We are in your hands, Phao," said Nur An. "If there is to be fighting, though, I should like to accompany Hadron."

"If we succeed there will be no fighting," replied the girl. She stepped quickly across the room to a door, which she opened, revealing a large closet. "Here, Nur An," she said, "is where you must remain until we return. There is no reason why anyone should open this door, and in so far as I know, it never has been opened since I have occupied these quarters, except by me."

"I do not like the idea of hiding," said Nur An with a grimace, "but—I have had to do many things recently that I did not like," and without more words he crossed the apartment and entered the closet. Their eyes met for an instant before Phao closed the door, and I read in the depth of both that which made me wonder, remembering as I did the story that Nur An had told me of the other woman whom Tul Axtar had stolen from him. But such matters were no concern of mine, nor had they any bearing upon the business at hand.

"Here is my plan, warrior," said Phao as she returned to my side. "When you entered this apartment you came saying that you were looking for the prisoner Tavia. Although she was not here, I believed you. We will go, therefore, to Yo Seno, the keeper of the keys, and you will tell him the same story, that you have been sent to fetch the prisoner Tavia. If Yo Seno believes you, all will be well, for he will go himself and release the prisoner, turning her over to you."

"And if he does not believe me?" I asked.

"He is a beast," she said, "who is better dead than alive. Therefore you will know what to do."

"I understand," I said. "Lead the way."

The office of Yo Seno, the keeper of the keys, was upon the fourth level of the palace, almost directly above the quarters of the infant prince. At the doorway Phao halted, and drawing my ear down to her lips, whispered her final instructions. "I shall enter first," she said, "upon some trivial errand. A moment later you may enter, but pay no attention to me. It must not appear that we have come together."

"I understand," I said, and walked a few paces along the corridor so that I should not be in sight when the door opened. She told me afterwards that she asked Yo Seno to have a new key made for one of the numerous doors in the apartment of the little prince.

I waited but a moment, and then I too entered the apartment. It was a gloomy room without windows. Upon its walls hung keys of every imaginable size and shape. Behind a large desk sat a coarse-looking man, who looked up quickly and scowled at the interruption as I entered.

"Well?" he demanded.

"I have come for the woman Tavia," I said, "the prisoner from Jahar."

"Who sent you? What do you want of her?" he demanded.

"I have orders to bring her to Haj Osis," I replied.

He looked at me suspiciously. "You bring a written order?" he asked.

"Of course not," I replied, "it is not necessary. She

is not to be taken out of the palace; merely from one apartment to another."

"I must have a written order," he snapped.

"Haj Osis will not be pleased," I said, "when he learns that you have refused to obey his command."

"I am not refusing," said Yo Seno. "Do not dare to say that I refuse. I cannot turn a prisoner over without a written order. Show me your authority and I will give you the keys."

I saw that the plan had failed; other measures must be taken. I whipped out my long sword. "Here is my authority!" I exclaimed, leaping towards him.

With an oath he drew his own sword, but instead of facing me with it he stepped quickly back, the desk still between us, and, turning, struck a copper gong heavily with the flat of his blade.

As I rushed towards him I heard the sound of hurrying feet and the clank of metal from an adjoining room. Yo Seno, still backing away, sneered sardonically, and then the lights went out and the windowless room was plunged into darkness. Soft fingers grasped my left hand and a low voice whispered in my ear, "Come with me."

Quickly I was drawn to one side and through a narrow aperture just as a door upon the opposite side of the chamber was flung open, revealing the forms of half a dozen warriors silhouetted against the light from the room behind them. Then the door closed directly in front of my face and I was again in utter darkness, but Phao's fingers still grasped my hand.

"Silence!" a soft voice whispered.

From beyond the panels I heard angry and excited voices. Above the others one voice rose in tones of authority. "What is wrong here?"

There were muttered exclamations and curses as men bumped against pieces of furniture and ran into one another.

"Give us a light," cried a voice, and a moment later, "That is better."

"Where is Yo Seno? Oh, there you are, you fat rascal. What is amiss?"

"By Issus! he is gone." The voice was that of Yo Seno.

"Who is gone?" demanded the other voice. "Why did you summon us?"

"I was attacked by a warrior," explained Yo Seno, "who came demanding the key to the apartment where Haj Osis keeps the daughter of——" I could not hear the rest of the sentence.

"Well, where is the man?" demanded the other.

"He is gone—and the key too. The key is gone." Yo Seno's voice rose almost to a wail.

"Quick, then, to the apartment where the girl is kept," cried the first speaker, doubtless the officer of the guard, and almost at once I heard them hasten from the apartment.

The girl at my side moved a little and I heard a low laugh. "They will not find the key," she said.

"Why?" I asked.

"Because I have it," she replied.

"Little good it will do us," I said ruefully. "They will keep the door well guarded now and we cannot use the key.

Phao laughed again. "We do not need the key," she said. "I took it to throw them off the track. They will watch the door while we enter elsewhere."

"I do not understand," I said.

"This corridor leads between the partitions to the room where the prisoner is kept. I know that because, when I was a prisoner in that room, Yo Seno came thus to visit me. He is a beast. I hope he has not visited this girl—I hope it for your sake, if you love her."

"I do not love her," I said. "She is only a friend." But I scarcely knew what I was saying, the words seemed to come mechanically, for I was in the grip of such an emotion as I never before had experienced or endured. It had seized me the instant that Phao had suggested that Yo Seno might have visited Tavia through this secret corriedor. I experienced a sensation that was almost akin to a convulsion—a sensation that left me a changed man. Before, I could have killed Yo Seno with my sword and been glad; now I wanted to tear him to pieces; I wanted to mutilate him and make him suffer. Never before in my life had I experienced such a bestial desire. It was hideous, and yet I gloated in its possession.

"What is the matter?" exclaimed Phao. "I thought I felt you tremble then."

"I trembled," I said.

"For what?" she asked.

"For Yo Seno," I replied; "but let us hasten. If this corridor leads to the apartment where Tavia is in prison, I cannot reach her too soon, for when Haj Osis learns that the key has been stolen he will have her removed to another prison."

"He will not learn it if Yo Seno and the padwar of the guard can prevent," said Phao, "for if this reached the ears of Haj Osis it might easily cost them both their lives. They will wait for you to come that they may kill you and get the key, but they will wait outside the prison door and you will not come that way."

As she spoke she started to walk along the narrow, dark corridor, leading me by the hand behind her. It was slow work, for Phao had to grope her way slowly because the corridor turned sharply at right angles as it followed the partitions of the apartments between which it passed, and there were numerous stairways that led up over doorways and finally a ladder to the level above.

Presently she halted. "We are there," she whispered, "but we must listen first to make sure that no one has entered the apartment with the prisoner."

I could see absolutely nothing in the darkness, and how Phao knew that she had reached her destination I could not guess.

"It is all right," she said presently, and simultaneously she pushed a wooden panel ajar, and in the opening I saw a portion of the interior of a circular apartment with narrow windows heavily barred. Opposite the opening, upon a pile of sleeping-silks and furs, I saw a woman reclining. Only a bare shoulder, a tiny ear and a head of tousled hair were visible. At the first glance I knew that they were Tavia's.

As we stepped into the apartment Phao closed the panel behind us. Attracted by the sound of our entrance, quietly executed though it was, Tavia sat up and looked at us and then, as she recognized me, sprang to her feet. Her eyes were wide with surprise and there was an exclamation upon her lips, which I silenced by a warning forefinger placed against my own. I crossed the apartment towards her, and she came to meet me, almost running. As I looked into her eyes I saw an expression there that I have never seen in the eyes of any other woman—at least not for me—and if I had ever doubted Tavia's friendship, such a doubt would have vanished in that instant, but I had not doubted it and I was only surprised now to realize the depth of it. Had Sanoma Tora ever looked at me like that I should have read love in the expression, but I had never spoken of love to Tavia and so I knew that it was only friendship that she felt. I had always been too much engrossed in my profession to make any close friendships, so that I had never realized until that moment what a wonderful thing friendship might be.

As we met in the centre of the room her eyes, moist with tears, were upturned to mine. "Hadron," she whispered, her voice husky with emotion, and then I put my arm about her slender shoulders and drew her to me, and something that was quite beyond my volition impelled me to kiss her upon the forehead. Instantly she disengaged herself and I feared that she had misunderstood that impulsive kiss of friendship, but the next words reassured me.

"I thought never to see you again, Hadron of Hastor," she said. "I feared that they had killed you.

How comes it that you are here and in the metal
of a warrior of Tjanath?"

I told her briefly of what had occurred to me since
we had been separated and of how I had temporarily,
at least, escaped The Death. She asked me what The
Death was, but I could not tell her.

"It is very horrible," said Phao.

"What is it?" I asked.

"I do not know," replied the girl, "only that it is
horrible. There is a deep pit, some say a bottomless
pit, beneath the lower pits of the palace; horrible
noises—groans and moans—arise perpetually from it,
and into this pit those that are to die The Death are
cast, but in such a way that the fall will not kill them.
They must reach the bottom alive to endure all the
horrors of The Death that await them there. That the
torture is almost interminable is evidenced by the fact
that the moans and groans of the victims never cease,
no matter how long a period may have elapsed between
executions."

"And you have escaped it," exclaimed Tavia. "My
prayers have been answered. For days and nights have
I been praying to my ancestors that you might be
spared. Now if you can but escape from this hateful
place! Have you a plan?"

"We have a plan that with the help of Phao here
may prove successful. Nur An, of whom I told you,
is hiding in a closet in one of the apartments of the
little prince. We shall return to that apartment at the
first opportunity, and there Phao will hide all three
of us until some opportunity for escape presents itself."

"And we should lose no more time in returning,"
said Phao. "Come, let us go at once."

As we turned towards the panel through which we
had entered I saw that it was ajar, though I was
confident that Phao had closed it after us when we
entered, and simultaneously I could have sworn that
I saw an eye glued to the narrow crack, as though
someone watched us from the dark interior of the secret
corridor.

In a single bound I was across the room and had drawn the panel aside. My sword was ready in my hand, but there was no one in the corridor beyond.

CHAPTER VII

THE DEATH

WITH PHAO IN THE LEAD and Tavia between us, we traversed the dark corridor back towards the apartment of Yo Seno. When we reached the panel marking the end of our journey, Phao halted and together we listened intently for any sound that might evidence the presence of an occupant in the room beyond. All was silent as the tomb.

"I believe," said Phao, "that it will be safer if you and Tavia remain here until night. I shall return to my apartment and go about my duties in the usual manner, and after the palace has quieted down these levels will be almost deserted; then I can come and get you with far less danger of detection than were I to take you to the apartment now."

We agreed that her plan was a good one, and bidding us a temporary farewell, she opened the panel sufficiently to permit her to survey the apartment beyond. It was quite empty. She stepped from the corridor, closing the panel behind her, and once again Tavia and I were plunged into darkness.

The long hours of our wait in the darkness of the corridor should have seemed interminable, but they did not. We made ourselves as comfortable as possible upon the floor, our backs against one of the walls, and, leaning close together so that we might converse in low whispers, we found more entertainment than I should have guessed possible, both in our conversation and in the long silences that broke it, so that it really did not seem a long time at all before the panel was swung open and we saw Phao in the subdued light of the apartment beyond. She motioned us to follow her, and in silence we obeyed. The corridor beyond the chamber of Yo Seno was deserted, as also was the ramp leading to the level below and the corridor upon which it opened. Fortune seemed to favour us at every step and there was a prayer of thanksgiving upon my lips as Phao pushed open the door leading into the apartment of the prince and motioned us to enter.

But at the same instant my heart sank within me, for, as I entered the apartment with Tavia, I saw warriors standing upon either side of the room awaiting us. With an exclamation of warning I drew Tavia behind me and backed quickly towards the door, but as I did so I heard a rush of feet and the clank of accountrements in the corridor behind me, and, casting a quick glance over my shoulder, I saw other warriors running from the doorway of an apartment upon the opposite side of the corridor.

We were surrounded. We were lost, and my first thought was that Phao had betrayed us, leading us into this trap from which there could be no escape. They hustled us back into the room and surrounded us, and for the first time I saw Yo Seno. He stood there, a sneering grin upon his face, and but for the fact that Tavia had assured me that he had not harmed her I should have leaped upon him there, though a dozen swords had been at my vitals the next instant.

"So!" sneered Yo Seno. "You thought to fool me, did you? Well, I am not so easily fooled. I guessed the truth and I followed you through the corridor and overheard all your plans as you discussed them with the woman Tavia. We have you all now," and turning to one of the warriors, he motioned to the closet upon the opposite side of the chamber. "Fetch the other," he commanded.

The fellow crossed to the door and, opening it,

revealed Nur An lying bound and gagged upon the floor.

"Cut his bonds and remove the gag," ordered Yo Seno. "It is too late now for him to thwart my plans by giving the others a warning."

Nur An came towards us, with a firm step, his head high and a glance of haughty contempt for our captors.

The four of us stood facing Yo Seno, the sneer upon whose face had been replaced by a glare of hatred.

"You have been sentenced to die The Death," he said. "It is the death for spies. No more terrible punishment can be inflicted. Could there be, it would be meted to you two," as he looked first at me and then at Nur An, "that you might suffer more for the murder of our two comrades."

So they had found the warriors we had dispatched. Well, what of it? Evidently it had not rendered our position any worse than it had been before. We were to die The Death, and that was the worst that they could accord us.

"Have you anything to say?" demanded Yo Seno.

"We still live!" I exclaimed, and laughed in his face.

"Before long you will be beseeching your first ancestors for death," hissed the keeper of the keys. "But you will not have death too soon, and remember that no one knows how long it takes to die The Death. We cannot add to your physical suffering, but for the torment of your mind let me remind you that we are sending you to The Death without letting you know what the fate of your accomplices will be," and he nodded towards Tavia and Phao.

That was a nice point, well chosen. He could not have hit upon any means more certain to inflict acute torture upon me than this, but I would not give him the satisfaction of witnessing my true emotion, and so, once again, I laughed in his face. His patience had about reached the limit of its endurance, for he turned abruptly to a padwar of the guard and ordered him to remove us at once.

As we were hustled from the room, Nur An called a brave good-bye to Phao.

"Good-bye, Tavia!" I cried, "and remember that we still live."

"We still live, Hadron of Hastor!" she called back. "We still live!" and then she was swept from my view as we were pushed along down the corridor.

Down ramp after ramp we were conducted to the uttermost depths of the palace pits and then into a great chamber where I saw Haj Osis sitting upon a throne, surrounded again by his chiefs and his courtiers as he had been upon the occasion that he had interviewed me. Opposite the Jed, and in the middle of the chamber, hung a great iron cage, suspended from a heavy block set in the ceiling. Into this cage we were roughly pushed; the door was closed and secured with a large lock. I wondered what it was all about and what this had to do with The Death, and while I wondered a dozen men pushed a huge trap-door from beneath the cage. A rush of cold, clammy air enveloped us and I experienced a chill that seemed to enter my marrow, as though I lay in the cold arms of death. Hollow moans and groans came faintly to my ears and I knew that we were above the pits where The Death lay.

No word was spoken within the chamber, but at a signal from Haj Osis strong men lowered the cage slowly into the aperture beneath us. Here the cold and the damp were more obvious and penetrating than before, while the ghastly sounds appeared to redouble in volume.

Down, down we slid into an abyss of darkness. The horror of the silence in the chamber above was forgotten in the horror of the pandemonium of uncanny sounds that rose from beneath.

How far we were lowered thus I may not even guess, but to Nur An it seemed at least a thousand feet, and then we commenced to detect a slight luminosity about us. The moaning and the groaning had become a constant roar. As we approached, it seemed less like moans and groans and more like the sound of wind and rushing waters.

Suddenly, without the slightest warning, the bottom of the cage, which evidently must have been hinged upon one side, and held by a catch that could be sprung from above, swung downward. It happened so quickly that we hardly had time for conjecture before we were plunged into rushing water.

As I rose to the surface I discovered that I could see. Wherever we were, it was not shrouded in impenetrable darkness, but was lighted dimly.

Almost immediately Nur An's head bobbed up at arm's length from me. A strong current was bearing us onward, and I realized at once that we were in the grip of a great underground river, one of those to which the remaining waters of dying Barsoom have receded. In the distance I descried a shore-line dimly visible in the subdued light, and, shouting to Nur An to follow me, I struck out towards it. The water was cold, but not sufficiently so to alarm me and I had no doubt but that we would reach the shore.

By the time that we had attained our goal and crawled out upon the rocky shore, our eyes had become accustomed to the dim light of the interior, and now, with astonishment, we gazed about us. What a vast cavern! Far, far above us its ceiling was discernible in the light of the minute radium particles with which the rock that formed its walls and ceiling was impregnated, but the opposite bank of the rushing torrent was beyond the range of our vision.

"So this is The Death!" exclaimed Nur An.

"I doubt if they know what it is themselves," I replied. "From the roaring of the river and the moaning of the wind, they have conjured something horrible in their own imaginations."

"Perhaps the greatest suffering that the victim must endure lies in his anticipation of what awaits him in these seemingly horrid depths," suggested Nur An, "whereas the worst that realization might bring would be death by drowning."

"Or by starvation," I suggested.

Nur An nodded. "Nevertheless," he said, "I wish I might return just long enough to mock them and witness their disappointment when they find that The Death is not so horrible after all."

"What a mighty river!" he added after a moment's silence. "Could it be a tributary of Iss?"

"Perhaps it is Iss herself," I said.

"Then we are bound upon the last long pilgrimage down to the lost sea of Korus in the valley Dor," said Nur An gloomily. "It may be a lovely place, but I do not wish to go there yet."

"It is a place of horror," I replied.

"Hush," he cautioned; "that is sacrilege."

"It is sacrilege no longer since John Carter and Tars Tarkas snatched the veil of secrecy from the valley Dor and disposed of the myth of Issus, Goddess of Life Eternal."

Even after I had told him the whole tragic story of the false gods of Mars, Nur An remained sceptical, so closely are the superstitions of religion woven into every fibre of our being.

We were both a trifle fatigued after our battle with the strong current of the river, and perhaps, too, we were suffering from reaction from the nervous shock of the ordeal through which we had passed. So we remained there, resting upon the rocky shore of the river of mystery. Eventually our conversation turned to what was uppermost in the minds of both and yet which each hesitated to mention—the fate of Tavia and Phao.

"I wish that they, too, had been sentenced to The Death," I said, "for then at least we might be with them and protect them."

"I am afraid that we shall never see them again," said Nur An gloomily. "What a cruel fate that I should have found Phao only to lose her again irretrievably so quickly!"

"It is indeed a strange trick of fate that after Tul Axtar stole her from you, that he should have lost her too, and then that you should find her in Tjanath."

He looked at me with a slightly puzzled expression for a moment and then his face cleared. "Phao is not the woman of whom I told you in the dungeon at Tjanath," he said. "Phao I loved long before; she was my first love. After I lost her I thought that I never could care for a woman again, but this other one came into my life and, knowing that Phao was gone for ever, I found some consolation in my new love, but I realize now that it was not the same, that no love could ever displace that which I felt for Phao."

"You lost her irretrievably once before," I reminded him, "but you found her again; perhaps you will find her once more."

"I wish that I might share your optimism," he said.

"We have little else to buoy us up," I reminded him.

"You are right," he said, and then with a laugh, added, "we still live!"

Presently, feeling rested, we set out along the shore in the direction that the river ran, for we had decided that that would be our course if for no other reason than that it would be easier going down hill than up. Where it would lead, we had not the slightest idea; perhaps to Korus; perhaps to Omean, the buried sea where lay the ships of the First Born.

Over tumbled rock masses we clambered and along level stretches of smooth gravel we pursued our rather aimless course, knowing not whither we were going, having no goal towards which to strive. There was some vegetation, weird and grotesque, but almost colourless for want of sunlight. There were tree-like plants with strange, angular branches that snapped off at the lightest touch, and as the trees did not look like trees, there were blossoms that did not look like flowers. It was a world as unlike the outer world as the figments of imagination are unlike realities.

But whatever musing upon the flora of this strange land I may have been indulging in was brought

to a sudden termination as we rounded the shoulder
of a jutting promontory and came face to face with
as hideous a creature as ever I had set my eyes upon.
It was a great white lizard with gaping jaws large
enough to engulf a man at a single swallow. At sight
of us it emitted an angry hiss and advanced menacingly
towards us.

Being unarmed and absolutely at the mercy of any
creature that attacked us, we pursued the only plan
that our intelligence could dictate—we retreated—and
I am not ashamed to admit that we retreated rapidly.

Running quickly around the end of the promontory,
we turned sharply up the bank away from the river.
The bottom of the cavern rose sharply, and as I
clambered upward I glanced behind me occasionally
to note the actions of our pursuer. He was now in
plain sight, having followed us around the end of the
promontory, and there he stood looking about as though
in search of us. Though we were not far from him,
he did not seem to see us, and I soon became convinced that his eyesight was faulty; but not wishing
to depend upon this I kept on climbing until presently
we came to the top of the promontory, and, looking
down upon the other side, I saw a considerable stretch
of smooth gravel, stretching out into the dim distance
along the river shore. If we could clamber down the
opposite side of the barrier and reach this level
stretch of gravel, I felt that we might escape the attentions of the huge monster. A final glance at him
showed him still standing, peering first in one direction
and then in another as though in search of us.

Nur An had followed close behind me and now
together we slipped over the edge of the escarpment,
and, though the rough rocks scratched us severely,
we finally reached the gravel below, whereupon, having
eluded our menacer, we set out upon a brisk run down
the river. We had covered scarcely more than fifty
paces when Nur An stumbled over an obstacle, and
as I stooped to give him a hand up, I saw that the
thing that had tripped him was the rotting harness

of a warrior, and a moment later I saw the hilt of a sword protruding from the gravel. Seizing it, I wrenched it from the ground. It was a good long sword, and I may tell you that the feel of it in my hand did more to restore my self-confidence than aught else that might have transpired. Being made of non-corrosive metal, as are all Barsoomian weapons, it remained as sound to-day as the moment that it had been abandoned by its owner.

"Look," said Nur An, pointing, and there at a little distance we saw another harness and another sword. This time there were two, a long sword and a short sword, and these Nur An took. No longer did we run. I have always felt that there is little upon Barsoom that two well-armed warriors need run from.

As we continued along our way across the level stretch of gravel we sought to solve the mystery of these abandoned weapons, a mystery that was still further heightened by our discovery of many more. In some cases the harness had rotted away entirely, leaving nothing but the metal parts, while in others it was comparatively sound and new. Presently we discerned a white mound ahead of us, but in the dim light of the cavern we could not at first determine of what it consisted. When we did, we were filled with horror, for the white mound was of the bones and skulls of human beings. Then, at last, I thought I had an explanation of the abandoned harness and weapons. This was the lair of the great lizard. Here he took his toll of the unhappy creatures that passed down the river; but how was it that armed men had come here? We had been cast into the cavern unarmed, as I was positive all of the condemned prisoners of Tjanath must have been. From whence came the others? I do not know, doubtless I shall never know. It was a mystery from the first. It will remain a mystery to the last.

As we passed on we found harness and weapons scattered all about, but there was infinitely more harness than weapons.

I had added a good short sword to my equipment, as well as a dagger, as had also Nur An, and I was stooping to examine another weapon which we had found—a short sword with a beautifully ornamented hilt and guard—when Nur An suddenly voiced an exclamation of warning.

"On guard," he cried, "Hadron! It comes!"

Leaping to my feet. I wheeled about, the short sword still in my hand, and there, bearing down upon us at considerable speed and with wide distended jaws, came the great white lizard, hissing ominously. He was a hideous sight, a sight such as to make even a brave man turn and run, which I am now convinced is what practically all of his victims did; but here were two who did not run. Perhaps he was so close that we realized the futility of flight without giving the matter conscious thought, but be that as it may, we stood there—Nur An with his long sword in his hand, I with the ornately carved short sword that I had been examining, though instantly I realized that it was not the weapon with which to defend myself against this great hulking brute.

Yet I could not bear to waste a weapon already in my hand, especially in view of an accomplishment of mine in which I took considerable pride.

In Helium, both officers and men often wager large amounts upon the accuracy with which they can hurl daggers and short swords, and I have seen considerable sums change hands within an hour, but so proficient was I that I had added considerably to my pay through my winning until my fame had spread to such an extent that I could find no one willing to pit his skill against mine.

Never had I hurled a weapon with a more fervent prayer for the accuracy of my throw than now as I launched the short sword swiftly at the mouth of the oncoming lizard. It was not a good throw. It would have lost me money in Helium, but in this instance, I think, it saved my life. The sword, instead of speeding in a straight line, point first, as it should have, turned slowly upward until it was travelling at an angle of about forty-five degrees, with the point forward and downward. In this position the point struck just inside of the lower jaw of the creature, while the heavy hilt, carried forward by its own momentum, lodged in the roof of the monster's mouth.

Instantly it was helpless; the point of the sword had passed through its tongue into the bony substance of its lower jaw, while the hilt was lodged in its upper jaw behind its mighty fangs. It could not dislodge the sword, either forward or backward, and for an instant it halted in hissing dismay, and simultaneously Nur An and I leaped to opposite sides of its ghastly white body. It tried to defend itself with its tail and talons, but we were too quick for it, and presently it was lying in a pool of its own purple blood in the final spasmodic muscular reaction of dissolution.

There was something peculiarly disgusting and loathsome about the purple blood of the creature, not only in its appearance, but in its odour, which was almost nauseating, and Nur An and I lost no time in quitting the scene of our victory. At the river we washed our blades and then continued on upon our fruitless quest.

As we had washed our blades we had noticed fish in the river, and after we had put sufficient distance between the lair of the lizard and ourselves, we determined to bend our energies for awhile towards filling our larder and our stomachs.

Neither of us had ever caught a fish or eaten one, but we knew from history that they could be caught and that they were edible. Being swordsmen, we naturally looked to our swords as the best means for procuring our flesh, and so we waded into the river with drawn long swords prepared to slaughter fish to our hearts' content, but wherever we went there were no fish. We could see them elsewhere, but not within reach of our swords.

"Perhaps," said Nur An, "fish are not such fools

as they appear. They may see us approaching and question our motives."

"I can readily believe that you are right," I replied. "Suppose we try strategy."

"How?" he asked.

"Come with me," I said, "and return to the bank." After a little search down stream I found a rocky ledge overhanging the river. "We will lie here at intervals," I said, "with only our eyes and the points of our swords over the edge of the bank. We must not talk or move, lest we frighten the fish. Perhaps in this way we shall procure one," for I had long since given up the idea of a general slaughter.

To my gratification my plan worked and it was not long before we each had a large fish.

Naturally, like other men, we prefer our flesh cooked, but being warriors we were accustomed to it either way, and so we broke our long fast upon raw fish from the river of mystery.

Both Nur An and I felt greatly refreshed and strengthened by our meal, however unpalatable it might have been. It had been some time since we had slept, and though we had no idea whether it was still night upon the outer surface of Barsoom, or whether dawn had already broken, we decided that it would be best for us to sleep, and so Nur An stretched out where we were while I watched. After he awoke, I took my turn. I think that neither of us slept more than a single zode, but the rest did us quite as much good as the food that we had eaten, and I am sure that I have never felt more fit than I did when we set out again upon our goalless journey.

I do not know how long we had been travelling after our sleep, for by now the journey was most monotonous, there being little change in the dimly seen landscape surrounding us and only the ceaseless roar of the river and the howling of the wind to keep us company.

Nur An was the first to discern the change; he seized my arm and pointed ahead. I must have been walking with my eyes upon the ground in front of me, else I must have seen what he saw simultaneously.

"It is daylight," I exclaimed. "It is the sun."

"It can be nothing else," he said.

There, far ahead of us, lay a great archway of light. That was all that we could see from the point at which we discovered it, but now we hastened on almost at a run, so anxious were we for a solution, so hopeful that it was indeed the sunlight and that in some inexplicable and mysterious way the river had found its way to the surface of Barsoom. I knew that this could not be true and Nur An knew it, and yet each knew how great his disappointment would be when the true explanation of the phenomenon was revealed.

When we approached the great patch of light it became more and more evident that the river had broken from its dark cavern out into the light of day, and when we reached the edge of that mighty portal we looked out upon a scene that filled our hearts with warmth and gladness, for there, stretching before us, lay a valley—a small valley it is true—a valley hemmed in, as far as we could see, by mighty cliffs, but yet a valley of life and fertility and beauty bathed in the hot light of the sun.

"It is not quite the surface of Barsoom," said Nur An, "but it is the next best thing."

"And there must be a way out," I said. "There must be. If there is not, we will make one."

"Right you are, Hadron of Hastor," he cried. "We will make a way. Come!"

Before us the banks of the roaring river were lined with lush vegetation; great trees raised their leafy branches far above the waters; the brilliant, scarlet sward was lapped by the little wavelets and everywhere bloomed gorgeous flowers and shrubs of many hues and shapes. Here was a vegetation such as I had never seen before upon the surface of Barsoom. Here were forms similar to those with which I was familiar and others totally unknown to me, yet all were lovely, though some were bizarre.

Emerging, as we had, from the dark and gloomy bowels of the earth, the scene before us presented a view of wondrous beauty, and, while doubtless enhanced by contrast, it was nevertheless such an aspect as is seldom given to the eyes of a Barsoomian of to-day to view. To me it seemed a little garden spot upon a dying world preserved from an ancient era when Barsoom was young and meteorological conditions were such as to favour the growth of vegetation that has long since become extinct over practically the entire area of the planet. In this deep valley, surrounded by lofty cliffs, the atmosphere doubtless was considerably denser than upon the surface of the planet above. The sun's rays were reflected by the lofty escarpment, which must also hold the heat during the colder periods of night, and, in addition to this, there was ample water for irrigation which nature might easily have achieved through percolation of the waters of the river through and beneath the top soil of the valley.

For several minutes Nun An and I stood spellbound by the bewitching view, and then, espying luscious fruit hanging in great clusters from some of the trees, and bushes loaded with berries, we subordinated the aesthetic to the corporeal and set forth to supplement our meal of raw fish with the exquisite offerings which hung so temptingly before us.

As we started to move through the vegetation we became aware of thin threads of a gossamer-like substance festooned from tree to tree and bush to bush. So fine as to be almost invisible, they were yet so strong as to impede our progress. It was surprisingly difficult to break them, and when there were a dozen or more at a time barring our way, we found it necessary to use our daggers to cut a way through them.

We had taken only a few steps into the deeper vegetation, cutting our way through the gossamer strands, when we were confronted by a new and surprising obstacle to our advance—a large, venomous-looking spider that scurried towards us in an inverted position, clinging with a dozen legs to one of the gossamer strands, which served both as its support and its pathway, and if its appearance was any index of its venomousness it must, indeed, have been a deadly insect.

As it came towards me, apparently with the most sinister intentions, I hastily returned my dagger to its scabbard and drew my short sword, with which I struck at the fearsome-looking creature. As the blow descended, it drew back so that my point only slightly scratched it, whereupon it opened its hideous mouth and emitted a terrific scream so out of proportion to its size and to the nature of such insects with which I was familiar that it had a most appalling effect upon my nerves. Instantly the scream was answered by an unearthly chorus of similar cries all about us, and immediately a swarm of these horrid insects came racing towards us upon their gossamer threads. Evidently this was the only position which they assumed in moving about and their webs the only means to that end, for their twelve legs grew upward from their backs, giving them a most uncanny appearance.

Fearing that the creatures might be poisonous, Nur An and I retreated hastily to the mouth of the cavern, and as the spiders could not go beyond the ends of their threads, we were soon quite safe from them, and now the luscious fruit looked more tempting than ever, since it seemed to be denied to us.

"The road down the river is well guarded," said Nur An with a rueful smile, "which might indicate a most desirable goal."

"At present that fruit is the most desirable thing in the world to me," I replied, "and I am going to try to discover some means of obtaining it."

Moving to the right, away from the river, I sought for an entrance into the forest that would be free from the threads of the spiders, and presently I came to a point where there was a well-defined trail about four or five feet wide, apparently cut by man from the vegetation. Across the mouth of it, however, were strung thousands of gossamer strands. To touch them, we know, would be the signal for myriads of the angry spiders to swarm upon us. While our greatest fear was, of course, that the insects might be poisonous, their cruelly fanged mouths also suggested that, poisonous or not, they might in their great numbers constitute a real menace.

"Did you notice," I said to Nur An, "that these threads seem stretched across the entrance to the pathway only? Beyond them I cannot detect any, though of course they are so tenuous that they might defy one's vision even at a short distance."

"I do not see any spiders here," said Nur An. "Perhaps we can cut our way through with impunity at this point."

"We shall experiment," I said, drawing my long sword.

Advancing, I cut a few strands, when immediately there swarmed out of the trees and bushes upon either side great companies of the insects, each racing along its own individual strand. Where the strands were intact the creatures crossed and recrossed the trail, staring at us with their venomous, beady eyes, their powerful, gleaming fangs bared threateningly towards us.

The cut strands floated in the air until borne down by the weight of the approaching spiders, who followed to the severed ends but no further. Here they either hung glaring at us or else clambered up and down excitedly, but not one of them ever ventured from his strand.

As I watched them, their antics suggested a plan. "They are helpless when their web is severed," I said to Nur An. "Therefore if we cut all their webs they cannot reach us." Whereupon, advancing, I swung my long sword above my head and cut downwards through the remaining strands. Instantly the creatures set up their infernal screaming. Several of them, torn from their webs by the blow of my sword, lay upon the ground upon their bellies, their feet sticking straight up into the air. They seemed utterly helpless, and though they screamed loudly and frantically waved their legs, they were clearly unable to move; nor could those hanging at either side of the trail reach us. With my sword I destroyed those that lay in the path and then, followed by Nur An, I entered the forest. Ahead of us I could see no webs; the way seemed clear, but before we advanced further into the forest I turned about to have a last look at the discomfited insects to see what they might be about. They had stopped screaming now and were slowly returning into the foliage, evidently to their lairs, and as they seemed to offer no further menace, we continued upon our way. The trees and bushes along the pathway were innocent of fruit or berries, though just beyond reach we saw them growing in profusion, behind a barrier of those gossamer webs that we had so quickly learned to avoid.

"This trail appears to have been made by man," said Nur An.

"Whoever made it, or when," I said, "there is no doubt but that some creature still uses it. The absence of fruit along it would alone be ample proof of that."

We moved cautiously along the winding trail, not knowing at what moment we might be confronted by some new menace in the form of man or beast. Presently we saw ahead of us what appeared to be an opening in the forest, and a moment later we emerged into a clearing. Looming in front of us at a distance of perhaps less than a haad was a towering pile of masonry. It was a gloomy pile, apparently built of black volcanic rock. For some thirty feet above the ground there was a blank wall, pierced by but a single opening—a small doorway almost directly in front of us. This part of the structure appeared to be a wall, beyond it rose buildings of weird and grotesque outlines, and dominating all was a lofty tower, from the summit of which a wisp of smoke curled upward into the quiet air.

From this new vantage-point we had a better view of the valley than had at first been accorded us, and now more marked than ever were the indications that it was the crater of some gigantic and long-extinct volcano. Between us and the buildings, which suggested a small walled city, the clearing contained a few scattered trees, but most of the ground was given over to cultivation, being traversed by irrigation ditches of an archaic type which had been abandoned upon the surface for many ages, having been superseded by a system of sub-irrigation when the diminishing water supply necessitated the adoption of conservation measures.

Satisfied that no further information could be gained by remaining where we were, I started boldly into the clearing towards the city. "Where are you going?" asked Nur An.

"I am going to find out who dwells in that gloomy place," I replied. "Here are fields and gardens, so they must have food, and that, after all, is the only favour that I shall ask of them."

Nur An shook his head. "The very sight of the place depresses me," he said. But he came with me as I knew he would, for Nur An is a splendid companion upon whose loyalty one may always depend.

We had traversed about two-thirds of the distance across the clearing towards the city before we saw any signs of life, and then a few figures appeared at the top of the wall above the entrance. They carried long, thin scarfs, which they seemed to be waving in greeting to us, and when we had come yet closer I saw that they were young women. They leaned over the parapet and smiled and beckoned to us.

As we came within speaking distance below the wall, I halted. "What city is this," I asked, "and who is Jed here?"

"Enter, warriors," cried one of the girls, "and we

will lead you to the Jed." She was very pretty and she was smiling sweetly, as were her companions.

"This is not such a depressing place as you thought," I said in a low voice to Nur An.

"I was mistaken," said Nur An. "They seem to be a kindly, hospitable people. Shall we enter?"

"Come," called another of the girls; "behind these gloomy walls lie food and wine and love."

Food! I would have entered a far more forbidding place than this for food.

As Nur An and I strode towards the small door, it slowly withdrew to one side. Beyond, across a black-paved avenue, rose buildings of black volcanic rock. The avenue seemed deserted as we stepped within. We heard the faint click of a lock as the door slid into place behind us and I had a sudden foreboding of ill that made my right hand seek the hilt of my long sword.

CHAPTER VIII

THE SPIDER OF GHASTA

FOR A MOMENT we stood undecided in the middle of the empty avenue, looking about us, and then our attentions was attracted to a narrow stairway running up the inside of the wall, upon the summit of which the girls had appeared and welcomed us.

Down the stairway the girls were coming. There were six of them. Their beautiful faces were radiant with happy smiles of welcome that instantly dispelled the gloom of the dark surroundings as the rising sun figures. As they approached a vision of Tavia sprang with light and warmth and happiness.

Beautifully wrought harness, enriched by many a

sparkling jewel, accentuated the loveliness of faultless figures. As they approached a vision of Tavia sprang to my mind. Beautiful as these girls unquestionably were, how much more beautiful was Tavia!

I recall distinctly, even now, that in that very instant, with all that was transpiring to distract my attention, I was suddenly struck by wonder that it should have been Tavia's face and figure that I saw rather than those of Sanoma Tora. You may believe that I brought myself up with a round turn and thereafter it was a vision of Sanoma Tora that I saw, and that, too, without any disloyalty to my friendship for Tavia—that blessed friendship which I looked upon as one of my proudest and most valuable possessions.

As the girls reached the pavement they came eagerly towards us. "Welcome, warriors," cried one, "to happy Ghasta. After your long journey you must be hungry. Come with us and you shall be fed, but first the great Jed will wish to greet you and welcome you to our city, for visitors to Ghasta are few."

As they led us along the avenue I could not but note the deserted appearance of the city. There was no sign of life about any of the buildings that we passed nor did we see another human being until we had come to an open plaza, in the centre of which rose a mighty building surmounted by the lofty tower that we had seen when we first emerged from the forest. Here we saw a number of people, both men and women —sad, dejected-looking people, who moved with bent shoulders and downcast eyes. There was no animation in their step and their whole demeanour seemed that of utter hopelessness. What a contrast they presented to the gay and happy girls who so joyously conducted us towards the main entrance of what I assumed to be the palace of the Jed! Here, burly warriors were on guard—fat, oily-looking fellows, whose appearance was not at all to my liking. As we aproached them an officer emerged from the interior of the building. If possible, he was even fatter and more greasy-looking than his men, but he smiled and bowed as he welcomed us.

"Greetings!" he exclaimed. "May the peace of Ghasta be upon the strangers who enter her gates."

"Send word to Ghron, the great Jed," said one of the girls to him, "that we are bringing two strange warriors who wish to do honour to him before partaking of the hospitality of Ghasta."

As the officer dispatched a warrior to notify the Jed of our coming, we were escorted into the interior of the palace. The furnishings were striking, but extremely fantastic in design and execution. The native wood of the forests had been used to fine advantage in the construction of numerous pieces of beautifully carved furniture, the grain of the woods showing lustrously in their various natural colours, the beauties of which were sometimes accentuated by delicate stain and by high polishes, but perhaps the most striking feature of the interior decorations was the gorgeously painted fabric that covered the walls and ceilings. It was a fabric of unbelievable lightness, which gave the impression of spun silver. So closely woven was it that, as I was to learn later, it would hold water and of such great strength that it was almost impossible to tear it.

Upon it were painted in brilliant colours the most fantastic scenes that imagination might conceive. There were spiders with the heads of beautiful women, and women with the heads of spiders. There were flowers and trees that danced beneath a great red sun, and great lizards, such as we had passed within the gloomy cavern on our journey down from Tjanath. In all the figures that were depicted there was nothing represented as nature had created it. It was as though some mad mind had conceived the whole.

As we waited in the great entrance hall of the palace of the Jed, four of the girls danced for our entertainment—a strange dance such as I had never before seen upon Barsoom. Its steps and movements were as weird and fantastic as the mural decorations of the room in which it was executed, and yet with all there was a certain rhythm and suggestiveness in the undulations of those lithe bodies that imparted to us a feeling of well-being and content.

The fat and greasy padwar of the guard moistened his thick lips as he watched them, and though he had doubtless seen them dance upon many occasions, he seemed to be much more affected than we, but perhaps he had no Phao or Sanoma Tora to occupy his thoughts.

Sanoma Tora! The chiselled beauty of her noble face stood out clearly upon the screen of memory for a brief instant and then slowly it began to fade. I tried to recall it, to see again the short, haughty lip and the cold, level gaze, but it receded into a blur from which there presently emerged a pair of wondrous eyes, moist with tears, a perfect face and a head of tousled hair.

It was then that the warrior returned to say that Ghron, the Jed, would receive us at once. Only the girls accompanied us, the fat padwar remaining behind, though I could have sworn that it was not through choice.

The room in which the Jed received us was upon the second level of the palace. It was a large room, even more grotesquely decorated than those through which we had passed. The furniture was of weird shapes and sizes, nothing harmonized with anything else and yet the result was a harmony of discord that was not at all unpleasing.

The Jed sat upon a perfectly enormous throne of volcanic glass. It was perhaps the most ornate and remarkable piece of furniture that I have ever seen and was the outstanding specimen of craftsmanship in the entire city of Ghasta, but if it caught my eye at the time it was only for an instant, as nothing could for long distract one's attention from the Jed himself. In the first glance he looked more like a hairy ape than a man. He was massively built with great, heavy, stooping shoulders and long arms covered with shaggy black hair, the more remarkable, perhaps, because there is no race of hairy men upon Barsoom. His face was broad and flat and his eyes were so far apart that they seemed literally to be set in the corners of his face. As we were halted before him, he twisted his mouth into what I imagined at the time was intended for a smile, but which only succeeded in making him look more horrible than before.

As is customary, we laid our swords at his feet and announced our names and our cities.

"Hadron of Hastor, Nur An of Jahar," he repeated. "Ghron, the Jed, welcomes you to Ghasta. Few are the visitors who find their way to our beautiful city. It is an event, therefore, when two such illustrious warriors honour us with a visit. Seldom do we receive word from the outer world. Tell us, then, of your journey and of what is transpiring upon the surface of Barsoom above us."

His words and his manner were those of a most solicitous host bent upon extending a proper and cordial welcome to strangers, but I could not rid myself of the belying suggestion of his repulsive countenance, though I could do no less than play the part of a grateful and appreciative guest.

We told our stories and gave him much news of those portions of Barsoom with which each of us was familiar, and as Nur An spoke I looked about me at the assemblage in the great chamber. They were mostly women and many of them were young and beautiful. The men, for the most part, were gross-looking, fat and oily, and there were certain lines of cruelty about their eyes and their mouths that did not escape me, though I tried to attribute it to the first depressing impression that the black and sombre buildings and the deserted avenues had conveyed to my mind.

When we had finished our recitals, Ghron announced that a banquet had been prepared in our honour, and in person he led the procession from the throne-room down a long corridor to a mighty banquet hall, in the centre of which stood a great marble table, down the entire length of which was a magnificient decoration consisting entirely of the fruits and flowers of the forest through which we had passed. At one end of the table was the Jed's throne and at the other were smaller thrones, one for Nur An and one for me. Seated on either side of us were the girls who had welcomed us to the city and whose business, it seemed, now was to entertain us.

The design of the dishes with which the table was set was quite in keeping with all the other mad designs of the palace of Ghron. No two plates or goblets or platters were of the same shape or size or design and nothing seemed suited to the purpose for which it was intended. My wine was served in a shallow, triangular-shaped saucer, while my meat was crammed into a tall, slender-stemmed goblet. However, I was too hungry to be particular, and, I hoped, too well conversant with the amenities, of polite society to reveal the astonishment that I felt.

Here, as in other parts of the palace, the wall coverings were of the gossamer-like silver fabric that had attracted my attention and admiration the moment that I had entered the building, and so fascinated was I by it that I could not refrain from mentioning it to the girl who sat at my right.

"There is no such fabric anywhere else in Barsoom," she said. "It is made here and only here."

"It is very beautiful," I said. "Other nations would pay well for it."

"If we could get it to them," she said, "but we have no intercourse with the world above us."

"Of what is it woven?" I asked.

"When you entered the valley Hohr," she said, "you saw a beautiful forest, running down to the banks of the river Syl. Doubtless you saw fruit in the forest and, being hungry, you sought to gather it, but you were set upon by huge spiders that sped along silver threads, finer than a woman's hair."

"Yes," I said, "that is just what happened."

"It is from this web, spun by those hideous spiders,

that we weave our fabric. It is as strong as leather and as enduring as the rocks of which Ghasta is built."

"Do women of Ghasta spin this wonderful fabric?" I asked.

"The slaves," she said, "both men and women."

"And from whence come your slaves," I asked, "if you have no intercourse with the upper world?"

"Many of them come down the river from Tjanath, where they have died The Death, and there are others who come from further up the river, but why they come or from whence we never know. They are silent people, who will not tell us, and sometimes they come from down the river but these are few and usually are so crazed by the horrors of their journey that we can glean no knowledge from them."

"And do any ever go on down the river from Ghasta?" I asked; for it was in that direction that Nur An and I hoped to make our way in search of liberty, as deep within me was the hope that we might reach the valley Dor and the lost sea of Korus, from which I was convinced I could escape, as did John Carter and Tars Tarkas.

"A few, perhaps," she said, "but we never know what becomes of these, for none returns."

"You are happy here?" I asked.

She forced a smile to her beautiful lips, but I thought that a shudder ran through her frame.

The banquet was elaborate and the food delicious. There was a great deal of laughter at the far end of the table where the Jed sat, for those about him watched him closely, and when he laughed, which he always did at his own jokes, the others all laughed uproariously.

Towards the end of the meal a troupe of dancers entered the apartment. My first view of them almost took my breath away, for, with but a single exception, they were all horribly deformed. That one exception was the most beautiful girl I have ever seen—the most beautiful girl I have ever seen, with the saddest face that I have ever seen. She danced divinely and about her hopped and crawled the poor, unhappy creatures whose sad afflictions should have made them the objects of sympathy rather than ridicule, and yet it was obvious that they had been selected for their part for the sole purpose of giving the audience an opportunity to vent its ridicule upon them. The sight of them seemed to incite Ghron to a pitch of frenzied mirth, and, to add to his own pleasure and to the discomforts of the poor, pathetic performers, he hurled food and plates at them as they danced about the banquet table.

I tried not to look at them, but there was a fascination in their deformities which attracted my gaze, and presently it became apparent to me that the majority of them were artificially deformed, that they had been thus broken and bent at the behest of some malign mind, and as I looked down the long board at the horrid face of Ghron, distorted by maniacal laughter, I could not but guess the author of their disfigurement.

When at last they were gone, three large goblets of wine were borne into the banquet hall by a slave; two of them were red goblets and one was black. The black goblet was set before Ghron and the red ones before Nur An and me. Then Ghron rose and the whole company followed his example.

"Ghron, the Jed, drinks to the happiness of his honoured guests," announced the ruler, and, raising the goblet to his lips, he drained it to the bottom.

It seemed obvious that this little ceremony would conclude the banquet and that it was intended Nur An and I should drink to the health of our host. I, therefore, raised my goblet. It was the first time that anything had been served to me in the proper receptacle, and I was glad that at last I might drink without incurring the danger of spilling most of the contents of the receptacle into my lap.

"To the health and power of the great Jed, Ghron," I said, and following my host's example, drained the contents of the goblet.

As Nur An followed my example with some appropriate words, I felt a sudden lethargy stealing over me and in the instant before I lost consciousness I realized that I had been given drugged wine.

When I regained consciousness I found myself lying on the bare floor of a room of a peculiar shape that suggested it was the portion of the arc of a circle lying between the peripheries of two concentric circles. The narrow end of the room curved inward, the wider end outward. In the latter was a single grated window; no door or other openings appeared in any of the walls, which were covered with the same silver fabric that I had noticed upon the walls and ceilings of the palace of the Jed. Near me lay Nur An, evidently still under the influence of the opiate that had been administered to us in the wine.

Again I looked about the room. I arose and went to the window. Far below me I saw the roofs of the city. Evidently we were imprisoned in the lofty tower that rose from the center of the palace of the Jed, but how had we been brought into the room? Certainly not through the window, which must have been fully two hundred feet above the city. While I was pondering this seemingly unanswerable problem, Nur An regained consciousness. At first he did not speak; he just lay there looking at me with a rueful smile upon his lips.

"Well?" I asked.

Nur An shook his head. "We still live," he said dismally, "but that is about the best that one may say."

"We are in the palace of a maniac, Nur An," I said. "There is no doubt in my mind as to that. Everyone here lives in constant terror of Ghron, and from what I have seen to-day they are warranted in feeling terror."

"Yet I believe we saw little or nothing of that," said Nur An.

"I saw enough," I replied.

"Those girls were so beautiful," he said after a moment's silence. "I could not believe that such beauty and such duplicity could exist together."

"Perhaps they were the unwilling tools of a cruel master," I suggested.

"I shall always like to think so," he said.

The day waned and night fell; no one came near us, but in the meantime I discovered something. Accidentally leaning against the wall at the narrow end of our room I found that it was very warm, in fact quite hot, and from this I inferred that the flue of the chimney from which we had seen the smoke issuing rose through the centre of the tower and the wall of the chimney formed the rear wall of our apartment. It was a discovery, but at the moment it meant nothing to us.

There were no lights in our apartment, and, as only Cluros was in the heavens and he upon the opposite side of the tower, our prison was in almost total darkness. We were sitting in gloomy contemplation of our predicament, each wrapped in his own unhappy thoughts, when I heard footsteps apparently approaching from below. They came nearer and nearer until finally they ceased in an adjoining apartment, seemingly the one next to ours. A moment later there was a scraping sound and a line of light appeared at the bottom of one of the side walls. It kept growing in width until I finally realized that the entire partition wall was rising. In the opening we saw at first the sandalled feet of warriors, and finally, little by little, their entire bodies were revealed—two stalwart, brawny men, heavily armed. They carried manacles, and with them they fastened our wrists behind our backs. They did not speak, but with a gesture one of them directed us to follow him, and, as we filed out of the room, the second warrior fell in behind us. In silence we entered a steep, spiral ramp, which we descended to the main body of the palace, but yet our escorts conducted us still lower until I knew that we must be in the pits beneath the palace.

The pits! Inwardly I shuddered. I much preferred the tower, for I have always possessed an inherent horror of the pits. Perhaps these would be utterly dark and doubtless overrun by rats and lizards.

The ramp ended in a gorgeously decorated apartment in which was assembled about the same company of men and women that had partaken of the banquet with us earlier in the day. Here, too, was Ghron upon a throne. This time he did not smile as we entered the room. He did not seem to realize our presence. He was sitting, leaning forward, his eyes fixed upon something at the far end of the room, over which hung a deadly silence that was suddenly shattered by a piercing scream of anguish. The scream was but a prelude to a series of similar cries of agony.

I looked quickly in the direction from which the screams came, the direction in which Ghron's gaze was fastened. I saw a naked woman chained to a grill before a hot fire. Evidently they had just placed her there as I had entered the room, and it was her first shrill scream of agony that had attracted my attention.

The grill was mounted upon wheels so that it could be removed to any distance from the fire that the torturer chose, or completely turned about presenting the other side of the victim to the blaze.

As my eyes wandered back to the audience I saw that most of the girls sat there glaring straight ahead, their eyes fixed with horror upon the horrid scene. I do not believe that they enjoyed it; I know that they did not. They were equally the unwilling victims of the cruel vagaries of Ghron's diseased mind, but like the poor creature upon the grill they were helpless.

Next to the torture itself, the most diabolical conceit of the mind that had directed it was the utter silence enjoined upon all spectators, against the background of which the shrieks and moans of the tortured victim evidently achieved their highest effectiveness upon the crazed mind of the Jed.

The spectacle was sickening. I turned my eyes away. Presently one of the warriors who had fetched us touched me on the arm and motioned me to follow him.

He led us from this apartment to another, and there we witnessed a scene infinitely more terrible than the grilling of the human victim. I cannot describe it; it tortures my memory even to think of it. Long before we reached that hideous apartment we heard the screams and curses of its inmates. In utter silence our guard ushered us within. It was the chamber of horrors in which the Jed of Ghasta was creating abnormal deformities for his cruel dance of the cripples.

Still in silence we were led from this horrid place, and now our guide conducted us upward to a luxuriously furnished apartment. Upon divans lay two of the beautiful girls who had welcomed us to Ghasta.

For the first time since we had left our room in the tower one of our escort broke the silence. "They will explain," he said, pointing to the girls. "Do not try to escape. There is only one exit from this room. We will be waiting outside." He then removed our manacles and with his companion left the apartment, closing the door after them.

One of the occupants of the room was the same girl who had sat at my right during the banquet. I had found her most gracious and intelligent and to her I now turned.

"What is the meaning of this?" I demanded. "Why are we made prisoners? Why have we been brought here?"

She beckoned me to come to the divan on which she reclined, and as I approached she motioned to me to sit down beside her.

"What you have seen to-night," she said, "represents the three fates that lie in store for you. Ghron has taken a fancy to you and he is giving you your choice."

"I do not yet quite understand," I said.

"You saw the victim before the grill?" she asked.

"Yes," I replied.

"Would you care to suffer that fate?"

"Scarcely."

"You saw the unhappy ones being bent and broken for the dance of the cripples," she pursued.

"I did," I answered.

"And now you see this luxurious room—and me. Which would you choose?"

"I cannot believe," I replied, "that the final alternative is without conditions, which might make it appear less attractive than it now seems, for otherwise there could be no possible question as to which I would choose."

"You are right," she said. "There are conditions."

"What are they?" I asked.

"You will become an officer in the palace of the Jed, and as such you will conduct tortures similar to those you have witnessed in the pits of the palace. You will be guided by whatever whim may possess your master."

I drew myself to my full height. "I choose the fire," I said.

"I knew that you would," she said sadly, "and yet I hoped that you might not."

"It is not because of you," I said quickly. "It is the other conditions which no man of honour could accept."

"I know," she said, "and had you accepted them I must eventually have despised you as I despise the others."

"You are unhappy here?" I asked.

"Of course," she said. "Who but a maniac could be happy in this horrid place? There are, perhaps, six hundred people in the city and there is not one who knows happiness. A hundred of us form the court of the Jed; the others are slaves. As a matter of fact, we are all slaves, subject to every mad whim or caprice of the maniac who is our master."

"And there is no escape?" I asked.

"None."

"I shall escape," I said.

"How?"

"The fire," I replied.

She shuddered. "I do not know why I should care so much," she said, "unless it is that I liked you from the first. Even while I was helping to lure you into the city for the human spider of Ghasta, I wished that I might warn you not to enter, but I was afraid, just as I am afraid to die. I wish that I had your courage to escape through the fire."

I turned to Nur An, who had been listening to our conversation. "You have reached your decision?" I asked.

"Certainly," he said. "There could be but one decision for a man of honour."

"Good!" I exclaimed, and then I turned to the girl. "You will notify Ghron of our decision?" I asked.

"Wait," she said; "ask for time in which to consider it. I know that it will make no difference in the end, but yet—— Oh, even yet there is a germ of hope within me that even utter hopelessness cannot destroy."

"You are right," I said, "There is always hope. Let him think that you have half persuaded us to accept the life of luxury and ease that he has offered as an alternative to death or torture, and that if you are given a little more time you may succeed. In the meantime we may be able to work out some plan of escape."

"Never," she said.

CHAPTER IX

PHOR TAK OF JHAMA

BACK IN OUR QUARTERS in the chimney tower, Nur An and I discussed every mad plan of escape that entered our brains. For some reason our fetters had not been replaced, which gave us at least as much freedom of action as our apartment afforded, and you may rest assured that we took full advantage of it, examining

minutely every square inch of the floor and the walls
as far up as we could reach, but our combined efforts
failed to reveal any means for raising the partition
which closed the only avenue of escape from our
prison, with the exception of the window, which,
while heavily barred and some two hundred feet above
the ground, was by no means, therefore, eliminated
from our plans.

The heavy vertical bars which protected the window
withstood our combined efforts when we sought to
bend them, though Nur An is a powerful man, while
I have always been lauded for my unusual muscular development. The bars were set a little too close together
to permit our bodies to pass through, but the removal
of one of them would leave an opening of ample size;
yet to what purpose? Perhaps the same answer was in
Nur An's mind that was in mine—that when hope
was gone and the sole alternative remaining was the
fire within the grill, we might at least cheat Ghron
could we but hurl ourselves from this high-flung window to the ground far below.

But whatever end each of us may have had in view,
he kept it to himself, and when I started digging at
the mortar at the bottom of one of the bars with the
prong of a buckle from my harness, Nur An asked
no questions but set to work similarly upon the mortar
at the top of the same bar. We worked in silence and
with little fear of discovery, as no one had entered
our prison since we had been incarcerated there. Once
a day the partition was raised a few inches and food
was slipped in to us beneath it, but we did not see the
person who brought it, nor did anyone communicate
with us from the time that the guards had taken us
to the palace that first night up to the moment that we
had finally succeeded in loosening the bar so that it
could be easily removed from its seat.

I shall never forget with what impatience we awaited
the coming of night, that we might remove the bar
and investigate the surrounding surface of the tower,
for it had occurred to me that it might offer a means

of descent to the ground below, or rather to the roof
of the building which it surmounted, from where we
might hope to make our way to the summit of the
city wall undetected. Already, in view of this possibility, I had planned to tear strips from the fabric
covering our walls wherewith to make a rope down
which we might lower ourselves to the ground beyond
the city wall.

As night approached I commenced to realize how
high I had built my hopes upon this idea. It already
seemed as good as accomplished, especially when I
had utilized the possibilities of the rope to its fullest
extent, which included making one of sufficient length
to reach from our window to the bottom of the tower.
Thus every obstacle was overcome. It was then, just
at dusk, that I explained my plan to Nur An.

"Fine," he exclaimed. "Let us start at once making
our rope. We know how strong this fabric is and that
a slender strand of it will support our weight. There
is enough upon one wall to make all the rope we
need."

Success seemed almost assured as we started to remove the fabric from one of the larger walls, but here
we met our first obstacle. The fabric was fastened at
the top and at the bottom with large-headed nails, set
close together, which withstood our every effort to tear
it loose. Thin and light in weight, this remarkable
fabric appeared absolutely indestructible, and we were
almost exhausted by our efforts when we were finally
forced to admit defeat.

The quick Barsoomian night had fallen and we
might now, with comparative safety, remove the bar
from the window and reconnoitre for the first time
beyond the restricted limits of our cell; but hope was
now low within our breasts and it was with little anticipation of encouragement that I drew myself to the sill
and projected my head and shoulders through the
aperture.

Below me lay the sombre, gloomy city, its blackness
relieved by a few dim lights, most of which shone

faintly from the palace windows. I passed my palm over the surface of the tower that lay within arm's reach, and again my heart sank within me. Smooth, almost glass-like volcanic rock, beautifully cut and laid, offered not the slightest handhold—indeed an insect might have found it difficult to have clung to its polished surface.

"It is quite hopeless," I said as I drew my head back into the room. "The tower is as smooth as a woman's breast."

"What is above?" asked Nur An.

Again I leaned out, this time looking upward. Just above me were the eaves of the tower—our cell was at the highest level of the structure. Something impelled me to investigate in that direction—an insane urge, perhaps, born of despair.

"Hold my ankles, Nur An," I said, "and in the name of your first ancestor, hold tightly!"

Clinging to two of the remaining bars I raised myself to a standing position upon the window ledge, while Nur An clung to my ankles. I could just reach the top of the eaves with my extended fingers. Lowering myself again to the sill, I whispered to Nur An. "I am going to attempt to reach the roof of the tower," I exclaimed.

"Why?" he asked.

I laughed. "I do not know," I admitted, "but something within my inner consciousness seems insistently to urge me on."

"If you fall," he said, "you will have escaped the fire—and I will follow you. Good luck, my friend from Hastor!"

Once again I raised myself to a standing position upon the sill and reached upward until my fingers bent above the edge of the lofty roof. Slowly I drew myself upward; below me, two hundred feet, lay the palace roof and death. I am very strong—only a very strong man could have hoped to succeed, for I had at best but a precarious hold upon the flat roof above me, but at last I succeeded in getting an elbow over and then I drew my body slowly over the edge until, at last, I lay panting upon the basalt flagging that topped the slender tower.

Resting a few moments, I arose to my feet. Mad, passionate Thuria raced across the cloudless sky; Cluros, her cold spouse, swung his aloof circle in splendid isolation; below me lay the valley of Hohr like some enchanted fairyland of ancient lore; above me frowned the beetling cliff that hemmed in this madman's world.

A puff of hot air struck me suddenly in the face, recalling to my mind that far below in the pits of Ghasta an orgy of torture was occurring. Faintly a scream arose from the black mouth of the flue behind me. I shuddered, but my attention was centered upon the yawning opening now and I approached it. Almost unbearable waves of heat were billowing upward from the mouth of the chimney. There was little smoke, so perfect was the combustion, but what there was shot into the air at terrific velocity. It almost seemed that were I to cast myself upon it I should be carried far aloft.

It was then that a thought was born—a mad, impossible idea, it seemed, and yet it clung to me as I lowered myself gingerly over the outer edge of the tower and finally regained the greater security of my cell.

I was about to explain my insane plan to Nur An when I was interrupted by sounds from the adjoining chamber and an instant later the partition started to rise. I thought they were bringing us food again, but the partition rose further than was necessary for the passing of food receptacles beneath it, and a moment later we saw the ankles and legs of a woman beneath the base of the rising wall. Then a girl stooped and entered our cell. In the light from the adjoining room I recognized her—she who had been selected by Ghron to lure me to his will. Her name was Sharu.

Nur An had quickly replaced the bar in the window, and when the girl entered there was nothing to in-

dicate that aught was amiss, or that one of us had
so recently been outside our cell. The partition remained half raised, permitting light to enter the apartment, and the girl, looking at me, must have noticed
my gaze wandering to the adjoining room.

"Do not let your hopes rise," she said with a rueful
smile. "There are guards waiting at the level next
below."

"Why are you here, Sharu?" I asked.

"Ghron sent me," she replied. "He is impatient for
your decision."

I thought quickly. Our only hope lay in the sympathy
of this girl, whose attitude in the past had at least
demonstrated her friendliness. "Had we a dagger and
a needle," I said in a low whisper, "we could give
Ghron his answer upon the morning of the day after
to-morrow."

"What reason can I give him for this further delay?" she asked after a moment's thought.

"Tell him," said Nur An, "that we are communing
with our ancestors and that upon their advice shall
depend our decision."

Sharu smiled. She drew a dagger from its sheath at
her side and laid it upon the floor, and from a pocket
pouch attached to her harness she produced a needle,
which she laid beside the dagger. "I shall convince
Ghron that it is best to wait," she said. "My heart had
hoped, Hadron of Hastor, that you would decide to
remain with me, but I am glad that I have not been
mistaken in my estimate of your chracter. You will
die, my warrior, but at least you will die as a brave
man should and undefiled. Good-bye! I look upon you
in life for the last time, but until I am gathered to my
ancestors your image shall remain enshrined within my
heart."

She was gone; the partition dropped, and again we
had the two things that I most desired—a dagger and
a needle.

"Of what good are those?" asked Nur An as I
gathered the two articles from the floor.

"You will see," I replied, and immediately I set to work cutting the fabric from the walls of our cell and then, standing upon Nur An's shoulders, I removed also that which covered the ceiling. I worked quickly, for I knew that we had little time in which to accomplish that which I had set out to do. A mad scheme it was, and yet withal within the realms of practicability.

Working in the dark, more by sense of feel than by sight, I must have been inspired by some higher power to have accomplished with any degree of perfection the task that I had set myself.

The balance of that night and all of the following day Nur An and I laboured without rest until we had fashioned an enormous bag from the fabric that had covered the walls and ceiling of our cell, and from the scraps that remained we fashioned long ropes and when night fell again our task was completed.

"May luck be with us," I said.

"The scheme is worthy of the mad brain of Ghron himself," said Nur An; "yet it has within it the potentialities of success."

"Night has fallen," I said; "we need not delay longer. Of one thing, however, we may be sure: Whether we succeed or fail we shall have escaped the fire, and in either event may our ancestors look with love and compassion upon Sharu, whose friendship has made possible our attempt."

"Whose love," corrected Nur An.

Once again I made the perilous ascent to the roof, taking one of our new-made ropes with me. Then, from the summit, I lowered it to Nur An, who fastened the great bag to it; after which I drew the fruits of our labours carefully to the roof beside me. It was as light as a feather, yet stronger than the well-tanned hide of a zitidar. Next, I lowered the rope and assisted Nur An to my side, but not until he had replaced the bar that we had removed from the window.

Attached to the bottom of our bag, which was open, were a number of long cords, terminating in loops. Through these loops we passed the longest rope that

we had made—a rope so long that it entirely encircled
the circumference of the tower when we lowered it
below the projecting eaves. We made it fast there, but
with a slip knot that could be instantly released with a
single jerk.

Next, we slid the loops at the end of the ropes
attached to the bottom of the bag along the cord that
encircled the tower below the eaves until we had
maneuvered the opening of the bag directly over the
mouth of the flue leading down into the furnace of
death in the pits of Ghasta. Standing upon either
side of the flue, Nur An and I lifted the bag until it
commenced to fill with the hot air rushing from the
chimney. Presently it was sufficiently inflated to remain in an erect position, whereupon, leaving Nur An
to steady it, I moved the loops until they were at equal
distances from one another, thus anchoring the bag
directly over the centre of the flue. Then I passed
another rope loosely through the loops and secured its
ends together, and to opposite sides of this rope Nur
An and I snapped the boarding hooks that are a part
of the harness of every Barsoomian warrior, the pri-
mary purpose of which is to lower boarding parties
from the deck of one ship to that of another directly
below, but which in practice are used in countless
ways and numerous emergencies.

Then we waited; Nur An ready to slip the knot that
held the rope around the tower beneath the eaves, and
I, upon the opposite side, with Sharu's sharp dagger
prepared to cut the rope upon my side.

I saw the great bag that we had made filling with
hot air. At first, loosely inflated, it rocked and swayed,
but presently, its sides distended, it strained upward.
Its fabric stretched tightly until I thought that it would
burst. It tugged and pulled at its restraining cords, and
yet I waited.

Down in the valley of Hohr there was little or no
wind, which greatly facilitated the carrying out of our
rash venture.

The great bag, almost as large as the room in which

we had been confined, bellied above us. It strained upon its guy ropes in its impatience to be aloft until I wondered that they held, and then I gave the word.

Simultaneously Nur An slipped his knot and I severed the rope upon the opposite side. Freed, the great bag leaped aloft, snapping us in its wake. It shot upward with a velocity that was astounding until the valley of Hohr was but a little hollow in the surface of the great world that lay below us.

Presently a wind caught us, and you may be assured that we gave thanks to our ancestors as we realized that we were at last drifting from above the cruel city of Ghasta. The wind increased until it was blowing rapidly in a north-easterly direction, but little did we care where it wafted us as long as it took us away from the river Syl and the valley of Hohr.

After we had passed beyond the crater of the ancient volcano, which formed the bed of the valley in which lay sombre Ghasta, we saw below us, in the moonlight, a rough volcanic country that presented a weird and impressive appearance of unreality; deep chasms and tumbled piles of basalt seemed to present an insurmountable barrier to man, which may explain why in this remote and desolate corner of Barsoom the valley of Hohr had lain for countless ages undiscovered.

The wind increased. Floating at a great altitude we were being carried at considerable speed, yet I could see that we were very slowly falling as the hot air within our bag cooled. How much longer it would keep us up I could not guess, but I hoped it would bear us at least beyond the uninviting terrain beneath us.

With the coming of dawn we were floating but a few hundred feet above the ground; the volcanic country was far behind us, and as far as we could see stretched lovely, rolling hills, sparsely timbered with the drought-resisting skeel upon which it has been said the civilization of Barsoom has been erected.

As we topped a low hill, passing over it by a scant fifty sofads, we saw below us a building of gleaming white. Like all the cities and isolated buildings of Barsoom, it was surrounded by a lofty wall, but in other respects it differed materially from the usual Barsoomian type of architecture. The edifice, which was made up of a number of buildings, was not surmounted by the usual towers, domes and minarets that mark all Barsoomian cities and which only in recent ages have been giving way slowly to the flat landing-stages of an aerial world. The structure below us was composed of a number of flat-roofed buildings of various heights, none of which, however, appeared to rise over four levels. Between the buildings and the outer walls and in several open courts between the buildings there was a profusion of trees and shrubbery with scarlet sward and well-kept paths. It was, in fact, a striking and beautiful sight, yet having so recently been lured to near destruction by the beauties of Hohr and the engaging allurements of her beautiful women, we had no mind to be deceived again by external appearances. We would float over the palace of enchantment and take our chances in the open country beyond.

But fate willed otherwise. The wind had abated; we were dropping rapidly; beneath us we saw people in the garden of the building, and simultaneously, as they discovered us, it was evident that they were filled with consternation. They hastened quickly to the nearest entrances, and there was not a human being in sight when we finally came to rest upon the roof of one of the taller sections of the structure.

As we extricated ourselves from the loops in which we had been sitting, the great bag, relieved of our weight, rose quickly into the air for a short distance, turned completely over and dropped to the ground just beyond the outer wall. It had served us well and now it seemed like a living thing that had given up its life for our salvation.

We were to have little time, however, for sentimental regrets, for almost immediately a head appeared through a small opening in the roof upon which we stood. The head was followed by the body of a man, whose harness was so scant as to leave him almost nude. He was an old man with a finely shaped head, covered with scant, grey locks.

Apparent physical old age is so rare upon Barsoom as always to attract immediate attention. In the natural span of life we live often to a thousand years, but during that long period our appearance changes but little. It is true that most of us meet violent death long before we reach old age, but there are some who pass the allotted span of life and others who do not care for themselves so well, and those few constitute the physically old among us; evidently of such was the little old man who confronted us.

At sight of him Nur An voiced an exclamation of pleased surprise. "Phor Tak!" he cried.

"Heigh-oo!" cackled the old man in a high falsetto. "Who cometh from the high heavens who knows old Phor Tak?"

"It is I—Nur An!" exclaimed my friend.

"Heigh-oo!" cried Phor Tak. "Nur An—one of Tul Axtar's pets."

"As you once were, Phor Tak."

"But not now—not now," almost screamed the old man. "The tyrant squeezed me like some juicy fruit and then cast the empty rind aside. Heigh-oo! He thought it was empty, but I pray daily to all my ancestors that he may live to know that he was wrong. I can say this with safety to you, Nur An, for I have you in my power, and I promise you that you shall never live to carry word of my whereabouts to Tul Axtar."

"Do not fear, Phor Tak," said Nur An. "I, too, have suffered from the villainy of the Jeddak of Jahar. You were permitted to leave the capital in peace, but all my property was confiscated and I was sentenced to death."

"Heigh-oo! Then you hate him too," exclaimed the old man.

"Hate is a weak word to describe my feeling for Tul Axtar," replied my friend.

"It is well," said Phor Tak. "When I saw you descending from the skies I thought that my ancestors had sent you to help me, and now I know that it was indeed true. Be this another warrior from Jahar?" he added, nodding his old head towards me.

"No, Phor Tak," replied Nur An. "This is Hadron of Hastor, a noble of Helium, but he, too, has been wronged by Jahar."

"Good!" exclaimed the old man. "Now there are three of us. Heretofore I have had only slaves and women to assist me, but now with two trained warriors, young and strong, the goal of my triumph appears almost in sight."

As the two men conversed I had recalled that part of the story that Nur An had told me in the pits of Tjanath which related to Phor Tak and his invention of the rifle that projected the disintegrating rays which had proved so deadly against the patrol boat above Helium the night of Sanoma Tora's abduction. Strange, indeed, was the fate that it should have brought me into the palace of the man who held the secret that might mean so much to Helium and to all Barsoom. Strange, too, and devious had been the path along which fate had led me, yet I knew that my ancestors were guiding me and that all must have been arranged to some good end.

When Phor Tak had heard only a portion of our story he insisted that we must be both fatigued and hungry and, like the good host that he proved to be, he conducted us down to the interior of his palace and, summoning slaves, ordered that we be bathed and fed and then permitted to retire until we were rested. We thanked him for his kindess and consideration, of which we were glad to avail ourselves.

The days that followed were both interesting and profitable. Phor Tak, surrounded only by a few faithful slaves who had followed him into his exile, was delighted with our company and with the assistance which we could give him in his experiment, which, once assured of our loyalty, he explained to us in detail.

He told us the story of his wanderings after he had left Jahar and of how he had stumbled upon this long-deserted castle, whose builder and occupants had left no record other than their bones. He told us that when he discovered it skeletons had strewn the courtyard, and in the main entrance were piled bones of a score of warriors, attesting the fierce defence that the occupants had waged against some unknown enemy, while in many of the upper rooms he had found other skeletons—the skeletons of women and children.

"I believe," he said, "that the place was beset by members of some savage horde of green warriors that left not a single survivor. The courts and gardens were overgrown with weeds and the interior of the building was filled with dust, but otherwise little damage had been done. I call it Jhama, and here I am carrying on my life's work."

"And that?" I asked.

"Revenge upon Tul Axtar," said the old man. "I gave him the disintegrating ray; I gave him the insulating paint that protects his own ships and weapons from it, and now some day I shall give him something else—something that will be as revolutionary in the art of war as the disintegrating ray itself; something that will cast the fleet of Jahar broken wrecks upon the ground; something that will search out the palace of Tul Axtar and bury the tyrant beneath its ruins."

We had not been long at Jhama before both Nur An and I became convinced that Phor Tak's mind was at least slightly deranged from long brooding over the wrongs inflicted upon him by Tul Axtar; though naturally possessed of a kindly disposition he was obsessed by a maniacal desire to wreck vengeance upon the tyrant with utter disregard of the consequences to himself and to others. Upon this single subject he was beyond the influence of reason, and having established to his own satisfaction that Nur An and I were potential factors in the successful accomplishment of his design, he would fly into a perfect frenzy of rage whenever I broached the subject of our departure.

Fretting as I was beneath the urge to push on to Jahar and the rescue of Sanoma Tora, I could but ill brook this enforced delay, but Phor Tak was adamant —he would not permit me to depart—and the absolute loyalty of his slaves made it possible for him to enforce his will. In our hearing he explained to them that we were guests, honoured guests as long as we made no effort to depart without his permission, but should they discover us in an attempt to leave Jhama surreptitiously they were to destroy us.

Nur An and I discussed the matter at length. We had discovered that four thousand haads of difficult and unfriendly country lay between us and Jahar. Being without a ship and without thoats there was little likelihood that we should be able to reach Jahar in time to be of service to Sanoma Tora, if we ever reached it at all, and so we agreed to bide our time, impressing Phor Tak with our willingness to aid him in the hope that eventually we should be able to enlist his aid and support, and so successful were we that within a short time we had so won the confidence of the old scientist that we began to entertain hope that he would take us into his innermost confidence and reveal the nature of the instrument of destruction which he was preparing for Tul Axtar.

I must admit that I was principally interested in his invention because I was confident that in order to utilize it against Tul Axtar he must find some means of transporting it to Jahar, and in this I saw an opportunity for reaching the capital of the tyrant myself.

We had been in Jhama about ten days, during which time Phor Tak exhibited signs of extreme nervousness and irritability. He kept us with him practically all of the time that he was not closeted in the innermost recesses of his secret laboratory.

During the evening meal upon the tenth day Phor Tak seemed more distraught than ever. Talking, as usual, interminably about his hated of Tul Axtar, his countenance assumed an expression of maniacal fury.

"But I am helpless," he almost screamed at last. "I am helpless because there is no one to whom I may entrust my secret, who also has the courage and intelligence to carry out my plan. I am too old, too weak to undergo the hardships that would mean nothing to young men like you, but which must be undergone if I am to fulfil my destiny as the saviour of Jahar. If I could but trust you! If I could but trust you!"

"Perhaps you can, Phor Tak," I suggested.

The words or my tone seemed to soothe him. "Heigh-oo!" he exclaimed. "Sometimes I almost think that I can."

"We have a common aim," I said; "or at least different aims which converge at the same point—Jahar. Let us work together then. We wish to reach Jahar. If you can help us, we will help you."

He sat in silent thought for a long moment. "I'll do it," he said. "Heigh-oo! I'll do it. Come," and rising from his chair, he led us towards the locked doorway that barred the entrance to his secret laboratory.

CHAPTER X

THE FLYING DEATH

PHOR TAK'S LABORATORY occupied an entire wing of the building and consisted of a single, immense room fully fifty feet in height. His benches, tables, instruments and cabinets, located in one corner, were lost in the great interior. Near the ceiling and encircling the room was a single track from which was suspended a miniature cruiser, painted the ghastly blue of Jahar. Upon one of the benches was a cylindrical object about as long as one's hand. These were the only noticeable features of the laboratory other than its immense emptiness.

As Phor Tak ushered us within he closed the door behind him and I heard the ominous click of the ponderous lock. There was something depressing in the suggestiveness of the situation, induced, perhaps, by our knowledge that Phor Tak was mad and accentuated by the eerie mystery of the vast chamber.

Leading us to the bench upon which lay the cylindrical object which had attracted my attention, he lifted it carefully, almost caressingly, from its resting-place. "This," he said, "is a model of the device that will destroy Jahar. In it you behold the concentrated essence of scientific achievement. In appearance it is but a small metal cylinder, but within it is a mechanism as delicate and as sensitive as the human brain, and you will perceive that it functions almost as though animated by a mind within itself, but it is purely mechanical and may be produced in quantities quickly and at low cost. Before I explain it further I shall demonstrate one phase of its possibilities. Watch!"

Still holding the cylinder in his hand, Phor Tak stepped to a shallow cabinet against the wall, and opening it revealed an elaborate equipment of switches, levers and push-buttons. "Now watch the miniature flier suspended from the track near the ceiling," he directed, at the same time closing a switch. Immediately the flier commenced to travel along the track at considerable speed. Now Phor Tak pressed a button upon the top of the cylinder, which immediately sped from his extended palm, turned quickly in the air and rushed straight for the speeding flier. Slowly the distance between the two closed; the cylinder, curving gradually into the line of flight of the flier, was now trailing directly behind it, its pointed nose but a few feet from the stern of the miniature ship. Then Phor Tak pulled a tiny lever upon his switchboard and the flier leaped forward at accelerated speed. Instantly the speed of the cylinder increased and I could see that it was gaining in velocity much more rapidly than the flier. Half-way around the room again its nose struck the stern of the fleeing craft with sufficient severity to cause the ship to tremble from stem to stern; then the cylinder fell away and floated gently toward the floor. Phor Tak opened a switch that stopped the flier in its flight and then, running forward, caught the descending cylinder in his hand.

"This model," he explained, as he returned to where we stood, "is so constructed that when it makes contact with the flier it will float gently downward to the floor, but, as you have doubtless fully realized ere this, the finished product in practical use will explode upon contact with the ship. Note these tiny buttons with which it is covered. When any one of these comes in contact with an object the model stops and descends, whereas the full-sized device, properly equipped, will explode, absolutely demolishing whatever it may have come in contact with. As you are aware, every substance in the universe has its own fixed vibratory rate. This mechanism can be so attuned as to be attracted by the vibratory rate of any substance. The model, for example, is attracted by the blue protective paint with which the flier is covered. Imagine a fleet of Jaharian warships moving majestically through the air in battle formation. From an enemy ship or from the ground and at a distance so far as to be unobservable by the ships of Jahar, I release as many of these devices as there are ships in the fleet, allowing a few moments to elapse between launchings. The first torpedo rushes towards the fleet and destroys the nearest ship. All the torpedoes in the rear, strung out in line, are attracted by the combined masses of all the blue protecting coverings of the entire fleet. The first ship is falling to the ground, and though all of its paint may not have been destroyed, it has not the power to deflect any of the succeeding torpedoes, which one by one destroy the nearest of the remaining ships until the fleet has been absolutely erased. I have destroyed a great fleet without risking the life of a single man of my own following."

"But they will see the torpedoes coming," suggested Nur An, "and they will devise some defence. Even gunfire might stop many of them."

"Heigh-oo! But I have thought of that," cackled Phor Tak. He laid the torpedo upon a bench and opened another cabinet.

In this cabinet were a number of receptacles, some tightly sealed and others opened, revealing their contents, which appeared to be different coloured paints. From a number of these receptacles protruded the handles of paint brushes. One such handle, however, appeared to hang in mid-air, a few inches above one of the shelves, while just beneath it was a section of the rim of a receptacle that also appeared to be resting upon nothing. Phor Tak placed his open hand directly beneath this floating rim, and when he removed his hand from the cabinet, the rim of the receptacle and the handle of the paint brush floating just above it, followed, hovering just over his extended fingers, which were cupped in the position that they might assume were they holding a glass jar, such as would ordinarily have belonged to a rim like that which I could see floating about an inch above his fingers.

Going to the bench where he had laid the cylinder, Phor Tak went through the motions of setting a jar upon it, and, though there was no jar visible other than the floating rim, I distinctly heard a noise that was identical with the sound which the bottom of a glass jar would have made in coming in contact with the bench.

I can assure you that I was greatly mystified, but still more so by the events immediately following. Phor Tak seized the handle of the paint brush and made a pass a few inches above the metal torpedo. Instantly a portion of the torpedo, about an inch wide and three or four inches long, disappeared. Pass after pass he made until finally the whole surface of the torpedo had disappeared. Where it had rested the bench was empty. Phor Tak returned the handle of the paint brush to its floating position just above the floating jar rim, and then he turned to us with an expression of childlike pride upon his face, as much as to say, "Well, what do you think of that? Am I not wonderful?" And I was certainly forced to concede that it was wonderful and that I was entirely baffled and mystified by what I had seen.

"There, Nur An," exclaimed Phor Tak, "is the answer to your criticism of The Flying Death."

"I do not understand," said Nur An with a puzzled expression upon his face.

"Heigh-oo!" cried Phor Tak. "Have you not seen me render the device invisible?"

"But it is gone," said Nur An.

Phor Tak laughed his high crackling laugh. "It is still there," he said, "but you cannot see it. Here," and he took Nur An's hand and guided it towards the spot where the device had been.

I could see Nur An's fingers apparently feeling over the surface of something several inches above the top of the table. "By my first ancestor, it is still there!" he exclaimed.

"It is wonderful," I exclaimed. "You did not even touch it; you merely made passes above it with the handle of a paint brush and it disappeared."

"But I did touch it," insisted Phor Tak. "The brush was there, but you did not see it because it was covered with the substance which renders The Flying Death invisible. Notice this transparent glass receptacle in which I keep the compound of invisibility, and all that you can see of it is that part of the rim which, by chance, has not been coated with the compound."

"Marvellous!" I exclaimed. "Even now, although I have witnessed it with my own eyes, I can scarce conceive of the possibility of such a miracle."

"It is no miracle," said Phor Tak. "It is merely the application of scientific principles well known to me for hundreds of years. Nothing moves in straight lines;

light, vision, electro-magnetic forces follow lines that curve. The compound of invisibility merely bows outward the reflected light, which, entering our eyes and impinging upon our optic nerves, results in the phenomenon which we call vision, so that they pass around any object which is coated with the compound. When I first started to apply the compound to The Flying Death, your line of vision was deflected around the small portions so coated, but when I coated the entire surface of the torpedo, the curve of your vision passed completely around it on both sides so that you could plainly see the bench upon which it was resting precisely as though the device had not been there."

I was astounded at the apparent simplicity of the explanation, and naturally, being a soldier, I saw the tremendous advantage that the possession of these two scientific secrets would impart to the nation which controlled them. For the safety; yes, for the very existence of Helium I must possess them, and if that were impossible, then Phor Tak must be destroyed before the secret of this infernal power could be passed on to any other nation. Perhaps I could so ingratiate myself with old Phor Tak as to be able to persuade him to turn these secrets over to Helium in return for Helium's assistance in the work of wreaking his vengeance upon Tul Axtar.

"Phor Tak," I said, "you hold here within your grasp two secrets which in the hands of a kindly and beneficient power would bring eternal peace to Barsoom."

"Heigh-oo!" he cried. "I do not want peace. I want war. War! War!"

"Very well," I agreed, realizing that my suggestion had not been in line with the mad processes of his crazed brain. "Let us have war then, and what country upon Barsoom is better equipped to wage war than Helium? If you want war, form an alliance with Helium."

"I do not need Helium," he cried. "I do not need to form alliances. I shall make war—I shall make war

alone. With the invisible Flying Death I can destroy
whole navies, whole cities, entire nations. I shall start
with Jahar. Tul Axtar shall be the first to feel the
weight of my devastating powers. When the fleet of
Jahar has tumbled upon the roofs of Jahar and the
walls of Jahar have fallen about the ears of Tul Axtar,
then shall I destroy Tjanath. Helium shall know me
next. Proud and mighty Helium shall tremble and bow
at the feet of Phor Tak. I shall be Jeddak of Jeddaks,
ruler of a world." As he spoke his voice rose to a
piercing shriek and he trembled in the grip of the
frenzy that held him.

He must be destroyed, not alone for the sake of
Helium, but for the sake of all Barsoom; this mad
mind must be removed if I found that it was impossible
to direct or cajole it to my own ends. I determined,
however, to omit no sacrifice that might tend to bring
about a satisfactory conclusion to this strange adventure. I knew that mad minds were sometimes fickle
minds, and I hoped that in a moment of insane caprice
Phor Tak might reveal to me the secret of The Flying
Death and the compound of invisibility. This hope
was his temporary reprieve from death; its fulfilment
would be his pardon, but I knew that I must work
warily—that at the slightest suggestion of duplicity,
Phor Tak's suspicions would be aroused and that I
should then be the one to be destroyed.

I tossed long upon my sleeping-silks and furs that
night in troubled thought and planning. I felt that I
must possess these secrets; yet how? That they existed
within his brain alone, I knew, for he had told me that
there were no written formulas or plans or specifica-
tions for either of them. Somehow I must wheedle
them out of him, and the best way to start was to ingratiate myself with him. To this end I must further
his plans in so far as I possibly could.

Just before I fell asleep my thoughts reverted to
Sanoma Tora and to the urgent mission that had led
me to enter upon what had developed into the strang-
est adventure of my career. I felt a twinge of self-

reproach as I suddenly realized that Sanoma Tora had not been uppermost in my mind while I had lain there making plans for the future, but now with recollection of her a plan was suggested whereby I might not only succour her but also advance myself in the good graces of Phor Tak at the same time, and, thus relieved, I fell asleep.

It was late the following morning before I had an opportunity to speak with the old inventor, when I immediately broached the subject that was uppermost in my mind. "Phor Tak," I said, "you are handicapped by lack of knowledge of conditions existing in Jahar and the size and location of the fleet. Nur An and I will go to Jahar for you and obtain the information that you must have if your plans are to be successful. In this way, Nur An and I will also be striking a blow at Tul Axtar, while we will be in a position to attend to those matters which require our presence in Jahar."

"But how will you get to Jahar?" demanded Phor Tak.

"Could you not let us take a flier?" I asked.

"I have none," replied Phor Tak. "I know nothing about them. I am not interested in them. I could not even build one."

To say that I was both surprised and shocked would be putting it mildly, but if I had previously entertained any doubts that Phor Tak's brain was abnormally developed, it would have vanished with his admission that he knew nothing about fliers, for it seemed to me that there was scarcely a man, woman or child in any of the flying nations of Barsoom but could have constructed some sort of a flier.

"But how without fliers did you expect to transport The Flying Death to the vicinity of the Jaharian fleet? How did you expect to demolish the palace of Tul Axtar, or reduce the city of Jahar to ruins?"

"Now that you and Nur An are here to help me, I can set my slaves to work under you and easily turn out a dozen torpedoes a day. As these are completed they will immediately be launched, and eventually they will find their way to Jahar and the fleet. Of that there is no doubt; even if it takes a year they will eventually find their prey."

"If nothing chances to get in their way," I suggested; "but even so what pleasure will you derive from your revenge if you are unable to witness any part of it?"

"Heigh-oo! I have thought of that," replied Phor Tak, "but one may not have everything."

"You may have that," I told him.

"And how?" he demanded.

"By taking your torpedoes aboard a ship and flying to Jahar," I replied.

"No," he exclaimed stubbornly, "I shall do it my own way. What right have you to interfere with my plans?"

"I merely want to help you," I said, attempting to mollify him by a conciliatory tone and attitude.

"And there is another thought," said Nur An, "that suggests that it might be expedient to follow Hadron's plans."

"You are both against me," said Phor Tak.

"By no means," Nur An assured him. "It is our keen desire to aid you that prompts the suggestion."

"Well, what is yours then?" asked the old man.

"Your plan contemplates the destruction of the navies of Tjanath and Helium following the fall of Jahar," exclaimed Nur An. "This, at least in respect to the navy of Helium, you cannot possibly hope to accomplish at so great a distance and without any knowledge of the number of ships to be destroyed, nor will your torpedoes be similiarly attracted to them as they are to the ships of Jahar because the ships of these other nations are not protected by the blue paint of Jahar. It will therefore be necessary for you to proceed to the vicinity of Tjanath and later to Helium, and for your own protection you will use the blue paint of Jahar upon your ship, for you may never be certain unless you are on the ground at the time that you have destroyed all of the navy of Jahar, or all of their disintegrating-ray rifles."

"That is true," said Phor Tak thoughtfully.

"And furthermore," continued Nur An, "if you dispatch more than the necessary number of torpedoes, those that remain at large will certainly be attracted by the blue paint of your own ship and you will be destroyed by your own devices."

"You will ruin all my plans," screamed Phor Tak. "Why did you think of this?"

"If I had not thought of it you would have been destroyed," Nur An reminded him.

"Well, what am I to do about it? I have no ship. I cannot build a ship."

"We can get one," I said.

"How?"

The conversation between Nur An and Phor Tak had suggested a plan to me and this I now explained roughly to them. Nur An was enthusiastic over the idea, but Phor Tak was not particularly keen for it. I could not understand the grounds for his objection, nor, as a matter of fact, did they interest me greatly, since he finally admitted that he would be compelled to act in accordance with my suggestion.

Immediately adjacent to Phor Tak's laboratory was a well-equipped machine shop, and here Nur An and I laboured for weeks, utilizing the services of a dozen slaves until we had succeeded in constructing what I am sure was the most remarkable-looking airship that it had ever fallen to my lot to behold. Briefly, it was a cylinder pointed at each end and closely resembled the model of the Flying Death. Within the outer shell was another smaller cylinder; between the walls of these two we placed the buoyancy tanks. The tanks and the sides of the two envelopes were pierced by observation ports along each side of the ship and at the bow and stern. These ports could be completely covered by shutters hinged upon the outside, but operated from within. There were two hatchways in the keel and two above which led to a narrow walkway along the top of the cylinder. In turrets, forward and aft, were mounted two disintegrating-ray rifles.

Above the controls was a periscope that transmitted an image of all that came within its range to a ground-glass plate in front of the pilot. The entire outside of the ship was first painted the ghastly blue that would protect it from the disintegrating-ray rifles of Jahar, while over this was spread a coating of the compound of invisibility. The shutters that covered the ports being similarly coated, the ship could attain practically total invisibility by closing them, the only point remaining visible being the tiny eye of the periscope.

Not possessing sufficient technical knowledge to enable me to build one of the new type motors, I had to content myself with one of the old types of much less efficiency.

At last the work was done. We had a ship that would accommodate four with ease, and it was uncanny to realize this fact and yet, at the same time, be unable to see anything but the tiny eye of the periscope when the covers were lowered over the ports, and even the eye of the periscope was invisible unless it was turned in the direction of the observer.

As the work neared completion I had noticed that Phor Tak's manner became more marked by nervousness and irritability. He found fault with everything and on several occasions he almost stopped the work upon the ship.

Now, at last, we were ready to sail. The ship was stocked with ammunition, water and provisions, and at the last minute I installed a destination control compass, for which I was afterwards to be devoutly thankful.

When I suggested immediate departure, however, Phor Tak demurred, but would give me no reason for his objection. Presently, however, I lost patience and told the old man that we were going anyway whether he liked it or not.

He did not fly into a rage as I had expected, but laughed instead, and there was something in the laugh that seemed more terrible than anger.

"You think I am a fool," he said, "and that I will let you go and carry my secrets to Tul Axtar, but you are mistaken."

"So are you," I snapped. "You are mistaken in thinking that we would betray you and you are also mistaken in thinking that you can prevent our departure."

"Heigh-oo!" he cackled. "I do not need to prevent your departure, but I can prevent your arrival at Jahar or elsewhere. I have not been idle while you worked upon this ship. I have constructed a full-size Flying Death. It is attuned to search out this ship. If you depart against my wishes, it will follow and destroy you. Heigh-oo! What do you think of that?"

"I think that you are an old fool," I cried in exasperation. "You have the opportunity to enlist the loyal aid of two honorable warriors and yet you choose to turn them into enemies."

"Enemies who cannot harm me," he reminded me. "I hold your lives in the hollow of my hand. Well have you concealed your thoughts from me, but not quite well enough. I have read enough of them to know that you think me mad and I have also received the impression that you would stop at nothing to prevent me from using my power against Helium. I have no doubt but that you will help me against Jahar, and against Tjanath too, perhaps, but Helium, the mightiest and proudest empire of Barsoom, is my real goal. Helium shall proclaim me Jeddak of Jeddaks if I have to wreck a world to accomplish my design."

"Then all our work has been for nothing?" I demanded. "We are not going to use the ship we have constructed?"

"We may use it," he said, "but under my terms."

"And what are they?" I asked.

"You may go alone to Jahar, but I shall keep Nur An here as hostage. If you betray me, he dies."

There was no moving him; no amount of argument could alter his determination. I tried to convince him that one man could accomplish little, that, in fact, he might not be able to accomplish anything, but he was adamant—I should go alone or not at all.

CHAPTER XI

"LET THE FIRE BE HOT!"

AS I AROSE that night into the starlit splendour of a Barsoomian night, the white castle of Phor Tak lay a lovely gem below me bathed in the soft light of Thuria. I was alone; Nur An remained behind, the hostage of the mad scientist. Because of him I must return to Jhama. Nur An had exacted no promise from me, but he knew that I would return.

Twenty-five hundred haads to the east lay Jahar and Sanoma Tora. Fifteen hundred haads to the south-west were Tjanath and Tavia. I turned the nose of my flier towards the goal of duty, towards the woman I loved, and, with throttle wide, my invisible craft sped towards distant Jahar.

But my thoughts I could not control. Despite my every effort to keep them concentrated upon the purpose of my adventure, they persisted in wandering to a prison tower, to a tousled head of refractory hair, to a rounded shoulder that had once pressed mine. I shook myself to be rid of the vision as I sped through the night, but it constantly returned, and in its wake came harrowing thoughts of the fate that might have overtaken Tavia during my absence.

I set my destination control compass upon Jahar, the exact position of which I had obtained from Phor Tak, and, thus relieved of the necessity of constantly remaining at the controls, I busied myself about the interior of the ship. I looked to the ammunition of the disintegrating-ray rifles and rearranged it to suit my own ideas.

Phor Tak had equipped me with three types of rays; one would distintegrate metal, another would disintegrate wood and the third would disintegrate human flesh. I had also brought along something which Phor Tak had refused me when I asked him for it. I pressed the pocket pouch in which I had placed it to make sure that I still had the vial, the contents of which I imagined might prove of inestimable value to me.

I raised all the port shutters and adjusted the ventilators, for at best the interior of this strange ship seemed close and stuffy to one who was accustomed to the open deck of the fast scout fliers of Helium. Then I spread my sleeping-silks and furs and settled myself down to rest, knowing that when I arrived at Jahar my destination control compass would stop the ship and an alarm would awaken me if I still slept. But sleep would not come. I thought of Sanoma Tora. I visualized her cold and stately beauty, but always her haughty eyes dissolved into the eyes of Tavia, sparkling with the joy of life, soft with the light of friendship.

I was far from Jhama when at last I sprang determinedly from my sleeping-silks and furs, and going to the controls, I cut off the destination control compass and with a single swift turn swung the nose of the flier towards Tjanath.

The die was cast. I felt that I should experience remorse and self-loathing, but I experienced neither. I joyed in the thought that I was rushing to the service of a friend, and I knew in the most innermost recesses of my heart that of the two, Tavia had more claim upon my friendship than had Sanoma Tora, from whom I had received at best only scant courtesy.

I did not again try to sleep. I did not feel like sleeping; instead I remained at the controls and watched the desolate landscape as it rushed forward to pass beneath me. With the coming of dawn I saw Tjanath directly ahead of me, and as I approached the city it was difficult for me to realize that I could do so with utter impunity and that my ship with its closed ports was entirely invisible. Moving slowly now, I circled above the palace of Haj Osis. Those portions of the palace that were topped by flat roofs revealed sleepy guardsmen. At the main hangar a single guardsman watched.

I floated above the east tower; beneath me, cuddled in her sleeping silks and furs, I could picture Tavia. How surprised she would be could she know that I hovered thus close above her.

Dropping lower I circled the tower, coming to a stop finally opposite the windows of the room in which Tavia had been confined. I manœuvred the ship to bring one of the ports opposite the window and close enough to give me a view of the interior of the room. But though I remained there for some time, I could see no one, and at last I became convinced that Tavia had been removed to other quarters. I was disappointed, for this must necessarily greatly complicate my plans for rescue. I had foreseen but little difficulty in transferring Tavia by night through the tower window to the flier; now I must make my plans all anew. Everything hinged, of course, upon my ability to locate Tavia. To do that it was evident that I must enter the palace. The moment that I quitted the invisibility of my flier, I should be menaced by the greatest danger at every turn, and, clothed as I was in home-made harness fashioned by the hands of the slaves of Phor Tak, I should arouse the active suspicion of the first person who set eyes upon me.

I must enter the palace, and to do it in any degree of safety I must have a disguise.

All my ports were now closed, the periscope being my only eye. I turned it slowly about as I tried to plan some method of procedure that might have within it some tiny seed of success.

As the panorama slowly unfolded itself upon the ground glass before me there appeared the main palace hanger and the single warrior upon watch. Here my periscope came to rest, for there was an entrance to the palace and here a disguise.

Slowly manœuvring my ship in the direction of the hangar, I brought it down upon the roof of that structure. I should have been glad to moor it, but here there were no means at hand. I must depend upon its own weight and hope that no high wind would rise.

Realizing that the instant that I emerged from the interior of the flier I should be entirely visible, I waited, watching through my periscope until the warrior upon the roof just below me turned his back; then I emerged quickly from the ship through one of the upper hatches and dropped to the roof upon the side closest to the warrior. I was about four feet from the edge of the roof and he was standing almost below me, his back towards me. Should he turn he would discover me instantly and would give an alarm before I could be upon him. My only hope of success, therefore, was to silence him before he realized that he was menaced.

I have learned from the experience of John Carter that first thoughts are often inspirations, while sober afterthought may lead to failure, or so delay action as to nullify all its effect.

Therefore, in this instance, I acted upon inspiration. I did not hesitate. I stepped quickly to the edge of the roof and hurled myself straight at the broad shoulders of the sentry. In my hand was a slim dagger.

The end came quickly. I think the poor fellow never knew what happened to him. Dragging his body to the interior of the hangar I stripped the harness from it; at the same time, though almost mechanically, I noted the ships within the hangar. With the exception of one, a patrol boat, they all bore the personal insignia of the Jed of Tjanath. They were the king's ships—an ornate cruiser heavily armed, two smaller pleasure craft, a two-man scout flier and a one-man scout flier. They were not much, of course, by comparison with the ships of Helium, but I was quite sure that they were absolutely the best that Tjanath could afford.

However, having my own ship, I was not particularly concerned with these other than that I am always interested in ships of all descriptions.

Not far from where I stood was the entrance to a ramp leading down into the palace. Realizing that only through boldness might I succeed, I walked directly to the ramp and entered it. As I rounded the first turn I was appalled to see that the ramp passed directly through a guard-room. Upon the floor fully a score of warriors were stretched upon their sleeping-silks and furs.

I did not dare to pause; I must keep on. Perhaps I could pass them without arousing their curiosity. I had but a brief glimpse of the room before I entered it, and in that glimpse I had seen only men apparently wrapped in sleep, and an instant later, as I emerged into the room itself, I saw that it contained only those whom I had first seen. No one within it was awake, but I heard voices in an adjoining room. Hurrying quickly across the apartment I entered the ramp upon the opposite side.

I think my heart had stood still as I strode silently across that room among those sleeping men, for had a single one of them awakened he would have inevitably known that I was no fellow-member of the guard.

Further down within the palace itself I should be in less danger, for so great is the number of retainers in the palace of a Jed that no one may know them all by sight, so that strange and unfamiliar faces are almost as customary as they are upon the avenues of a city.

My plan was to try to reach the tower room in which Tavia had been confined, for I was positive that from my position in the flier I could not see the entire interior, and it was just possible that Tavia was there.

Owing to the construction of my ship I had been unable to attract her attention without raising a hatch and taking the chance of revealing my presence, which would, I felt, have jeopardized Tavia's chances of escape far too greatly to warrant my doing so.

Perhaps I should have waited until night; perhaps

I was over-anxious and in my zeal might be running far greater risks than were necessary. I thought of these things now and perhaps I upbraided myself, but I had gone too far now to retreat. I was properly in for it, whatever might follow.

As I followed the ramp down to different levels I tried to discover some familiar landmark that might lead me to the east tower, and as I emerged into a corridor at one of the levels I saw almost directly in front of me a door which I instantly recognized—it was the door to the office of Yo Seno, the keeper of the keys.

"Good!" I thought. "Fate certainly has led me here."

Crossing to the door I opened it and stepped quickly within the room, closing the door behind me. Yo Seno was sitting at his desk. He was alone. He did not look up. He was one of those arrogant men—a small man with a little authority—who liked to impress his importance upon all inferiors. Therefore, doubtless it was his way to ignore his visitors for a moment or two. This time he made a mistake. After quietly locking the door behind me I crossed to the door at the opposite end of the room and bolted it too.

It was then that, doubtless compelled by curiosity, Yo Seno looked up. At first he did not recognize me. "What do you want?" he demanded gruffly.

"You, Yo Seno," I said.

He looked at me steadily for a moment with growing astonishment, then with his eyes wide he leaped to his feet. "You?" he screamed. "By Issus, no! You are dead!"

"I have returned from the grave, Yo Seno. I have come back to haunt you," I said.

"What do you want?" he demanded. "Stand aside! You are under arrest."

"Where is Tavia?" I asked.

"How do I know?" he demanded.

"You are the keeper of the keys, Yo Seno. Who

should know better than you where the prisoners are?"

"Well, what if I do know? I shall not tell," he said.

"You shall tell, Yo Seno, or you shall die," I warned him.

He had walked from behind his desk and was standing not far from me when, without warning and with far greater celerity than I gave him credit for possessing, he snatched his long sword from its scabbard and was upon me.

I was forced to jump backward quickly to avoid his first cut, but when he swung the second time my own sword was out and I was on my guard. Yo Seno proved himself no mean antagonist. He was clever with the sword and he knew that he was fighting for his life. I wondered at first why he did not call for help, and then I came to the conclusion that it was because there were no warriors in the adjoining room, as there had been upon my previous visit to Yo Seno's quarters. We fought in silence, only the din of metal upon metal reflecting the deadliness of the combat.

I was in a hurry to be done with him and I was pressing him closely when he resorted to a trick which came near to proving my undoing. I had backed him up against his desk and thought that I had him where he could not escape. I could not see his left hand behind him, nor the heavy vase for which it was groping, but an instant later I saw the thing flying straight at my head and I also saw the opening which Yo Seno made in the instant that he cast the missle, for so occupied was he with his aim that he let his point drop. Stooping beneath the vase I sprang into close quarters, driving my sword through the heart of Yo Seno.

As I wiped the blood from my blade upon the hair of my victim I could not repress a feeling of elation that it had been my hand that had cut down the seducer of Phao and in some measure avenged the honour of my friend, Nur An.

Now, however, was no time for meditation. I heard

footsteps approaching in the corridor without, and hastily seizing the harness of the corpse, I dragged it towards the panel which hid the entrance to the secret corridor that led to the room in the east tower—that familiar corridor where I had passed happy moments alone with Tavia.

With more haste than reverence I dumped the corpse of Yo Seno into the dark interior and then, closing the panel after me, I groped my way through the darkness towards the tower room, my heart high with the hope that I might find Tavia still there.

As I approached the panel at the tower end of the corridor I could feel my heart beating rapidly—a sensation to which I was unaccustomed and which I could not explain. I was positive that I was in excellent physical condition, and, while it is not at all unusual that surprise or imminent danger causes the heart of some men to palpitate, even though they may be endowed with exceptional courage, yet, for my part, I had never experienced such a sensation and I must admit that I was deeply mystified.

The anticipation of seeing Tavia again soon caused me to forget the unpleasant sensation, and as I stopped behind the panel my whole mind was occupied with pleasurable consideration of what I hoped awaited me beyond—the longed-for reunion with this best of friends.

I was upon the point of springing the catch and opening the panel when my attention was attracted by voices from the room beyond. I heard a man's voice and that of a woman, but I could understand no words. Cautiously I opened the panel sufficiently to permit me to view the interior of the apartment.

The scene that met my gaze sent the hot fighting blood surging through my frame. In the centre of the room a young warrior in rich trappings had Tavia in his grasp and was dragging her across the room towards the doorway. Tavia struggled, striking at him.

"Don't be a fool," snarled the man. "Haj Osis has

given you to me. You will lead a better life as my slave than most free women live."

"I prefer prison or death," replied Tavia.

Phao was standing helplessly at one side, her eyes filled with compassion for Tavia. It was obvious that she could do nothing to defend her friend, for the trappings of the warrior proclaimed him of high rank, but just what that rank was I did not discern at the time, for I was not interested. In a bound I was in the centre of the room, and seizing the warrior roughly by the shoulder, I hurled him backward so heavily that he fell sprawling to the floor. I heard gasps of astonishment from both Phao and Tavia and my name breathed in the soft accents of the latter.

As I drew my sword the warrior scrambled to his feet, but did not draw. "Fool! Idiot! Knave!" he shrieked. "Do you not realize what you have done? Do you not know who I am?"

"In a moment it will be 'who you were,'" I told him in a low voice. "On guard!"

"No," he cried, backing away. "You wear the harness and the metal of a warrior of the guard. You cannot dare draw your sword against the son of Haj Osis. Back, fellow, I am Prince Haj Alt."

"I could pray to Issus that you might be Haj Osis himself," I replied, "but at least there will be some recompense in the knowledge that I have destroyed his spawn. On guard, you fool, unless you wish to die like a sorak."

He was still backing away and now he looked about him with every evidence of terror written upon his weak countenance. He espied the panel door that I had inadvertently left open, and before I could prevent he had darted through and closed it behind him. I leaped in pursuit, but the lock had clicked and I did not know where to find the mechanism to release it.

"Quick, Phao!" I cried. "You know the secret of the panel. Open it for me. We must not permit this fellow to escape or he will sound the alarm and we shall all be lost."

Phao ran quickly to my side and placed her thumb upon a button cleverly hidden in the ornate carving of the wood panelling that covered the wall. I waited in breathless expectancy, but the panel did not open. Phao pushed frantically again and again, and then she turned to me with a gesture of helplessness and defeat.

"He has tampered with the lock upon the other side," she said. "He is a clever rogue and he would have thought of that."

"We must follow," I said, and raising my long sword I struck the panel a heavy blow that would have shattered much thicker planking, but I only made a scratch upon it, tearing away a little piece scarce thicker than a fingernail, but the scar that I had made revealed the harrowing truth—the panel was constructed of forandus, the hardest and the lightest metal known to Barsoomians. I turned away. "It is useless," I said, "to attempt to pierce forandus with cold steel."

Tavia had crossed to us and was standing in silence, looking up into my face. Her eyes were bathed with unshed tears and I saw her lips tremble. "Hadron!" she breathed. "You have come back from the dead. Oh, why did you come? For this time they will make no mistake."

"You know why I came, Tavia," I told her.

"Tell me," she said, very soft and low.

"For friendship, Tavia," I replied; "for the best friend that a man ever had."

At first she seemed surprised and then an odd little smile curved her lips. "I would rather have the friendship of Hadron of Hastor," she said, "than any other gift the world might give me."

It was a nice thing for her to say and I certainly appreciated it, but I did not understand that little smile. However, I had no time then in which to solve riddles; the problem of our safety was the all-important question, and then it was that I thought of the vial in my pocket pouch. I looked quickly about the room. In one corner I espied a pile of sleeping-silks and furs;

something there might answer my purpose; the contents of the vial might yet give us all freedom if I had but time enough. I ran quickly across the room and searched rapidly until I had found three pieces of fabric that were at least better suited to my purpose than any of the others. I opened my pocket pouch to withdraw the vial and at the same instant I heard the pounding of running feet and the clank and clatter of arms.

Too late! They were already at the door. I closed my pocket pouch and waited. At first it was in my mind to take them on in combat as they entered, but I put that idea aside as worse than useless, since it could result in nothing but my death, whereas time might conjure an opportunity to use the contents of the vial.

The door swung open, fully fifty warriors were revealed in the corridor without. A padwar of the guard entered, followed by his men. "Surrender!" he commanded.

"I have not drawn," I replied. "Come and take it."

"You admit that you are the warrior who attacked the prince, Haj Alt?" he demanded.

"I do," I replied.

"What have these women to do with it?"

"Nothing. I do not know them. I followed Haj Alt here because I thought that it would give me the opportunity that I have long sought to kill him."

"Why did you want to kill him?" demanded the padwar. "What grievance have you against the prince?"

"None," I replied. "I am a professional assassin and I was hired by others."

"Who are they?" he demanded.

I laughed at him, for I knew that he knew better than to ask a professional assassin of Barsoom such a question as that. The members of this ancient fraternity are guided by a code of ethics which they scrupulously observe, and seldom, if ever, can anything persuade or force one of their number to divulge the name of his principal.

I saw Tavia's eyes upon me and it seemed to me

that there was a little questioning expression in them, but I knew that she must know that I was lying thus to protect her and Phao.

I was hustled from the chamber, and as I was being conducted along the corridors and down the ramps of the palace, the padwar questioned me in an endeavour to learn my true identity. I was greatly relieved to discover that they did not recognize me and I hoped that I might continue to escape recognition; not that it would make any difference to my fate, for I realized that the direst would be inflicted upon one who had attempted to assassinate the prince of the house of Haj Osis, but I was afraid that were I to be recognized they might accuse Tavia of complicity in the attack upon Haj Alt and that she would be made to suffer accordingly.

Presently I found myself in the pits again and by chance in the very cell that Nur An and I had occupied. I experienced almost the sensations of a homecoming, but with variations. Once again I was alone, fettered to a stone wall, my only hope the vial which they had overlooked and which still reposed at the bottom of my pocket pouch. But this was no time or place to use its contents, nor had I the requisite materials at hand even had I been unfettered.

I was not long in the pits this time before warriors came and, unlocking my fetters, conducted me to the great throne-room of the palace, where Haj Osis sat upon his dais surrounded by the high officers and functionaries of his army and his court.

Haj Alt, the prince, was there and when he saw me being led up towards the throne he trembled with rage. As I was halted in front of the Jed, he turned to his son. "Is this the warrior who attacked you, Haj Alt?" he asked.

"This is the scoundrel," replied the younger man. "He took me by surprise and would have stabbed me in the back had I not managed to outwit him."

"He drew his sword against you," demanded Haj Osis—"against the person of a prince?"

"He did and he would have killed me with it, too, as he did kill Yo Seno, whose corpse I found in the corridor that leads from Yo Seno's office to the tower."

So they had found the body of Yo Seno. Well, they would not kill me any deader for that crime than for menacing the life of the prince.

As this juncture an officer entered the throne-room rather hurriedly. He was breathing rapidly as he stopped at the foot of the throne. He was standing close beside me and I saw him turn and look quickly at me, his eyes running rapidly up and down me between head and feet. Then he addressed the man upon the throne.

"Haj Osis, Jed of Tjanath," he said, "I came quickly to tell you that the body of a warrior of the hangar guard has just been found within the Jed's hangar. His harness had been stripped from him and his weapons, while strange harness and strange weapons were left beside his corpse, and as I approached your throne, Haj Osis, I recognized the harness of my dead warrior upon the body of this man here," and he pointed an accusing finger at me.

Haj Osis was scrutinizing me very carefully now. There was a strange look in his eyes that I did not like. It betokened half recognition, and then of a sudden I saw the dawning of full recognition there, and the Jed of Tjanath swore a loud oath that resounded through the great throne-room.

"Breath of Issus!" he shouted. "Look at him! Do you not know him? He is the spy from Jahar who called himself Hadron of Hastor. He died The Death. With my own eyes I saw him, and yet he is back here in my palace murdering my people and threatening my son, but this time he shall die." Haj Osis had risen from his throne, and with upraised hands that seemed to claw the air above me he appeared like some hideous corphal pronouncing a curse upon its victim. "But first we shall know who sent him here. He did not come of his own volition to kill me and my son; behind him is some malignant mind that yearns to destroy the Jed of Tjanath and his family. Burn him slowly, but do not let him die until he has divulged the name. Away with him! Let the fire be hot, but slow."

CHAPTER XII

THE CLOAK OF INVISIBILITY

AS HAJ OSIS, Jed of Tjanath, pronounced sentence of death upon me I knew that whatever I might do to save myself must be done at once, for the instant that the guards laid hold upon me again my final hope would have vanished, for it was evident that the torture and the death would take place immediately.

The warriors forming the guard that had escorted me from the pits were lined up several paces behind me. The dais upon which Haj Osis stood was raised but a little over three feet above the floor of the throne-room. Between me and the Jed of Tjanath there was no one, for as he had sentenced me he had advanced from his throne to the very edge of the platform.

The action that I took was not delayed as long as it has taken me to tell it. Had it been, it could never have been taken, for the guards would have been upon me. Instantly the last word fell from his mouth my plan was formulated, and in that instant I leaped cat-like to the dais, full upon Haj Osis, Jed of Tjanath. So sudden, so unexpected was my attack that there was no defence. I seized him by the throat with one hand and with the other I snatched his dagger from its sheath, and raising it above him I shouted my warning in a voice that all might hear.

"Stand back, or Haj Osis dies!" I cried.

They had started to rush me, but as the full import of my threat came home to them they halted.

"It is my life or yours, Haj Osis," I said, "unless you do what I tell you to do."

"What?" he asked, his face black with terror.

"Is there an ante-room behind the throne?" I asked.

"Yes," he replied. "What of it?"

"Take me there alone," I said. "Command your people to stand aside."

"And let you kill me when you get me there?" he demanded, trembling.

"I shall kill you now if you do not," I replied. "Listen, Haj Osis; I did not come here to kill you or your son. What I told the padwar of the guard was a lie. I came for another purpose, far transcending in importance to me the life of Haj Osis or that of his son. Do as I tell you and I promise that I shall not kill you. Tell your people that we are going into the ante-room and that I promise not to harm you if we are left alone there for five xats" (*about fifteen minutes*).

He hesitated.

"Make haste," I said, "I have no time to waste," and I let the point of his own dagger touch his throat.

"Don't!" he screamed, shrinking back. "I will do whatever you say. Stand back all of you!" he shouted to his people. "I am going to the ante-room with this warrior and I command you upon pain of death not to enter there for five xats. At the end of that time, come; but not before."

I took a firm hold upon Haj Osis' harness between his shoulders and I kept the point of his dagger pressed against the flesh beneath his left shoulder-blade as I followed him towards the ante-room, while those who had crowded the dais behind the throne fell back to make an aisle for us. At the doorway I halted and turned towards them.

"Remember," I said, "five full xats and not a tal before."

Entering the ante-room I closed and bolted the door,

and then, still forcing Haj Osis ahead of me, I crossed
the room and closed and bolted the only other door to
the chamber. Then I pushed the Jed to one side of the
room.

"Lie down here upon your face," I said.

"You promised not to kill me," he wailed.

"I shall not kill you unless they come before the five
xats are up and you do otherwise than as I bid you so
as to delay me. I am going to bind you, but it will
not hurt you."

With poor grace he lay down upon his belly, and
with his own harness I strapped his arms together behind his back. Then I blindfolded him and left him
lying there.

As I had first entered the room I had taken in its
contents with a single, quick glance and I had seen
there precisely the things that I most needed, and now
that I had disposed of Haj Osis I crossed quickly to
one of the windows and tore down a part of the silk
hangings that covered it. It was a full length of fine,
light silk and very wide, since it had been intended to
hang in graceful folds as an underdrape with heavier
hangings. At the ornate desk where the Jed of Tjanath
signed his decrees, I went to work. First I took the vial
from my pocket pouch and unstoppered it; then I wad-
ded the silk into a ball, and because of its wonderful
fineness I could compress it within my two hands.
Fastening the ball of silk into a loosely compressed
mass with strips torn from another hanging, I slowly
poured the contents of the vial over it, turning the ball
with the point of Haj Osis' dagger. Remembering Phor
Tak's warning, I was careful not to let any of the
contents of the vial come in contact with my flesh, and
I could readily see why one had to be careful as I
watched the ball of silk disappear before my eyes.

Knowing that the compound of invisibility would
dry almost as rapidly as it impregnated the silk, I
waited only a brief instant after emptying about half
the contents of the vial upon the ball. Then, groping
with my fingers, I found the strings that held it into

its roughly spherical shape and cut them, after which I shook the silk out as best I could. For the most part it was invisible, but there were one or two spots that the compound had not reached. These I quickly daubed with some of the liquid remaining in the vial, which I now restoppered and replaced in my pocket pouch.

So much depended upon the success of my experiment that I almost feared to put it to the test, but it must be tested, and there could be only a few xats remaining before the warriors of Haj Osis would burst into the ante-chamber.

By feel alone I draped the silk over my head so that it fell all about me. Through its thin and delicate meshes I could see objects at close range quite well enough to make my way about. I crossed to Haj Osis and took the blind from his eyes, at the same time stepping quickly back. He looked hurriedly and affrightedly about him.

"Who did that?" he demanded, and then half to himself, "He is gone." For a moment he was silent, rolling his eyes about in all directions, searching every nook and corner of the apartment. Then an expression that was part hope and part relief came to his eyes.

"Quick!" he shouted in a loud voice. "The guard! He has escaped!"

I breathed a sigh of relief—if Haj Osis could not see me, no one could—my plan had succeeded.

I dared not return to the throne-room and make my escape that way along corridors with which I was familiar, for I could already hear the rush of feet towards the ante-room door, and I was well aware that, although they could not see me, they could feel me and that unquestionably in the rush my mantle of invisibility, or at least a portion of it, would be torn from me, which would indubitably spell my doom.

I ran quickly to the other doorway and unbolted it, and as I opened it I looked back at Haj Osis. His eyes were upon the doorway and they were wide with incredulity and horror. For an instant I did not realize the cause and looked quickly behind me to see if I could see what had caused Haj Osis' fright, and then it dawned upon me and I smiled. He had seen and heard the bolt shot and the door open as though by ghostly hands.

He must have sensed a vague suspicion of the truth, for he turned quickly towards the other door and screamed a warning in a high falsetto voice. "Do not enter," he cried, "until the five xats are up. It is I who commands—Haj Osis, the Jed."

Closing the door after me and still smiling, I hastened along the corridor, searching for a ramp that would carry me to the upper levels of the palace from which I could easily locate the guard-room and the hanger where I had left my ship.

The corridor I had entered led directly into the royal apartments.

At first it was difficult to accustom myself to my invisibility, and as I suddenly entered an apartment in which there were several people, my first impulse was to turn and flee, but as I had stepped directly into the view of one of the occupants of the room and at a distance of little more than five or six feet without attracting his attention, although his eyes were apparently directly upon me, my confidence was quickly restored. I continued on across the room as nonchalantly as though I had been in my own quarters in Helium.

The royal apartments seemed interminable, and though I was constantly seeking a way out of them into one of the main corridors of the palace, I was instead constantly stumbling into places where I did not care to be and where I had no business, sometimes with considerable embarrassment, as when I entered a cosy, private apartment in the women's quarters at a moment when I was convinced they were not expecting strange gentlemen.

I would not turn back, however, for I had no time to lose, and crossing the room I followed another short corridor only to leap from the frying-pan into the fire—I had entered the forbidden apartment of the Jeddara herself. It is a good thing for the royal lady that it was I and not Haj Osis who came thus unexpectedly upon her, for her position was most compromising, and from his harness I judged that her good-looking companion was a slave. In disgust I retreated, for there was no other exit from the apartment, and presently I stumbled, entirely by accident, upon one of the main corridors of the palace—a busy corridor filled with slaves, warriors and courtiers, with men, women and children passing to and fro upon whatever business called them, or perhaps seated upon the carved benches that lined the walls.

I was not yet accustomed to my new and surprising state of invisibility. I could see the people about me and it seemed inevitable that I must be seen. For a moment I had hesitated in the doorway that had led me to the corridor. A slave girl, approaching along the corridor, turned suddenly towards the doorway where I stood. She was looking directly at me, yet her gaze appeared to pass entirely through me. For an instant I was filled with consternation, and then, realizing that she was about to collide with me, I stepped quickly to one side. She passed by me, but it was evident that she sensed my presence, for she paused and looked quickly about, an expression of surprise in her eyes. Then, to my immense relief, she passed on through the doorway. She had not seen me, though doubtless she had heard me as I stepped aside. With a feeling of renewed confidence I now joined the throng in the corridor, threading my way in and out among the people to avoid contact with them and searching diligently all the while for the entrance to a ramp leading upward. This I presently discovered, and it was not long thereafter that I reached the upper level of the palace, where a short search brought me to the guard-room at the foot of the ramp leading to the royal hangars.

Idling in the guard-room, the warriors then off duty were engaged in various pursuits. Some were cleaning their harness and polishing their metal; two were playing at jetan, while others were rolling tiny numbered spheres at a group of numbered holes—a fascinating game of chance, called yano, which is, I presume, almost as old as Barsoomian civilization. The room was filled with the laughter and oaths of fighting men. How alike are warriors the world over! But for their harness and their metal they might have been a detachment of the palace guard at Helium.

Passing among them I ascended the ramp to the roof where the hangars stood. Two warriors on duty at the top of the ramp almost blocked my further progress. It would be a narrow squeeze to pass between them and I feared detection. As I paused I could not but overhear their conversation.

"I tell you that he was struck from behind," said one. "He never knew what killed him," and I knew that they were talking about the guardsman I had killed.

"But from whence came his assassin?" demanded the other.

"The padwar believes it may have been a fellow member of the guard. There will be an investigation and we shall all be questioned."

"It was not I," said the other. "He was my best friend."

"Nor was it I."

"He had a way with women. Perhaps—"

My attention was distracted and their conversation terminated by the footsteps of a warrior running rapidly up the ramp. My position was now most precarious. The ramp was narrow and the man coming from behind might easily bump into me. I must therefore pass the sentries immediately and make my way to the roof. There was just sufficient room between the warrior at my left and the side wall of the ramp for me to pass through, if he did not step back, and with all the stealth that I could summon I edged myself slowly behind him, and you may rest assured that I breathed a sigh of relief when I had passed him.

The warrior ascending the ramp had now reached the two men. "The assassin of the hangar sentry has been discovered," he said. "He is none other than the spy from Jahar who called himself Hadron of Hastor and who, with the other spy, Nur An, was sentenced to die The Death. Through some miracle he escaped and has returned to the palace of Haj Osis. Besides the hangar sentry, he has slain Yo Seno, but he was captured after attacking the Prince, Haj Alt. Again he has escaped and he is now at large in the palace. The padwar of the guard has sent me to direct you to redouble your watchfulness. Great will be the reward of him who captures Hardon of Hastor, dead or alive."

"He'll never come here by daylight."

I smiled as I walked quickly towards the hangar. To reach the roof without disarranging my robe of invisibility was difficult, but I finally accomplished it. Before me lay the empty roof; no ship was in sight, but I smiled again to myself, knowing well that it was there. I looked about for the eye of the periscope that would reveal the craft's presence to me, but it was not visible. However, that did not concern me greatly, since I realized that it might be turned in the opposite direction. It was only necessary for me to walk to where I had left the ship, and this I did, feeling ahead of me with extended hands.

I crossed the roof from one side to the other, but found no ship. That I was perplexed goes without saying. I most certainly knew where I had left the ship, but it was no longer there. Perhaps a wind had moved it slightly, and with this thought in mind I searched another section of the roof, but with equal disappointment. By now I was truly apprehensive, and thereupon I set about a systematic search of the roof until I had covered every square foot of it and was convinced beyond doubt that the worst of disasters had befallen me—my ship was gone; but where? Indeed the compound of invisibility had its drawbacks. My ship might be and probably was at no great distance from me, yet I could not see it. A gentle wind was blowing from the south-west. If my ship had risen from the roof, it would drift in a north-easterly direction, but though I strained my eyes towards that point of the compass I could discern nothing of the tiny eye of the periscope.

I must admit that for a moment I was well-nigh discouraged. It seemed that always when success was about within my grasp some malign fate snatched it from me, but presently I shook this weak despondency from me and with squared shoulders faced the future and whatever it might bring.

For a few moments I considered my position in all its aspects and sought to discover the best solution of my problem. I must rescue Tavia, but I felt that it would be useless to attempt to do so without a ship, therefore I must have a ship, and I knew that ships were just beneath me in the royal hangars. At night these hangars would be closed and locked, and watched over by sentries into the bargain. If I would have a ship I must take it now and depend upon the swiftness and boldness of my act for its success.

Royal fliers are usually fast fliers, and if the ships of Haj Osis were no exception to this general Barsoomian rule, I might hope to outdistance pursuit could I but pass the hangar sentry.

Of one thing I was certain, I could not accomplish that by remaining upon the roof of the hangar, and so I cautiously descended, choosing a moment when the attention of the sentries was directed elsewhere, for there was always danger that my robe might blow aside, revealing my limbs.

Once on the roof again I slipped quickly into the hangar, and inspecting the ships I selected one that I was sure would carry four with ease, and which, from its lines, gave token of considerable speed.

Clambering to the deck I took my place at the controls; very gradually I elevated the ship about a foot from the floor; then I opened the throttle wide.

Directly ahead of me, through the open doorways of the hangar, the sentries were standing upon the

opposite side of the room. As the ship leaped into the
sunlight they voiced simultaneously a cry of surprise
and alarm. Like brave warriors they sprang forward
with drawn long swords and I could see that they were
going to try to board me before I could gain altitude,
but presently one of them halted wide-eyed and stood
aside.

"Blood of our first ancestor!" he cried "There is no
one at the controls."

The second man had evidently discovered this simultaneously, for he, too, shrank aside, and with whirling
propeller I shot upward from the royal hangar of the
Jed of Tjanath.

But only for an instant were the two sentries overwhelmed by astonishment. Immediately I heard the
shriek of sirens and the clang of great gongs, and
then, glancing behind, I saw that already they had
launched a flier in pursuit. It was a two-man flier, and
almost immediately I realized that it was far swifter
than the one I had chosen; and then to make matters
even worse for me I saw patrol boats arising from
hangars located elsewhere upon the palace roof. That
they all saw my ship and were converging upon it
was evident; escape seemed impossible; each way I
turned a patrol boat was approaching; already I had
been driven into an ascending spiral, my eyes constantly alert for any avenue of escape that might open
to me.

How hopeless it looked! My ship was too slow; my
pursuers too many.

It would not be long now, I thought, and at that
very instant I saw something off my port bow at a
little greater altitude that gave me one of the greatest
thrills I had ever experienced in my life. It was only
a little round eye of glass, but to me it meant life and
more than life, for it might mean also life and happiness for Tavia—and of course for Sanoma Tora.

A patrol boat coming diagonally from below was
almost upon me as I drew my flier beneath that floating eye, judging the distance so nicely that I just had

clearance for my head beneath the keel of my own ship. Locating one of the hatches, which were so constructed that they could be opened either from the inside or the out, I scrambled quickly into the interior of the Jhama, as Phor Tak had christened it.

Closing the hatch and springing to the controls, I rose quickly out of immediate danger. Then, standing to one side, I watched my former pursuers.

I could read the consternation in their faces as they came alongside the royal flier that I had stolen, and realized that it was unmanned. Not having seen either me or my ship, they must have been hard put to it to find any sort of an explanation for the phenomenon.

As I watched them I found it constantly necessary to change my position, owing to the number of patrol boats and other craft that were congregating. I did not wish to leave the vicinity of the palace entirely, for it was my intention to remain here until after dark, when I should make an attempt to take Tavia and Phao aboard the Jhama. I also had it in my mind to reconnoitre the east tower during the day and try to get into communication with Tavia if possible. It was already the fifty zode. In fifty xats (*three hours*) the sun would set.

I wished to initiate my plan of rescue as soon after dark as possible, as experience had taught me that plans do not always develop as smoothly in execution as they do in contemplation.

A warrior from one of the patrol ships had boarded the royal craft that I had purloined and was returning it to the hangar. Some of the ships were following and others were returning to their stations. A single patrol boat remained cruising about, and as I watched it I suddenly became aware that a young officer standing upon its deck had espied the eye of my periscope. I saw him pointing towards it, and immediately thereafter the craft altered its course and came directly toward me. This was not so good and I lost no time in moving to one side, turning the eye of my periscope away from them so that they could not see it or follow me.

I moved a short distance out of their course and then swung my periscope towards them again. To my astonishment I discovered that they, too, had altered their course and were following me.

Now I rose swiftly and took a new direction, but when I looked again the craft was bearing down upon me, and not only that, but she was training a gun on me.

What had happened? It was evident that something had gone wrong and that I was no longer clothed in total invisibility, but whatever it was, it was too late now to rectify it even if I could. I had but a single recourse and I prayed to my first ancestor that it might not now be too late to put it into execution. Should they fire upon me I was lost.

I brought the Jhama to a full stop and sprang quickly aft to where the rear rifle was mounted on a platform just within the after turret.

In that instant I had occasion to rejoice in the foresight that had prompted me to rearrange the projectiles properly against the necessity for instant use in such an emergency as this. Selecting one, I jammed it into the chamber and closed the breech-block.

The turret, crudely and hastily constructed though it had been, responded to my touch and an instant later my sight covered the approaching patrol vessel, and through the tiny opening provided for the sight I witnessed the effect of my first shot with Phor Tak's disintegrating-ray rifle.

I had used a metal disintegrating projectile and the result was appalling.

I loved a ship and it tore my heart to see that staunch craft fall apart in mid-air as its metal parts disappeared before the disintegrating ray.

But that was not all; as wood and leather and fabric sank with increasing swiftness towards the ground, brave warriors hurtled to their doom. It was horrifying.

I am a true son of Barsoom; I joy in battle; armed

conflict is my birthright and war the goal of my ambition, but this was not war; it was murder.

I took no joy in my victory as I had when I laid Lo Seno low in mortal combat, and now, more then ever, was I determined that this frightful instrument of destruction must in some way be for ever banned upon Barsoom. War with such a weapon completely hidden by the compound of invisibility would be too horrible to contemplate. Navies, cities, whole nations could be wiped out by a single battleship thus equipped. The mad dream of Phor Tak might easily come true and a maniac yet rule all Barsoom.

But meditation and philosophizing were not for me at this time. I had work to do, and though it necessitated wiping out all Tjanath, I purposed doing it.

Again the sirens and the gongs raised their wild alarm; again patrol boats gathered. I felt that I must depart until after nightfall, for I had no stomach to again be forced to turn that deadly rifle upon my fellow-men while any alternative existed.

As I started to turn back to the controls my eyes chanced to fall upon one of the stern ports, and, to my surprise, I saw that the shutter was raised. How this occurred I do not know; it has always remained a mystery, but at least it explained how it had been possible for the patrol boat to follow me. That round port-hole moving through the air must have filled them with wonder, but at the same time it was a clue to follow, and though they did not understand it, they, like the brave warriors that they were, followed it in the line of their duty.

I quickly closed it, and, after examining the others and finding them all closed, I was now confident that, wiht the exception of the small eye of my periscope, I was entirely surrounded by invisibility and hence under no immediate necessity for leaving the vicinity of the palace, as I could easily manœuvre the ship to keep out of the way of the patrol boats that were now again congregating near the royal hangar.

I think they were pretty much upset by what had

happened and evidently there was no unanimity of opinion as to what should be done. The patrol ships hovered about, evidently waiting orders, and it was not until almost dark that they set out in a systematic search of the air above the city; nor had they been long at this before I understood their orders as well as though I had read them myself. The lower ships moved at an altitude of not over fifty feet above the higher buildings; two hundred feet above these moved the second line. The ships at each level cruised in a series of concentric circles and in opposite directions, thereby combing the air above the city so closely that no enemy ship could possibly approach. The air below was watched by a thousand eyes; at every point of vantage sentries were on watch and upon the roof of every public building guns appeared as if by magic.

I began to be quite apprehensive that even the small eye of my periscope might not go undetected, and so I dropped my ship into a little opening among some lofty trees that grew within the palace garden, and here I waited some twenty feet above the ground, my periscope completely screened from view, unseen and, in consequence, myself unseeing, until the swift night of Barsoom descended upon Tjanath; then I rose slowly from my leafy retreat.

Above the trees I paused to have a look about me through the periscope. Far above me were the twinkling lights of the circling patrol boats and from a thousand windows of the palace shone other lights. Before me rose the dark outlines of the east tower silhouetted against the starry sky.

Rising slowly I circled the tower until I had brought the Jhama opposite Tavia's window.

My ship carried no lights, of course, and I had not switched on any of the lights within her cabin, so that I felt that I might with impunity raise one of the upper hatches, and this I did. The Jhama lay with her upper deck a foot or two beneath the sill of Tavia's window. Before venturing from below I replaced my cloak of invisibility about me.

There was no light in Tavia's room. I placed my ear close against the iron bars and listened. I could hear no sound. My heart sank within me. Could it be that they had removed her to some other part of the palace? Could it be that Haj Alt had come and taken her away? I shuddered at the mere suggestion and cursed the luck that had permitted him to escape my blade.

With all those eyes and ears straining through the darkness I feared to make the slightest sound, though I felt that there was little likelihood that the open hatch would be noticed in the surrounding darkness; yet I must ascertain whether or not Tavia was within that room. I leaned close against the bars and whispered her name. There was no response.

"Tavia!" I whispered, this time much louder, and it seemed to me that my voice went booming to high heaven in tones that the dead might hear.

This time I heard a response from the interior of the room. It sounded like a gasp, and then I heard someone moving—approaching the window. It was so dark in the interior that I could see nothing, but presently I heard a voice close to me.

"Hadron! Where are you?"

She had recognized my voice. For some reason I thrilled to the thought of it. "Here at the window, Tavia," I said.

She came very close. "Where?" she asked. "I cannot see you."

I had forgotten my robe of invisibility. "Never mind," I said. "You cannot see me, but I will explain that later. Is Phao with you?"

"Yes."

"And no one else?"

"No."

"I am going to take you with me, Tavia—you and Phao. Stand aside well out of line of the window so that you will not be hurt while I remove the bars. Then be ready to board my ship immediately."

"Your ship!" she said. "Where is it?"

"Never mind now. There is a ship here. Do just as I tell you. Do you trust me?"

"With my life, Hadron, for ever," she whispered.

Something within me sang. It was more than a mere thrill; I cannot explain it; nor did I understand it, but now there were other things to think of.

"Stand aside quickly, Tavia, and keep Phao away from the window until I call you again." Dimly I could see her figure for a moment and then I saw it withdraw from the window. Returning to the controls I brought the forward turret of the ship opposite the window, upon the bars of which I trained the rifle. I loaded it and pressed the button. Through the tiny sight aperture and because of the darkness I could see nothing of the result, but I knew perfectly well what had happened, and when I lowered the ship again and went on deck I found that the bars had vanished in thin air.

"Quick, Tavia," I said. "Come!"

With one foot upon the deck of the flier and the other upon the sill of the window, I held the ship close to the wall of the tower and as best I could I held the cloak of invisibility like a canopy to shield the girls from sight as they boarded the Jhama.

It was a difficult and risky business. I wished I might have had grappling hooks, but I had none, and so I must do the best I could, holding the cloak with one hand and assisting Tavia to the sill with the other.

"There is no ship," she said in a slightly frightened tone.

"There is a ship, Tavia," I said. "Think only of your confidence in me and do as I bid." I grasped her firmly by the harness where the straps crossed upon her back. "Have no fear," I said, and then I swung her out over the hatch and lowered her gently into the interior of the Jhama.

Phao was behind her and I must give her credit for being as courageous as Tavia. It must have been a terrifying experience to those two girls to feel that they were being lowered into thin air a hundred feet above the ground, for they could see no ship—only a darker hole within the darkness of the night.

As soon as they were both aboard, I followed them, closing the hatch after me.

They were huddled in the darkness on the floor of the cabin, weak and exhausted from the brief ordeal through which they had just passed, but I could not take the time then to answer the questions with which I knew their heads must be filled.

If we passed the watchers on the roofs and the patrol boats above, there would be plenty of time for questions and answers. If we did not, there would be no need of either.

CHAPTER XIII

TUL AXTAR'S WOMEN

WITH PROPELLERS MOVING only enough to give us headway, we moved slowly and silently from the tower. I did not dare to rise to the altitude of the circling fliers for fear of almost inevitable collision, owing to the limited range of visibility permitted by the periscope, and so I held to a course that carried me only above the roof of the lower part of the palace until I reached a broad avenue that led in an easterly direction to the outer wall of the city. I kept well down below the roofs of the buildings, where there was little likelihood of encountering other craft. Our only danger of detection now, and that was slight indeed, was that our propeller might be overheard by some of the watchers on the roofs, but the hum and drone of the propellers of the ships above the city must have drowned out whatever slight sound our slowly revolving blades gave forth, and at last we came to the gate at the end of the avenue, and rising to top its battlements, we passed out of Tjanath into the night beyond. The lights of the city and of the circling patrol boats above grew fainter and fainter as we left them far behind.

We had maintained absolute silence during our escape from the city, but as soon as our escape appeared assured, Tavia unlocked the flood-gates of her curiosity. Phao's first question was relative to Nur An. Her sigh of relief held as great assurance of her love for him as words could have done. The two listened in breathless attention to the story of our miraculous escape from The Death. Then they wanted to know all about the Jhama, the compound of invisibility and the disintegrating ray with which I had dissolved the bars from their prison window. Nor was it until their curiosity had been appeased that we were able to discuss our plans for the future.

"I feel that I should go at once to Jahar," I said.

"Yes," said Tavia in a low voice. "It is your duty. You must go there first and rescue Sanoma Tora."

"If there was only some place where I might leave you and Phao in safety, I should feel that I could carry on this mission with far greater peace of mind, but I know of no other place than Jhama, and I hesitate to return there and let Phor Tak know that I failed to go immediately to Jahar as I had intended. The man is quite insane. There is no telling what he might do if he learns the truth; nor am I certain that you two would be safe there in his power. He trusts only his slaves and he might easily become obsessed with an hallucination that you are spies."

"You need not think of me at all," said Tavia, "for no matter where you might find a place to leave us, I should not remain. The place of the slave is with her master."

"Do not say that, Tavia. You are not my slave."

"I am a slave girl," she replied. "I must be someone's slave. I prefer to be yours."

I was touched by her loyalty, but I did not like to

thing of Tavia as a slave; yet however much I might loathe the idea the fact remained that she was one. "I gave you your freedom, Tavia," I said.

She smiled. "I do not want it, and now that it is decided that I am to remain with you" (she had done all the deciding), "I wish to learn all that I can about navigating the Jhama, for it may be that in that way I may help you."

Tavia's knowledge of aerial navigation made the task of instructing her simple indeed; in fact she had no trouble whatsoever in handling the craft.

Phao also manifested an interest and it was not long before she, too, took her turn at the controls, while Tavia insisted upon being inducted into all the mysteries of the disintegrating-ray rifle.

Long before we saw the towers of Tul Axtar's capital we sighted a one-man scout flier painted the ghastly blue of Jahar, and then far to the right and to the left we saw others. They were circling slowly at a great altitude. I judged that they were scouts watching for the coming of an expected enemy fleet. We passed below them and a little later encountered the second line of enemy ships. These were all scout cruisers, carrying from ten to fifteen men. Approaching one of them quite closely I saw that it carried four disintegrating-ray rifles, two mounted forward and two aft. As far as I could see in either direction these ships were visible, and if, as I presumed, they formed a circle entirely about Jahar, they must have been numerous indeed.

Passing on beyond them we presently encountered the third line of Jaharian ships. Here were stationed huge battleships, carrying crews of a thousand men and more and fairly bristling with big guns.

While none of these ships was as large as the major ships of Helium, they constituted a most formidable force and it was obvious that they had been built in great numbers.

What I had already seen impressed me with the fact that Tul Axtar was entertaining no idle dream in

his contemplated subjection of all Barsoom. With but
a fraction of the ships I had already seen I would
guarantee to lay waste all of Barsoom, provided my
ships were armed with disintegrating-ray rifles, and I
felt sure that I had seen but a pitiful fraction of Tul
Axtar's vast armament.

The sight of all these ships filled me with the direst
forebodings of calamity. If the fleet of Helium had not
already arrived and been destroyed, it certainly must
be destroyed when it did arrive. No power on earth
could save it. The best that I could hope, had the fleet
already arrived, was that an encounter with the disintegrating-ray rifles of the first line might have proved
sufficient warning to turn the balance of the fleet back.

Far behind the line of battleships I could see the
towers of Jahar rising in the distance, and as we
reached the vicinity of the city I descried a fleet of
the largest ships I have ever seen, resting upon the
ground just outside the city wall. These ships, which
completely encircled the city wall that was visible to
us, must have been capable of accommodating at least
ten thousand men each, and from their construction
and their light armaments, I assumed them to be transports. These, doubtless, were to carry the hordes of
hungry Jaharian warriors upon the campaign of loot
and pillage that it was planned should destroy a world.

Contemplation of this vast armada prompted me to
abandon all other plans and hasten at once to Helium,
that the alarm might be spread and plans be made to
thwart the mad ambition of Tul Axtar. My mind was
a seething cauldron of conflicting urges. But duty and
honour presented conflicting demands upon me. Countless times had I risked my life to reach Jahar for but
a single purpose, and now that I had arrived I was
called upon to turn back for the fulfilment of another
purpose— a larger, a more important one, perhaps; but
I am only human and so I turned first to the rescue
of the woman that I loved, determined immediately
thereafter to throw myself wholeheartedly into the
prosecution of the other enterprise that duty and in-

clination demanded of me. I argued that the slight delay that would result would in no way jeopardize the greater cause, while should I abandon Sanoma Tora now there was little likelihood that I would ever be able to return to Jahar to her succour.

With the great ghastly blue fleet of Jahar behind us, we topped the city's walls and moved in the direction of the palace of the Jeddak.

My plans were well formulated. I had discussed them again and again with Tavia, who had grown up in the palace of Tul Axtar.

At her suggestion we were to manœuvre the Jhama to a point directly over the summit of a slender tower, upon which there was not room to land the flier, but through which I could gain ingress to the palace at a point close to the quarters of the women.

As we had passed through the three lines of Jaharian ships, protected by our coating of the compound of invisibility, so we passed the sentries on the city wall and the warriors upon watch in the towers and upon the ramparts of the palace of the Jeddak, and without incident worthy of note I stopped the Jhama just above the summit of the tower that Tavia indicated.

"In about ten xats" (*approximately thirty minutes*) "it will be dark," I said to Tavia. "If you find it impractical to remain here constantly, try to return when dark has fallen, for whether or not I am successful in finding Sanoma Tora I shall not attempt to return to the Jhama until night has fallen."

She had told me that there was a possibility that the women's quarters might be locked at sunset, and for this reason I was entering the palace by daylight, though I should have much preferred not to risk it until after nightfall. Tavia had also assured me that if I once entered the women's quarters I would have no difficulty in leaving even after they were locked, as the door could be opened from the inside, the precaution of locking being taken not for fear that the inmates would leave the quarters, but to protect them against the dangers of assassins and others with evil intent.

Adjusting the robe of invisibility about me, I raised the forward keel hatch, which was directly over the summit of the tower that had once been used as a look-out in some distant age before newer and loftier portions of the palace had rendered it useless for this purpose.

"Good-bye and good luck," whispered Tavia. "When you return I hope that you will bring your Sanoma Tora with you. While you are gone I shall pray to my ancestors for your success."

Thanking her, I lowered myself through the hatch to the summit of the tower, in which was set a small trap-door.

As I raised this door I saw below me the top of the ancient ladder that long-dead warriors had used and which evidently was seldom, if ever, used now, as was attested by the dust upon its rungs. The ladder led me down to a large room in the upper level of this portion of the palace—a room that had doubtless originally been a guard-room, but which was now the receptacle of odds and ends of discarded furniture, hangings and ornaments. Filled as it was with specimens of the craftsmanship of ancient Jahar, together with articles of more modern fabrication, it would have been a most interesting room to explore; yet I passed through it with nothing more than a single searching glance for living enemies. Closely following Tavia's instructions I descended two spiral ramps, where I found myself in a most ornately decorated corridor, opening upon which were the apartments of the women of Tul Axtar. The corridor was long, stretching away fully a thousand sofads to a great, arched window at the far end, through which I could see the waving foliage of trees.

Many of the countless doors that lined the corridor on either side were open or ajar, for the corridor itself was forbidden to all but the women and their slaves, with the exception of Tul Axtar. The foot of the single ramp leading to it from the level below was watched over by a guard of picked men, composed exclusively of eunuchs, and Tavia assured me that short shrift was made of any adventurous spirit who sought to investigate the precincts above; yet here was I, a man and an enemy, safely within the forbidden territory.

As I looked about me in an attempt to determine where to commence my investigation, several women emerged from one of the apartments and approached me along the corridor. They were beautiful women, young and richly trapped, and from their light conversation and their laughter I judged that they were not unhappy. My conscience pricked me as I realized the mean advantage that I was taking of them, but it could not be avoided, and so I waited and listened, hoping that I might overhear some snatch of conversation that would aid me in my quest for Sanoma Tora; but I learned nothing from them other than that they referred to Tul Axtar contemptuously as the old zitidar. Some of their references to him were extremely personal and none was complimentary.

They passed me and entered a large room at the end of the corridor. Almost immediately thereafter other women emerged from other apartments and followed the first party into the same apartment.

It soon became evident to me that they were congregating there, and I thought that perhaps this might be the best way in which to start my search for Sanoma Tora—perhaps she, too, might be among the company.

Accordingly I fell in behind one of the groups and followed it through the large doorway and a short corridor, which opened into a great hall that was so gorgeously appointed and decorated as to suggest the throne-room of a Jeddak, and in fact such appeared to have been a part of its purpose, for at one end rose an enormous, highly carved throne.

The floor was of highly polished wood, in the centre of which was a large pool of water. Along the sides of the room were commodious benches, piled with

pillows and soft silks and furs. Here it was that Tul-
Axtar occasionally held unique court, surrounded solely
by his women. Here they danced for him; here they
disported themselves in the limpid waters of the pool
for his diversion; here banquets were spread and to
the strains of music high revelry persisted long into
the night.

As I looked about me at those who had already
assembled I saw that Sanoma Tora was not among
them, and so I took my place close to the entrance
where I might scrutinize the face of each who entered.

They were coming in droves now. I believe that I
have never seen so many women alone together before.
As I watched for Sanoma Tora I tried to count them,
but I soon gave it up as hopeless, though I estimated
that fully fifteen hundred women were congregated in
the great hall when at last they ceased to enter.

They seated themselves upon the benches about the
room, which was filled with a babel of feminine voices.
There were women of all ages and of every type, but
there was none that was not beautiful. The secret
agents of Tul Axtar must have combed the world for
such an aggregation of loveliness as this.

A door at one side of the throne opened and a file
of warriors entered. At first I was surprised because
Tavia had told me that no men other than Tul Axtar
ever were permitted upon this level, but presently I
saw that the warriors were women dressed in the
harness of men, their hair cut and their faces painted
after the fashion of the fighting men of Barsoom.
After they had taken their places on either side of
the throne, a courtier entered by the same door—
another woman masquerading as a man.

"Give thanks!" she cried. "Give thanks! The Jeddak
comes!"

Instantly the women arose and a moment later Tul
Axtar, Jeddak of Jahar, entered the hall, followed by
a group of women disguised as courtiers.

As Tul Axtar lowered his great bulk into the throne,
he signalled for the women in the room to be seated.

Then he spoke in a low voice to a woman courtier at his side.

The woman stepped to the edge of the dais. "The great Jeddak deigns to honour you individually with his royal observation," she announced in stilted tones. "From my left you will pass before him, one by one. In the name of the Jeddak, I have spoken."

Immediately the first woman at the left arose and walked slowly past the throne, pausing in front of Tul Axtar long enough to turn completely about, and then walked slowly on around the apartment and out through the doorway beside which I stood. One by one in rapid succession the others followed her. The whole procedure seemed meaningless to me. I could not understand it—then.

Perhaps a hundred women had passed before the Jeddak and come down the long hall towards me when something in the carriage of one of them attracted my attention as she neared me, and an instant later I recognized Sanoma Tora. She was changed, but not greatly, and I could not understand why it was that I had not discovered her in the room previously. I had found her! After all these long months I had found her—the woman I loved. Why did my heart not thrill?

As she passed through the doorway leading from the great hall, I followed her and along the corridor to an apartment near the far end, and when she entered, I entered behind her. I had to move quickly, too, for she turned immediately and closed the door after her.

We were alone in a small room, Sanoma Tora and I. In one corner were her sleeping-silks and furs; between two windows was a carved bench upon which stood those toilet articles that are essential to a woman of Barsoom.

It was not the apartment of a Jeddara; it was little better than the cell of a slave.

As Sanoma Tora crossed the room listlessly towards a stool which stood before the toilet bench, her back was towards me and I dropped the robe of invisibility from about me.

"Sanoma Tora," I said in a low voice.

Startled, she turned towards me. "Hadron of Hastor!" she exclaimed; "or am I dreaming?"

"You are not dreaming, Sanoma Tora. It is Hadron of Hastor."

"Why are you here? How did you get here? It is impossible. No men but Tul Axtar are permitted upon this level."

"Here I am, Sanoma Tora, and I have come to take you back to Helium—if you wish to return."

"Oh, name of my first ancestor, if I could but hope," she cried.

"You may hope, Sanoma Tora," I assured her. "I am here and I can take you back."

"I cannot believe it," she said. "I cannot imagine how you gained entrance here. It is madness to think that two of us could leave without being detected."

I threw the cloak about me. "Where are you, Tan Hadron? What has become of you? What has happened?" cried Sanoma Tora.

"This is how I gained entrance," I explained. "This is how we shall escape." I removed the cloak from about me.

"What forbidden magic is this?" she demanded, and, as best I might in few words, I explained to her the compound of invisibility and how I had come by it.

"How have you fared here, Sanoma Tora?" I asked her. "How have they treated you?"

"I have not been ill treated," she replied; "no one has paid any attention to me." I could scent the wounded vanity in her tone. "Until to-night I had not seen Tul Axtar. I have just come from the hall where he holds court among his women."

"Yes," I said, "I know. I was there. It was from there that I followed you here."

"When can you take me away?" she asked.

"Very quickly now," I replied.

"I am afraid that it will have to be quickly," she said.

"Why?" I asked.

"When I passed Tul Axtar he stopped me for a moment and I heard him speak to one of the courtiers at his side. He told her to ascertain my name and where I was quartered. The women have told me what happens after Tul Axtar has noticed one of us, and I am afraid; but what difference does it make? I am only a slave."

What a change had come over the haughty Sanoma Tora! Was this the same arrogant beauty who had refused my hand? Was this the Sanoma Tora who had aspired to be a jeddara? She was humbled now— I read it in the droop of her shoulders, in the trembling of her lips, in the fear-haunted light that shone from her eyes.

My heart was filled with compassion for her, but I was astonished and dismayed to discover that no other emotion overwhelmed me. The last time that I had seen Sanoma Tora I would have given my soul to have been able to take her into my arms. Had the hardships that I had undergone so changed me? Was Sanoma Tora, a slave, less desirable to me than Sanoma Tora, daughter of the rich Tora Hatan? No; I knew that that could not be true. I had changed, but doubtless it was only a temporary metamorphosis induced by the nervous strain which I was undergoing consequent upon the responsibility imposed upon me by the necessity for carrying word to Helium in time to save her from destruction at the hands of Tul Axtar—to save not only Helium, but a world. It was a grave responsibility. How might one thus burdened have time for thoughts of love? No, I was not myself; yet I knew that I still loved Sanoma Tora.

Realizing the necessity for haste, I made a speedy examination of the room and discovered that I could easily effect Sanoma Tora's rescue by taking her through the window, just as I had taken Tavia and Phao from the east tower at Tjanath.

Briefly, but carefully, I explained my plan to her and bade her prepare herself while I was gone that there might be no delay when I was ready to take her aboard the Jhama.

"And now, Sanoma Tora," I said, "for a few moments, good-bye! The next that you will hear will be a voice at your window, but you will see no one nor any ship. Extinguish the light in your room and step to the sill. I will take your hand. Put your trust in me then and do as I bid."

"Good-bye, Hadron!" she said. "I cannot express now in adequate words the gratitude that I feel, but when we are returned to Helium there is nothing that you can demand of me that I shall not grant you, not only willingly, but gladly."

I raised her fingers to my lips and had turned towards the door when Sanoma Tora laid a detaining hand upon my arm. "Wait!" she said. "Someone is coming."

Hastily I resumed my cloak of invisibility and stepped to one side of the room as the door leading into the corridor was thrown open, revealing one of the female courtiers of Tul Axtar in gorgeous harness. The woman entered the room and stepped to one side of the door, which remained opened.

"The Jeddak! Tul Axtar, Jeddak of Jahar!" she announced.

A moment later Tul Axtar entered the room, followed by half a dozen of his female courtiers. He was a gross man with repulsive features, which reflected a combination of strength and weakness, of haughty arrogance, of pride and of doubt—an innate questioning of his own ability.

As he faced Sanoma Tora his courtiers formed behind him. They were masculine-looking women, who had evidently been selected because of this very characteristic. They were good-looking in a masculine way and their physiques suggested that they might prove a very effective bodyguard for the Jeddak.

For several minutes Tul Axtar examined Sanoma

Tora with appraising eyes. He came closer to her, and there was that in his attitude which I did not like, and when he laid a hand upon her shoulder, I could scarce restrain myself.

"I was not wrong," he said. "You are gorgeous. How long have you been here?"

She shuddered, but did not reply.

"You are from Helium?"

No answer.

"The ships of Helium are on their way to Jahar." He laughed. "My scouts bring word that they will soon be here. They will meet with a warm welcome from the great fleet of Tul Axtar." He turned to his courtiers. "Go!" he said, "and let none return until I summon her."

They bowed and retired, closing the door after them, and then Tul Axtar laid his hands again upon the bare flesh of Sanoma Tora's shoulder.

"Come!" he said. "I shall not war with all of Helium —with you I shall love—by my first ancestor, but you are worth the love of a Jeddak."

He drew her towards him. My blood boiled—so hot was my anger that it boiled over, and without thought of the consequences I let the cloak fall from me.

CHAPTER XIV

THE CANNIBALS OF U-GOR

AS I DROPPED the cloak of invisibility aside I drew my long sword, and as it slithered from its sheath, Tul Axtar heard and faced me. His craven blood rushed to his heart and left his face pale at the sight of me.

A scream was in his throat when my point touched him in warning.

"Silence!" I hissed.

"Who are you?" he demanded.

"Silence!"

Even in the instant my plans were formed. I made him turn with his back towards me, and then I disarmed him, after which I bound him securely and gagged him.

"Where can I hide him, Sanoma Tora?" I asked.

"There is a little closet here," she said, pointing towards a small door in one side of the room, and then she crossed to it and opened it, while I dragged Tul Axtar behind her and cast him into the closet—none too gently I can assure you.

As I closed the closet door I turned to find Sanoma Tora white and trembling. "I am afraid," she said. "If they come back and find him thus, they will kill me."

"His courtiers will not return until he summons them," I reminded her. "You heard him tell them that such were his wishes—his command."

She nodded.

"Here is his dagger," I told her. "If worst comes to worst you can hold them off by threatening to kill Tul Axtar," but the girl seemed terrified, she trembled in every limb and I feared that she might fail if put to the test. How I wished that Tavia were here. I knew that she would not fail, and, in the name of my first ancestor, how much depended upon success!

"I shall return soon," I said, as I groped about the floor for the robe of invisibility. "Leave that large window open, and when I return, be ready."

As I replaced the cloak about me I saw that she was trembling so that she could not reply; in fact she was even having difficulty in holding the dagger, which I expected momentarily to see drop from her nerveless fingers, but there was naught that I could do but hasten to the Jhama and try to return before it was too late.

I gained the summit of the tower without incident.

Above me twinkled the brilliant stars of a Barsoomian night, while just above the palace roof hung the gorgeous planet, Jasoom (Earth).

The Jhama, of course, was invisible, but so great was my confidence in Tavia that when I stretched a hand upward I knew that I should feel the keel of the craft, and sure enough I did. Three times I rapped gently upon the forward hatch, which was the signal that we had determined upon before I had entered the palace. Instantly the hatch was raised and a moment later I had clambered aboard.

"Where is Sanoma Tora?" asked Tavia.

"No questions now," I replied. "We must work quickly. Be ready to take over the controls the moment that I leave them."

In silence she took her place at my side, her soft shoulder touching my arm, and in silence I dropped the Jhama to the level of the windows in the women's quarters. In a general way I knew the location of Sanoma Tora's apartment, and as I moved slowly along I kept the periscope pointed towards the windows, and presently I saw the figure of Sanoma Tora upon the ground glass before me. I brought the Jhama close to the sill, her upper deck just below it.

"Hold her here, Tavia," I said. Then I raised the upper hatch a few inches and called to the girl within the room.

At the sound of my voice she trembled so that she almost dropped the dagger, although she must have known that I was coming and had been awaiting me.

"Darken your room," I whispered to her. I saw her stagger across to a button that was set in the wall and an instant later the room was enveloped in darkness. Then I raised the hatch and stepped to the sill. I did not wish to be bothered with the enveloping folds of the mantle of invisibility and so I had folded it up and tucked it into my harness, where I could have it instantly ready for use in the event of an emergency. I found Sonoma Tora in the darkness, and so weak with terror was she that I had to lift her in

my arms and carry her to the window, where with
Phao's help I managed to draw her through the open
hatch into the interior. Then I returned to the closet
where Tul Axtar lay bound and gagged. I stooped and
cut the bounds which held his ankles.

"Do precisely as I tell you, Tul Axtar," I said, "or
my steel will have its way yet and find your heart. It
thirsts for your blood, Tul Axtar, and I have difficulty
in restraining it, but if you do not fail me perhaps I
shall be able to save you yet. I can use you, Tul Axtar,
and upon your usefulness to me depends your life, for
dead you are of no value to me."

I made him rise and walk to the window, and there
I assisted him to the sill. He was terror-stricken when
I tried to make him step out into space, as he thought,
but when I stepped to the deck of the Jhama ahead of
him and he saw me apparently floating there in the air,
he took a little heart and I finally succeeded in getting
him aboard.

Following him I closed the hatch and lighted a
single dim light within the hull. Tavia turned and
looked at me for orders.

"Hold her where she is, Tavia," I said.

There was a tiny desk in the cabin of the Jhama
where the officer of the ship was supposed to keep his
log and attend to any other records or reports that it
might be necessary to make. Here were writing materials, and as I got them out of the drawer in which
they were kept, I called Phao to my side.

"You are of Jahar," I said. "You can write in the
language of your country?"

"Of course," she said.

"Then write what I dictate," I instructed her.

She prepared to do my bidding.

"If a single ship of Helium is destroyed," I dictated,
"Tul Axtar dies. Now sign it Hadron of Hastor, Padwar of Helium."

Tavia and Phao looked at me, and then at the prisoner, their eyes wide in astonishment, for in the dim

light of the ship's interior they had not recognized the prisoner.

"Tul Axtar of Jahar!" breathed Tavia incredulously. "Tan Hadron of Hastor, you have saved Helium and Barsoom to-night."

I could not but note how quickly her mind functioned, with what celerity she had seen the possibilities that lay in the possession of the person of Tul Axtar, Jeddak of Jahar.

I took the note that Phao had written, and, returning quickly to Sanoma Tora's room, I laid it upon her dressing-table. A moment later I was again in the cabin of the Jhama and we were rising swiftly above the roofs of Jahar.

Morning found us beyond the uttermost line of Jaharian ships, beneath which we had passed, guided by their lights—evidence to me that the fleet was poorly officered, for no trained man, expecting an enemy in force, would show lights aboard his ships at night.

We were speeding now in the direction of far Helium, following the course that I hoped would permit us to intercept the fleet of the Warlord in the event that it was already bound for Jahar, as Tul Axtar had announced.

Sanoma Tora had slightly recovered her poise and control of her nerves. Tavia's sweet solicitude for her welfare touched me deeply. She had soothed and quieted her as she might have soothed and quieted a younger sister, though she herself was younger than Sanoma Tora; but with the return of confidence Sanoma Tora's old haughtiness was returning and it seemed to me that she showed too little gratitude to Tavia for her kindliness, but I realized that that was Sanoma Tora's way, that it was born in her and that doubtless deep in her heart she was fully appreciative and grateful. However that may be, I cannot but admit that I wished at the time that she would show it by some slight word or deed. We were flying smoothly, slightly above the normal altitude of battleships. The destination control compass was holding the Jhama to her course, and after all that I had passed through I felt the need of sleep. Phao, at my suggestion, had rested earlier in the night, and as all that was needed was a lookout to keep a careful watch for ships, I entrusted this duty to Phao, and Tavia and I rolled up in our sleeping-silks and were soon asleep.

Tavia and I were about mid-ship, Phao was forward at the controls, constantly swinging the periscope to and fro searching the sky for ships. When I retired Sanoma Tora was standing at one of the starboard ports looking out into the night, while Tul Axtar lay down in the stern of the ship. I had long since removed the gag from his mouth, but he seemed too utterly cowed even to address us and lay there in morose silence, or perhaps he was asleep—I do not know.

I was thoroughly fatigued and must have slept like a log from the moment that I laid down until I was suddenly awakened by the impact of a body upon me. As I struggled to free myself, I discovered to my chagrin that my hands had been deftly bound while I slept, a feat that had been rendered simple by the fact that it is my habit to sleep with my hands together in front of my face.

A man's knee was upon my chest, pressing me heavily against the deck, and one of his hands clutched me by the throat. In the dim light of the cabin I saw that it was Tul Axtar and that his other hand held a dagger.

"Silence!" he whispered. "If you would live, make no sound," and then to make assurance doubly sure he gagged me and bound my ankles. Then he crossed quickly to Tavia and bound her, and as he did so my eyes moved quickly about the interior of the cabin in search of aid. On the floor, near the controls, I saw Phao lying bound and gagged as was I. Sanoma Tora crouched against the wall, apparently overcome by terror. She was neither bound nor gagged. Why had she not warned me? Why had she not come to my help?

If it had been Tavia who remained unbound instead of Sanoma Tora, how different would have been the outcome of Tul Axtar's bid for liberty and revenge.

How had it all happened? I was sure that I had bound Tul Axtar so securely that he could not possibly have freed himself, and yet I must have been mistaken, and I cursed myself for the carelessness that had upset all my plans and that might easily eventually spell the doom of Helium.

Having disposed of Phao, Tavia and me, Tul Axtar moved quickly to the controls, ignoring Sanoma Tora as he passed by her. In view of the marked terror that she displayed, I could readily understand why he did not consider her any menace to his plans—she was as harmless to him free as bound.

Putting the ship about he turned back towards Jahar, and though he did not understand the mechanism of the destination control compass and could not cut it out, this made no difference as long as he remained at the controls, the only effect that the compass might have being to return the ship to its former course should the controls be again abandoned while the ship was in motion.

Presently he turned towards me. "I should destroy you, Hadron of Hastor," he said, "had I not given the word of a jeddak that I would not."

Vaguely I had wondered to whom he had given his word that he would not kill me, but other and more important thoughts were racing through my mind, crowding all else into the background. Uppermost among them, of course, were plans for regaining control of the Jhama and, secondarily, apprehension as to the fate of Tavia, Sanoma Tora and Phao.

"Give thanks for the magnanimity of Tul Axtar," he continued, "who exacts no penalty for the affront you have put upon him. Instead you are to be set free. I shall land you." He laughed. "Free! I shall land you in the province of U-Gor!"

There was something nasty in the tone of his voice which made his promise sound more like a threat. I

had never heard of U-Gor, but I assumed that it was
some remote province from which it would be difficult
or impossible for me to make my way either to Jahar
or Helium. Of one thing I was confident—that Tul
Axtar would not set me free in any place that I might
become a menace to him.

For hours the Jhama moved on in silence. Tul Axtar
had not had the decency or the humanity to remove
our gags. He was engrossed with the business of the
controls, and Sanoma Tora, crouching against the
side of the cabin, never spoke; nor once in all that
time did her eyes turn towards me. What thoughts
were passing in that beautiful head? Was she trying to
find some plan by which she might turn the tables upon
Tul Axtar, or was she merely crushed by the hopeless
outlook—the prospect of being returned to the slavery
of Jahar? I did not know; I could not guess; she was
an enigma to me.

How far we travelled or in what direction I did not
know. The night had long since passed and the sun
was high when I became aware that Tul Axtar was
bringing the ship down. Presently the purring of the
motor ceased and the ship came to a stop. Leaving
the controls he walked back to where I lay.

"We have arrived in U-Gor," he said. "Here I shall
set you at liberty, but first give me the strange thing
that rendered you invisible in my palace."

The cloak of invisibility! How had he learned of
that? Who could have told him? There seemed but
one explanation, but every fibre of my being shrank
even from considering it. I had rolled it up into a
small ball and tucked it into the bottom of my pocket
pouch, its sheer silk permitting it to be compressed
into a very small space. He took the gag from my
mouth.

"When you return to your palace at Jahar," I said,
"look upon the floor beneath the window in the apartment that was occupied by Sanoma Tora. If you find
it there you are welcome to it. As far as I am concerned it has served its purpose well."

"Why did you leave it there?" he demanded.

"I was in a great hurry when I quit the palace and accidents will happen." I will admit that my lie may not have been very clever, but neither was Tul Axtar, and he was deceived by it.

Grumbling, he opened one of the keel hatches and very unceremoniously dropped me through it. Fortunately the ship lay close to the ground and I was not injured. Next he lowered Tavia to my side, and then he, himself, descended to the ground. Stopping, he cut the bonds that secured Tavia's wrists.

"I shall keep the other," he said. "She pleases," and somehow I knew that he meant Phao. "This one looks like a man and I swear that she would be as easy to subdue as a she banth. I know the type. I shall leave her with you." It was evident that he had not recognized Tavia as one of the former occupants of the women's quarters in his palace and I was glad that he had not.

He re-entered the Jhama, but before he closed the hatch he spoke to us again. "I shall drop your weapons when we are where you cannot use them against me, and you may thank the future Jeddara of Jahar for the clemency I have shown you!"

Slowly the Jhama rose. Tavia was removing the cords from her ankles, and when she was free she came and fell to work upon the bonds that secured me, but I was too dazed, too crushed by the blow that had been struck me to realize any other fact than that Sanoma Tora, the woman I loved, had betrayed me, for I fully realized now what anyone but a fool would have guessed before—that Tul Axtar had bribed her to set him free by the promise that he would make her Jeddara of Jahar.

Well, her ambition would be fulfilled, but at what a hideous cost. Never, if she lived for a thousand years, could she look upon herself or her act with aught but contempt and loathing, unless she was far more degraded than I could possibly believe. No; she would suffer, of that I was sure; but that thought gave me no pleasure. I loved her and could not even now wish her unhappiness.

As I sat there on the ground, my head bowed in misery, I felt a soft arm steal about my shoulders and a tender voice spoke close to my ear. "My poor Hadron!"

That was all; but those few words embodied such a wealth of sympathy and understanding that, like some miraculous balm, they soothed the agony of my tortured heart.

No one but Tavia could have spoken them. I turned, and taking one of her little hands in mine, I pressed it to my lips. "Loved friend," I said. "Thanks be to all my ancestors that it was not you."

I do not know what made me say that. The words seemed to speak themselves without my volition, and yet when they were spoken there came to me a sudden realization of the horror that I would have felt had it been Tavia who had betrayed me. I could not even contemplate it without an agony of pain. Impulsively I took her in my arms.

"Tavia," I cried, "promise me that you will never desert me. I could not live without you."

She put her strong young arms about my neck and clung to me. "Never this side of death," she whispered, and then she tore herself from me and I saw that she was weeping.

What a friend! I knew that I could never again love a woman, but what cared I for that if I could have Tavia's friendship for life?

"We shall never part again, Tavia," I said. "If our ancestors are kind and we are permitted to return to Helium, you shall find a home in the house of my father and a mother in my mother."

She dried her eyes and looked at me with a strange wistful expression that I could not fathom, and then, through her tears, she smiled—that odd, quizzical little smile that I had seen before and that I did not understand any more than I understood a dozen of her moods and expressions, which made her so dif-

ferent from other girls and which, I think, helped to
attract me towards her. Her characteristics lay not all
upon the surface—there were depths and undercur-
rents which one might not easily fathom. Sometimes
when I expected her to cry, she laughed; and when I
thought that she should be happy, she wept, but she
never wept as I have seen other women weep—never
hysterically, for Tavia never lost control of herself, but
quietly as though from a full heart rather than from
overwrought nerves, and through her tears there might
burst a smile at the end.

I think that Tavia was quite the most wonderful
girl that I had ever known, and as I had come to
know her better and see more of her, I had grown to
realize that despite her attempt at mannish disguise
to which she still clung, she was quite the most beautiful girl that I had ever seen. Her beauty was not like
that of Sanoma Tora, but as she looked up into my
face now the realization came to me quite suddenly,
and for what reason I do not know, that the beauty
of Tavia far transcended that of Sanoma Tora because
of the beauty of the soul that, shining through her
eyes, transfigured her whole countenance.

Tul Axtar, true to his promise, dropped our weapons through the lower hatch of the Jhama, and as we
buckled them on we listened to the rapidly diminishing
sound of the propellers of the departing craft. We were
alone and on foot in a strange and, doubtless, an unhospitable country.

"U-Gor!" I said. "I have never heard of it. Have
you, Tavia?"

"Yes," she said. "This is one of the outlying provinces of Jahar. Once it was a rich and thriving
agricultural country, but as it fell beneath the curse
of Tul Axtar's mad ambition for man-power, the
population grew to such enormous proportions that
U-Gor could not support its people. Then cannibalism
started. It began justly with the eating of the officials
that Tul Axtar had sent to enforce his cruel decrees.
An army was dispatched to subdue the province, but

the people were so numerous that they conquered the army and ate the warriors. By this time their farms were ruined. They had no seed and they had developed a taste for human flesh. Those who wished to till the ground were set upon by bands of roving men and devoured. For a hundred years they have been feeding upon one another until now it is no longer a populous province, but a waste-land inhabited by roving bands, searching for one another that they may eat."

I shuddered at her recital. It was obvious that we must escape from this accursed place as rapidly as possible. I asked Tavia if she knew the location of U-Gor, and she told me that it lay south-east of Jahar, about a thousand haads south-west of Xanator.

I saw that it would be useless to attempt to reach Helium from here. Such a journey on foot, if it could be accomplished at all, would require years. The nearest friendly city towards which we could turn was Gathol, which I estimated lay some seven thousand haads almost due north. The possibility of reaching Gathol seemed remote in the extreme, but it was our only hope, and so we turned our faces towards the north and set out upon our long and seemingly hopeless journey towards the city of my mother's birth.

The country about us was rolling, with here and there a range of low hills, while far to the north I could see the outlines of higher hills against the horizon. The land was entirely denuded of all but noxious weeds, attesting the grim battle for survival waged by its unhappy people. There were no reptiles; no insects; no birds—all had been devoured during the century of misery that had lain upon the land.

As we plodded onward through this desolate and depressing waste, we tried to keep up one another's spirits as best we could, and a hundred times I had reason to give thanks that it was Tavia who was my companion and no other.

What could I have done under like circumstances burdened with Sanoma Tora? I doubt that she could have walked a dozen haads, while Tavia swung along at my side with the lithe grace of perfect health and strength. It takes a good man to keep up with me on a march, but Tavia never lagged; nor did she show signs of fatigue more quickly than I.

"We are well matched, Tavia," I said.

"I had thought of that—a long time ago," she said quietly.

We continued on until almost dusk without seeing a sign of any living thing and were congratulating ourselves upon our good fortune when Tavia glanced back, as one of us often did.

She touched my arm and nodded towards the rear. "They come!" she said simply.

I looked back and saw three figures upon our trail. They were too far away for me to be able to do more than identify them as human beings. It was evident that they had seen us and they were closing the distance between us at a steady trot.

"What shall we do?" asked Tavia. "Stand and fight, or try to elude them until night falls?"

"We shall do neither," I said. "We shall elude them now without exerting ourselves in the least."

"How?" she asked.

"Through the inventive genius of Phor Tak, and the compound of invisibility that I filched from him."

"Splendid!" exclaimed Tavia. "I had forgotten your cloak. With it we should have no difficulty in eluding all dangers between here and Gathol."

I opened my pocket pouch and reached in to withdraw the cloak. It was gone! As was the vial containing the remainder of the compound. I looked at Tavia and she must have read the truth in my expression.

"You have lost it?" she asked.

"No, it has been stolen from me," I replied.

She came again and laid her hand upon my arm in sympathy, and I knew that she was thinking what I was thinking, that it could have been none other than Sanoma Tora who had stolen it.

I hung my head. "And to think that I jeopardized your safety, Tavia, to save such as she."

"Do not judge her hastily," she said. "We cannot know how sorely she may have been tempted, or what threats were used to turn her from the path of honour. Perhaps she is not as strong as we."

"Let us not speak of her," I said. "It is a hideous sensation, Tavia, to feel love turned to hatred."

She pressed my arm. "Time heals all hurts," she said, "and some day you will find a woman worthy of you, if such a one exists."

I looked down at her. "If such a one exists," I mused, but she interrupted my meditation with a question.

"Shall we fight or run, Hadron of Hastor?" she demanded.

"I should prefer to fight and die," I replied, "but I must think of you, Tavia."

"Then we shall remain and fight," she said; "but, Hadron, you must not die."

There was a note of reproach in her tone that did not escape me and I was ashamed of myself for having seemed to forget the great debt that I owed her for her friendship.

"I am sorry," I said. "Tavia, I could not wish to die while you live."

"That is better," she said. "How shall we fight? Shall I stand upon your right or upon your left?"

"You shall stand behind me, Tavia," I told her. "While my hand can hold a sword, you will need no other defence."

"A long time ago, after we first met," she said, "you told me that we should be comrades in arms. That means that we fight together, shoulder to shoulder, or back to back. I hold you to your word, Tan Hadron of Hastor."

I smiled, and, though I felt that I could fight better alone than with a woman at my side, I admired her courage. "Very well," I said; "fight at my right, for thus you will be between two swords."

The three upon our trail had approached us so closely by this time that I could discern what manner of creatures they were, and I saw before me naked savages with tangled, unkempt hair, filthy bodies and degraded faces. The wild light in their eyes, their snarling lips exposing yellow fangs, their stealthy, slinking carriage gave them more the appearance of wild beasts than men.

They were armed with swords, which they carried in their hands, having neither harness nor scabbard. They halted a short distance from us, eying us hungrily, and doubtless they were hungry, for their flabby bellies suggested that they went often empty and were then gorged when meat fell to their lot in sufficient quantities. Tonight these three had hoped to gorge themselves; I could see it in their eyes. They whispered together in low tones for a few minutes and then they separated and circled us. It was evident that they intended to rush us from different points simultaneously.

"We'll carry the battle to them, Tavia," I whispered. "When they have taken their positions around us, I shall give the word and then I shall rush the one in front of me and try to dispatch him before the others can set upon us. Keep close beside me that they cannot cut you off."

"Shoulder to shoulder until the end," she said.

CHAPTER XV

THE BATTLE OF JAHAR

GLANCING ACROSS MY shoulder I saw that the two circling to our rear were already further away from us than he who stood facing us, and realizing that the unexpectedness of our act would greatly enhance the chances of success, I gave the word.

"Now, Tavia," I whispered, and together we leaped forward at a run straight for the naked savage facing us.

It was evident that he had not expected this and it was also evident that he was a slow-witted beast, for as he saw us coming his lower jaw dropped and he just stood there, waiting to receive us; whereas if he had had any intelligence he would have fallen back to give his fellows time to attack us from the rear.

As our swords crossed I heard a savage growl from behind, such a growl as might issue from the throat of a wild beast. From the corner of my eye I saw Tavia glance back, and then before I could realize what she intended, she sprang forward and ran her sword through the body of the man in front of me as he lunged at me with his own weapon, and now, wheeling together, we faced the other two, who were running rapidly towards us, and I can assure you that it was with a feeling of infinite relief that I realized that the odds were no longer so greatly against us.

As the two engaged us, I was handicapped at first by the necessity of constantly keeping an eye upon Tavia, but not for long.

In an instant I realized that a master hand was wielding that blade. Its point wove in and out past the clumsy guard of the savage, and I knew, and I guessed he must have sensed, that his life lay in the hollow of the little hand that gripped the hilt. Then I turned my attention to my own antagonist.

These were not the best swordsmen that I have ever met, but they were far from being poor swordsmen. Their defence, however, far excelled their offence, and this, I think, was due to two things, natural cowardice and the fact that they usually hunted in packs which far outnumbered the quarry. Thus a good defence only was required, since the death-blow might always be struck from behind by a companion of the one who engaged the quarry from in front.

Never before had I seen a woman fight and I should have thought that I should have been chagrined to have one fighting at my side, but instead I felt a strange thrill that was partly pride and partly something else that I could not analyse.

At first, I think, the fellow facing Tavia did not realize that she was a woman, but he must have soon, as the scant harness of Barsoom hides little and certainly did not hide the rounded contours of Tavia's girlish body. Perhaps, therefore, it was surprise that was his undoing, or possibly when he discovered her sex he became over-confident, but at any rate Tavia slipped her point into his heart just an instant before I finished my man.

I cannot say that we were greatly elated over our victory. Each of us felt compassion for the poor creatures who had been reduced to their horrid state by the tyranny of cruel Tul Axtar, but it had been their lives or ours and we were glad that it had not been ours.

As a matter of precaution I took a quick look about us as the last of our antagonists fell, and I was glad that I had, for I immediately discerned three creatures crouching at the top of a low hill not far distant.

"We are not done yet, Tavia," I said. "Look!" and pointed in the direction of the three.

"Perhaps they do not care to share the fate of their fellows," she said. "They are not approaching."

"They can have peace if they want it as far as I am concerned," I said. "Come, let us go on. If they follow us, then will be time enough to consider them."

As we walked on towards the north we glanced back occasionally and presently we saw the three rise and come down the hill towards the bodies of their slain fellows, and as they did so we saw that they were women and that they were unarmed.

When they realized that we were departing and had no intention of attacking them, they broke into a run and, uttering loud, uncanny shrieks, raced madly towards the corpses.

"How pathetic," said Tavia sadly. "Even these poor

degraded creatures possess human emotions. They, too, can feel sorrow at the loss of loved ones."

"Yes," I said. "Poor things, I am sorry for them."

Fearing that in the frenzy of their grief they might attempt to avenge their fallen mates, we kept a close eye upon them or we might not have witnessed the horrid sequel of the fray. I wish that we had not.

When the three women reached the corpses they fell upon them, but not with weeping and lamentation—they fell upon them to devour them.

Sickened, we turned away and walked rapidly towards the north until long after darkness had descended.

We felt that there was little danger of attack at night since there were no savage beasts in a country where there was nothing to support them, and also that it was reasonable to assume that the hunting men would be abroad by day rather than by night, since at night they would be far less able to find quarry or follow it.

I suggested to Tavia that we rest for a short time and then push on for the balance of the night, find a place of concealment early in the day and remain there until night had fallen again, as I was sure that if we followed this plan we would make better time and suffer less exhaustion by travelling through the cool hours of darkness, and at the same time would greatly minimize the danger of discovery and attack by whatever hostile people lay between us and Gathol.

Tavia agreed with me and so we rested for a short time taking turns at sleeping and watching.

Later we pushed on and I am sure that we covered a great distance before dawn, though the high hills to the north of us still looked as far away as they had upon the previous day.

We now set about searching for some comfortable place of concealment where we might spend the daylight hours. Neither of us was suffering to any extent from hunger or thirst, as the ancients would have done under like circumstances, for with the gradual diminution of water and vegetable matter upon Mars during countless ages all her creatures have by a slow process of evolution been enabled to go for long periods without either food or drink, and we have also learned so to control our minds that we do not think of food or drink until we are able to procure it, which doubtless greatly assists us in controlling the cravings of our appetite.

After considerable search we found a deep and narrow ravine which seemed a most favourable place in which to hide, but scarcely had we entered it when I chanced to see two eyes looking down upon us from the summit of one of the ridges that flanked it. As I looked, the head in which the eyes were set was withdrawn below the summit.

"That puts an end to this place," I said to Tavia, telling her what I had seen. "We must move on and look for a new sanctuary."

As we emerged from the ravine at its upper end I glanced back, and again I saw the creature looking at us. As we moved on I kept glancing back and occasionally I would see him—one of the hunting men of U-Gor. He was stalking us as the wild beast stalks its prey. The very thought of it filled me with disgust. Had he been a fighting man stalking us merely to kill I should not have felt as I did, but the thought that he was stealthily trailing us because he desired to devour us was repellent—it was horrifying.

Hour after hour the thing kept upon our trail; doubtless he feared to attack because we outnumbered him or perhaps he thought we might become separated, or lie down to sleep or do one of the number of things that travellers might do that would give him the opportunity he sought, but after a while he must have given up hope. He no longer sought to conceal himself from us, and once, as he mounted a low hill, he stood there silhouetted against the sky, and throwing his head back, he gave voice to a shrill, uncanny cry that made the short hairs upon my neck stand erect. It was the hunting cry of the wild beast calling the pack to the kill.

I could feel Tavia shudder and press more closely to

me, and I put my arm about her in a gesture of protection, and thus we walked on in silence for a long time.

Twice again the creature voiced his uncanny cry, until at last it was answered ahead of us and to the right.

Again we were forced to fight, but this time only two, and when we pushed on again it was with a feeling of depression that I could not shake off—depression for the utter hopelessness of our situation.

At the summit of a higher hill than we had before crossed I halted. Some tall weeds grew there. "Let us lie down here, Tavia," I said. "From here we can watch; let us be the watchers for a while. Sleep, and when night comes we shall move on."

She looked tired, and that worried me, but I think she was suffering more from the nervous strain of the eternal stalking than from physical fatigue. I know that it affected me, and how much more might it affect a young girl than a trained fighting man. She lay very close to me, as though she felt safer thus, and was soon asleep, while I watched.

From this high vantage point I could see a considerable area of country about us and it was not long before I detected figures of men prowling about like hunting banths, and often it was apparent that one was stalking another. There were at least a half-dozen such visible to me at one time. I saw one overtake his prey and leap upon it from behind. They were at too great a distance from me for me to discern accurately the details of the encounter, but I judged that the stalker ran his sword through the back of his quarry and then, like a hunting banth, he fell upon his kill and devoured it. I do not know that he finished it, but he was still eating when darkness fell.

Tavia had had a long sleep, and when she awoke she reproached me for having permitted her to sleep so long and insisted that I must sleep.

From necessity I have learned to do with little sleep when conditions are such that I cannot spare the time, though I always make up for it later, and I have also learned to limit my sleep to any length of time that I choose, so that now I awoke promptly when my allotted time had elapsed and again we set out towards far Gathol.

Again this night, as upon the preceding one, we moved unmolested through the horrid land of U-Gor, and when morning dawned we saw the high hills rising close before us.

"Perhaps these hills mark the northern limits of U-Gor," I suggested.

"I think they do," replied Tavia.

"They are only a short distance away now," I said; "let us keep on until we have passed them. I cannot leave this accursed land behind me too soon."

"Nor I," said Tavia. "I sicken at the thought of what I have seen."

We had crossed a narrow valley and were entering the hills when we heard the hateful hunting cry behind us. Turning, I saw a single man moving across the valley towards us. He knew that I had seen him, but he kept steadily on, occasionally stopping to voice his weird scream. We heard an answer come from the east and then another and another from different directions. We hastened onward, climbing the low foothills that led upward towards the summit far above, and as we looked back we saw the hunting men converging upon us from all sides. We had never seen so many of them at one time before.

"Perhaps if we get well up into the mountains we can elude them," I said.

Tavia shook her head. "At least we have made a good fight, Hadron," she said.

I saw that she was discouraged; nor could I wonder; yet a moment later she looked up at me and smiled brightly. "We still lived, Hadron of Hastor!" she exclaimed.

"We still live and we have our swords," I reminded her.

As we climbed they pressed upward behind us, and

presently I saw others coming through the hills from
the right and from the left. We were turned from the
low saddle over which I had hoped to cross the summit of the range, for hunting men had entered it from
above and were coming down towards us. Directly
ahead of us now loomed a high peak, the highest in the
range as far as I could see, and only there, up its
steep side, were there no hunting men to bar our way.

As we climbed, the sides of the mountain grew
steeper until the ascent was not only most arduous,
but sometimes difficult and dangerous; yet there was
no alternative and we pressed onward towards the
summit, while behind us came the hunting men of U-
Gor. They were not rushing us, and from that I felt
confident that they knew that they had us cornered. I
was looking for a place in which we might make a
stand, but I found none, and at last we reached the
summit, a circular, level space perhaps a hundred feet
in diameter.

As our pursuers were yet some little distance below
us, I walked quickly around the outside of the table-
like top of the peak. The entire northern face dropped
sheer from the summit for a couple of hundred feet,
definitely blocking our retreat. At every other point
the hunting men were ascending. Our situation appeared hopeless; it *was* hopeless, and yet I refused to
admit defeat.

The summit of the mountain was strewn with loose
rock. I hurled a rock down at the nearest cannibal.
It struck him upon the head and sent him hurtling
down the mountain side, carrying a couple of his
fellows with him. Then Tavia followed my example,
and together we bombarded them, but more often we
scored misses than hits and there were so many of
them and they were so fierce and so hungry that we
did not even stem their advance. So numerous were
they now that they reminded me of insects, crawling
up there from below—huge, grotesque insects that
would soon fall upon us and devour us.

As they came nearer they gave voice to a new cry

that I had not heard before. It was a cry that differed from the hunting call, but was equally as terrible.

"Their war-cry," said Tavia.

On and on with relentless persistency the throng swarmed upward towards us. We drew our swords; it was our last stand. Tavia pressed closer to me and for the first time I thought I felt her tremble.

"Do not let them take me," she said. "It is not death that I fear."

I knew what she meant and I took her in my arms. "I cannot do it, Tavia," I said. "I cannot."

"You must," she replied in a firm voice. "If you care for me even as a friend, you cannot let these beasts take me alive."

I know that I choked then so that I could not reply, but I knew that she was right and I drew my daggar.

"Good-bye, Hadron—my Hadron!"

Her breast was bared to receive my dagger, her face was upturned towards mine. It was still a brave face with no fear upon it, and oh, how beautiful it was.

Impulsively, guided by a power I could not control, I bent and crushed my lips to hers. With half-closed eyes she pressed her own lips upward more tightly against mine.

"Oh, Issus!" she breathed as she took them away, and then, "They come! Strike now, Hadron, and strike deep!"

The creatures were almost at the summit. I swung my hand upward that I might bury the slim dagger deeply in that perfect breast. To my surprise my knuckles struck something hard above me. I glanced upward. There was nothing there; yet something impelled me to feel again, to solve that uncanny mystery even in that instant of high tragedy.

Again I felt above me. By Issus, there was something there! My fingers passed over a smooth surface—a familiar surface.

It could not be, and yet I knew that it must be— the Jhama. I asked no questions of myself nor of fate at that instant. The hunting men of U-Gor were almost upon us as my groping fingers found one of the mooring rings in the bow of the Jhama. Quickly I swung Tavia above my head..

"It is the Jhama. Climb to her deck," I cried.

The dear girl, as quick to seize upon the fortuitous opportunities as any trained fighting man, did not pause to question, but swung herself upward to the deck with the agility of an athlete, and as I seized the mooring ring and drew myself upward she lay flat upon her belly and reaching down assisted me; nor was the strength in that slender frame unequal to the task.

The leaders of the horde had reached the summit. They paused in momentary confusion when they saw us climb into thin air and stand there apparently just above their heads, but hunger urged them on and they leaped for us, clambering upon one another's backs and shoulders to seize us and drag us down.

Two almost gained the deck as I fought them all back single-handed while Tavia had raised a batch and leaped to the controls.

Another foul-faced thing reached the deck upon the opposite side, and only chance revealed him to me before he had run his sword through my back. The Jhama was already rising as I turned to engage him. There was little room there in which to fight, but I had the advantage in that I knew the extent of the deck beneath my feet, while he could see nothing but thin air. I think it frightened him, too, and when I rushed him he stepped backward out into space and, with a scream of terror, hurtled downward towards the ground.

We were saved, but how in the name of all our ancestors had the Jhama chanced to be at this spot.

Perhaps Tul Axtar was aboard! The thought filled me with alarm for Tavia's safety, and with my sword ready I leaped through the hatchway into the cabin, but only Tavia was there.

We tried to arrive at some explanation of the miracle

that had saved us, but no amount of conjecture brought forth anything that was at all satisfactory.

"She was there when we needed her most," said Tavia; "that fact should satisfy us."

"I guess it will have to for the time being at least," I said, "and now once more we can turn a ship's nose towards Helium."

We had passed but a short distance beyond the mountains when I sighted a ship in the distance, and shortly thereafter another and another until I was aware that we were approaching a great fleet moving towards the east. As we came closer I descried the hulls painted with the ghastly blue of Jahar and I knew that this was Tul Axtar's formidable armada.

And then we saw ships approaching from the east and I knew that it was the fleet of Helium. It could be no other; yet I must make certain, and so I sped in the direction of the nearest ship of this other fleet until I saw the banners and pennons of Helium floating from her upper works and the battle insignia of the Warlord painted upon her prow. Behind her came the other ships—a noble fleet moving to inevitable doom.

A Jaharian cruiser was moving towards the first great battleship as I raced to intercept them and bring one of my rifles into action.

I was forced to come close to my target, as was the Jaharian cruiser, since the effective range of the disintegrating-ray rifle is extremely limited.

Everything aboard the battleship of Helium was ready for action, but I knew why they had not fired a gun. It has ever been the boast of John Carter, Warlord of Barsoom, that he would not start a war. The enemy must fire the first shot. If I could have reached them in time he would have realized the fatal consequences of this magnanimous and chivalrous code, and the ships of Helium, with their long-range guns, might have annihilated Jahar's entire fleet before it could have brought its deadly rifles within range, but fate had ordained otherwise, and now the best that I could hope was that I might reach the Jaharian ship before it was too late.

Tavia was at the controls. We were racing towards the blue cruiser of Jahar. I was standing at the forward rifle. In another moment we should be within range, and then I saw the great battleship of Helium crumble in mid-air. Its wooden parts dropped slowly towards the ground and a thousand warriors plunged to a cruel death upon the barren land beneath.

Almost immediately the other ships of Helium were brought to a stop. They had witnesed the catastrophe that had engulfed the first ship of the line, and the commander of the fleet had realized that they were menaced by a new force of which they had no knowledge.

The ships of Tul Axtar, encouraged by this first success, were now moving swiftly to the attack. The cruiser that had destroyed the great battleship was in the lead, but now I was within range of it.

Realizing that the blue protective paint of Jahar would safeguard the ship itself against the disintegrating ray, I had rammed home a cartridge of another type in the chamber, and swinging the muzzle of the rifle so that it would rake the entire length of the ship, I pressed the button.

Instantly the men upon deck dissolved into thin air —only their harness and their metal and their weapons were left.

Directing Tavia to run the Jhama alongside, I raised the upper hatch and leaped to the deck of the cruiser, and a moment later I had raised the signal of surrender above her. One can imagine the consternation aboard the nearer ships of Jahar as they saw that signal flying from her forward mast, for there was none sufficiently close to have witnessed what actually transpired aboard her.

Returning to the cabin of the Jhama I lowered the hatch and went at once to the periscope. Far in the rear of the first line of Jaharian ships I could just discern the royal insignia upon a great battleship, which told me that Tul Axtar was there, but in a safe position. I should have liked to reach his ship next, but the fleet was moving forward towards the ships of Helium and I dared not spare the time.

By now the ships of Helium had opened fire and shells were exploding about the leading ships of the Jaharian fleet—shells so nicely timed that they can be set to explode at any point up to the extreme range of the gun that discharges them. It takes nice gunnery to synchronize the timing with the target.

As ship after ship of the Jaharian fleet was hit, the others brought their big guns into action. Temporarily, at least, the disintegrating-ray rifles had failed, but that they would succeed I knew if a single ship could get through the Heliumetic line, where among the great battleships she could destroy a dozen in the space of a few minutes.

The gunnery of the Jaharians was poor; their shells usually exploded high in air before they reached their target, but as the battle continued it improved; yet I knew that Jahar never could hope to defeat Helium with Helium's own weapons.

A great battleship of Tul Axtar's fleet was hit three times in succession almost alongside of me. I saw her drop by the stern and I knew that she was done for, and then I saw her commander rush to the bow and take the last long dive, and I knew that there were brave men in Tul Axtar's fleet as well as in the fleet of Helium, but Tul Axtar was not one of them, for in the distance I could see his flagship racing towards Jahar.

Despite the cowardice of the Jeddak, the great fleet pushed on to the attack. If they had the courage they could still win, for their ships outnumbered the ships of Helium ten to one, and as far as the eye could reach I could see them speeding from the north, from the south and from the west towards the scene of battle.

Closer and closer the ships of Helium were pressing towards the ships of Jahar. In his ignorance the Warlord was playing directly into the hands of the enemy. With their superior marksmanship and twenty battleships protected by the blue paint of Jahar, Helium could wipe out Tul Axtar's great armada; of that I was confident, and with that thought came an inspiration. It might be done and only Tan Hadron of Hastor could do it.

Shells were falling all about us. The force of the explosions rocked the Jhama until she tossed and pitched like an ancient ship upon an ancient sea. Again and again were we perilously close to the line of fire of the Jaharian disintegrating-ray rifles. I felt that I might no longer risk Tavia thus, yet I must carry out the plan that I had conceived.

It is strange how men change and for what seemingly trivial reasons. I had thought all my life that I would make any sacrifice for Helium, but now I knew that I would not sacrifice a single hair of that tousled head for all Barsoom. This, I soliloquized, is friendship.

Taking the controls I turned the bow of the Jhama towards one of the ships of Helium, that was standing temporarily out of the line of fire, and as we approached her side I turned the controls back over to Tavia, and, raising the forward hatch, sprang to the deck of the Jhama, raising both hands above my head in signal of surrender in the event that they might take me for a Jaharian.

What must they have thought when they saw me apparently floating upright upon thin air? That they were astonished was evident by the expressions on the faces of those nearest to me as the Jhama touched the side of the battleship.

They kept me covered as I came aboard, leaving Tavia to manœuvre the Jhama.

Before I could announce myself I was recognized by a young officer of my own umak. With a cry of surprise he leaped forward and threw his arms about me. "Hadron of Hastor!" he cried. "Have I witnessed your resurrection from death? But no, you are too real, too much alive to be any wraith of the other world."

"I am alive now," I cried, "but none of us will be

unless I can get word to your commander. Where is he?"

"I am alive now," I cried, "but none of us will be unless I can get word to your commander. Where is he?"

"Here," said a voice behind me, and I turned to see an old odwar who had been a great friend of my father's. He recognized me immediately, but there was no time even for greetings.

"Warn the fleet that the ships of Jahar are armed with disintegrating-ray rifles that can dissolve every ship as you saw the first one dissolve. They are only effective at short range. Keep at least a haad distance from them and you are relatively safe. And now if you will give me three men and direct the fire of your fleet away from the Jaharian ships on the south of their line, I will agree to have twenty ships for you in an hour—ships protected by the blue of Jahar in which you may face their disintegrating-ray rifles with impunity."

The odwar knew me well and upon his own responsibility he agreed to do what I asked.

Three padwars of my own class guaranteed to accompany me. I fetched Tavia aboard the battleship and turned her over to the protection of the old odwar, though she objected strenuously to being parted from me.

"We have gone through so much together, Hadron of Hastor," she said, "let us go on to the end together."

She had come quite close to me and spoken in a low voice that none might overhear. Her eyes, filled with pleading, were upturned to mine.

"I cannot risk you further, Tavia," I said.

"There is so much danger then, you think?" she asked.

"We shall be in danger, of course," I said; "this is war and one can never tell. Do not worry though. I shall come back safely."

"Then it is that you fear that I shall be in the way," she said, "and another can do the work better than I?"

"Of course not," I replied. "I am thinking only of your safety."

"If you are lost, I shall not live. I swear it," she said, "so if you can trust me to do the work of a man, let me go with you instead of one of those."

I hesitated. "Oh, Hadron of Hastor, please do not leave me here without you," she said.

I could not resist her. "Very well, then," I said, "come with me. I would rather have you than any other," and so it was that Tavia replaced one of the padwars on the Jhama, much to the officer's chagrin.

Before entering the Jhama I turned again to the old odwar. "If we are successful," I said, "a number of Tul Axtar's battleships will move slowly toward the Helium line beneath signals of surrender. Their crews will have been destroyed. Have boarding parties ready to take them over."

Naturally everyone aboard the battleship was intensely interested in the Jhama, though all that they could see of her was the open hatch and the eye of the periscope. Officers and men lined the rail as we went aboard our invisible craft, and as I closed the hatch a loud cheer rang out above me.

My first act thoroughly evidenced my need of Tavia, for I put her at the after turret in charge of the rifle there, while one of the padwars took the controls and turned the prow of the Jhama towards the Jaharian fleet.

I was standing in a position where I could watch the changing scene upon the ground glass beneath the periscope, and when a great battleship swung slowly into the miniature picture before me, I directed the padwar to lay a straight course for her, but a moment later I saw another battleship moving abreast of her. This was better, and we changed our course to pass between the two.

They were moving gallantly towards the fleet of Helium, firing their big guns now and reserving their disintegrating-ray rifles for closer range. What a magnificent sight they were, and yet how helpless.

The tiny, invisible Jhama, with her little rifles, constituted a greater menace to them than did the entire fleet of Helium. On they drove, unconscious of the inevitable fate bearing down upon them.

"Sweep the starboard ship from stem to stern," I called to Tavia. "I will take this fellow on our port," and then to the padwar at the controls, "Half speed!"

Slowly we passed their bows. I touched the button upon my rifle and through the tiny sighting aperture I saw the crew dissolve in the path of those awful rays, as the two ships passed. We were very close—so close that I could see the expressions of consternation and horror on the faces of some of the warriors as they saw their fellows disappear before their eyes, and then their turn would come and they would be snuffed out in the twinkling of an eye, their weapons and their metal clattering to the deck.

As we dropped astern of them, our work completed, I had the padwar bring the Jhama about and alongside one of the ships, which I quickly boarded, running up the signal of surrender. With the death of the officer at her controls she had fallen off with the wind, but I quickly brought her up again and, setting her at half speed, her bow towards the ships of Helium. I locked the controls and left her.

Returning to the Jhama, we crossed quickly to the other ship, and a few moments later it, too, was moving slowly towards the fleet of the Warlord, the signal of surrender fluttering above it.

So quickly had the blow been struck that even the nearer ships of Jahar were some time in realizing that anything was amiss. Perhaps they were unable to believe their own eyes when they saw two of their great battleships surrender before having been struck by a single shot, but presently the commander of a light cruiser seemed to awaken to the seriousness of the situation, even though he could not fully have understood it. We were already moving towards another battleship when I saw the cruiser speeding directly towards one of our prizes, and I knew that it would never reach the fleet of Helium if he boarded it, a thing which I must prevent at all costs. His course would bring him across our bow, and as he passed I raked him with the forward rifle.

I saw that it would be impossible for the Jhama to overtake this swift cruiser, which was moving at full speed, and so we had to let her go her way. At first I was afraid she would ram the nearer prize, and had she hit her squarely at the rate that she was travelling, the cruiser would have ploughed halfway through the hull of the battleship. Fortunately, she missed the great ship by a hair and went speeding on into the midst of the fleet of Helium.

Instantly she was the target for a hundred guns, a barrage of shells was bursting about her, and then there must have been a dozen hits simultaneously, for the cruiser simply disappeared—a mass of flying debris.

As I turned back to our work I saw the havoc being wrought by the big guns of Helium upon the enemy ships to the north of me. In the instant that I glanced I saw three great battleships take the final dive, while at least four others were drifting helplessly with the wind, but other ships of that mighty armada were swinging into action. As far as I could see they were coming from the north, from the south and from the west. There seemed no end to them, and now, at last, I realized that only a miracle could give victory to Helium.

In accordance with my suggestion our own fleet was holding off, concentrating the fire of its big guns upon the nearer ships of Jahar—constantly seeking to keep those deadly rifles out of range.

Again we fell to work—to the grim work that the god of battle had allotted to us. One by one, twenty great battleships surrendered their deserted decks to us, and as we worked I counted fully as many more destroyed by the guns of the Warlord.

In the prosecution of our work we had been compelled to destroy at least half a dozen small craft, such as scout fliers and light cruisers, and now these were racing erratically among the remaining ships of the Jaharian fleet, carrying consternation and doubtless terror to the hearts of Tul Axtar's warriors, for all the nearer ships must have realized long since that some strange new force had been loosed upon them by the ships of Helium.

By this time we had worked so far behind the Jaharian first line that we could no longer see the ships of Helium though bursting shells attested the fact that they were still there.

From past experience I realized that it would be necessary to protect the captured Jaharian ships from being retaken, and so I turned back, taking a position where I could watch as many of them as possible, and it was well that I did so, for we found it necessary to destroy the crews of three more ships before we reached the battle line of Helium.

Here they had already manned a dozen of the captured battleships of Jahar, and, with the banners and pennons of Helium above them, they had turned about and were moving into action against their sister ships.

It was then that the spirit of Jahar was broken. This I think, was too much for them, as doubtless the majority of them believed that these ships had gone over to the enemy voluntarily with all their officers and crews, for few, if any, could have known that the latter had been destroyed.

Their Jeddak had long since deserted them. Twenty of their largest ships had gone over to the enemy and now, protected by the blue of Jahar and manned by the best gunners of Barsoom, were ploughing through them, spreading death and destruction upon every hand.

A dozen of Tul Axtar's ships surrendered voluntarily and then the others turned and scattered; very few of them headed towards Jahar, and I knew by that they believed that the city must inevitably fall.

The Warlord made no effort to pursue the fleeing craft; instead he stationed the ships that we had captured from the enemy, more than thirty all told now, around the fleet of Helium to protect it from the disintegrating-ray rifles of the enemy in the event of a renewed attack, and then slowly we moved on Jahar.

CHAPTER XVI

DESPAIR

IMMEDIATELY AFTER THE close of the battle the Warlord sent for me, and a few moments later Tavia and I stepped aboard the flagship.

The Warlord himself came forward to meet us. "I knew," he said, "that the son of Had Urtur would give a good account of himself. Helium can scarcely pay the debt of gratitude that you have placed upon her to-day. You have been to Jahar; your work to-day convinces me of that. May we with safety approach and take the city?"

"No," I replied, and then briefly I explained the mighty force that Tul Axtar had gathered and the armament with which he expected to subdue the world. "But there is a way," I said.

"And what is that?" he asked.

"Send one of the captured Jaharian ships with a flag of truce and I believe that Tul Axtar will surrender. He is a coward. He fled in terror when the battle was still young."

"Will he honour the flag of truce?"

"If it is carried aboard one of his own ships, protected by the blue paint of Jahar, I believe that he will," I said; "but at the same time I shall accompany the ship in the invisible Jhama. I know how I may gain entrance to the palace. I have abducted Tul Axtar once and perchance I may be able to do it again. If you have him in your hands, you can dictate terms to the nobles, all of whom fear the terrific power of the hungry multitude that is held in check now only by the instinctive terror they feel for their Jeddak."

As we waited for the former Jaharian cruiser that was to carry the flag of truce to come alongside, John Carter told me what had delayed the expedition against Jahar for so many months.

The major-domo of Tor Hatan's palace to whom I had entrusted the message to John Carter and which would have led immediately to the descent upon Jahar, had been assassinated while on his way to the palace of the Warlord. Suspicion, therefore, did not fall upon Tul Axtar, and the ships of Helium scoured Barsoom for many months in vain search for Sanoma Tora.

It was only by accident that Kal Tavan the slave, who had overheard my conversation with the major-domo, learned that the ships of Helium had not been dispatched to Jahar, for a slave ordinarily is not taken into the confidences of his master, and the arrogant Tor Hatan was, of all men, least likely to do so; but Kal Tavan did hear eventually and he went himself to the Warlord and told his story.

"For his services," said John Carter, "I gave him his freedom, and as it was apparent from his demeanour that he had been born to the nobility in his native country, though he did not tell me this, I gave him service aboard the fleet. He has turned out to be an excellent man and recently I have made him a dwar. Having been born in Tjanath and served in Kobol, he was more familiar with this part of Barsoom than any other man in Helium. I therefore assigned him to duty with the navigating officer of the fleet and he is now aboard the flagship."

"I had occasion to notice the man immediately after Sanoma Tora's abduction," I said, "and I was much impressed by him. I am glad that he has found his freedom and the favour of the Warlord."

The cruiser that was to bear the flag of truce was now alongside. The officer in command reported to the Warlord and as he received his instructions, Tavia and I returned to the Jhama. We had decided to carry on our part of the plan alone, for if it became necessary to abduct Tul Axtar again I had hoped, also, that I might find Phao and Sanoma Tora, and if so the small cabin of the Jhama would be sufficiently crowded without the addition of the two padwars. They were reluctant to leave her, for I think they had had the most glorious experience of their lives during the short time that they had been aboard her, but I gained permission from the Warlord for them to accompany the cruiser to Jahar.

Once again Tavia and I were alone. "Perhaps this will be our last cruise aboard the Jhama," I said.

"I think I shall be glad to rest," she replied.

"You are tired?" I asked.

"More tired than I realized until I felt the safety and security of that great fleet of Helium about me. I think that I am just tired of being always in danger."

"I should not have brought you now," I said. "There is yet time to return you to the flagship."

She smiled. "You know better than that, Hadron," she said.

I did know better. I knew that she would not leave me. We were silent for a while as the Jhama slid through the air slightly astern of the cruiser. As I looked at Tavia's face, it seemed to reflect a great weariness and there were little lines of sadness there that I had not seen before. Presently she spoke again in a dull tone that was most unlike her own.

"I think that Sanoma Tora will be glad to come away with you this time," she said.

"I do not know," I said. "It makes no difference to me whether she wishes to come or not. It is my duty to fetch her."

She nodded. "Perhaps it is best," she said; "her father is a noble and very rich."

I did not understand what that had to do with it, and not being particularly interested further in either Sanoma Tora or her father, I did not pursue the conversation. I knew it was my duty to return Sanoma

Tora to Helium if possible, and that was the only interest that I had in the affair.

We were well within sight of Jahar before we encountered any warships, and then a cruiser came to meet ours which bore the flag of truce. The commanders of the two boats exchanged a few words, and then the Jaharian craft turned and led the way towards the palace of Tul Axtar. It moved slowly and I forged on ahead, my plans already made, and the Jhama, being clothed with invisibility, needed no escort. I steered directly to that wing of the palace which contained the women's quarters and slowly circled it, my periscope on a line with the windows.

We had rounded the end of the wing in which the great hall lay where Tul Axtar held court with his women, when the periscope came opposite the windows of a gorgeous apartment. I brought the ship to a stop before it, as I had before some of the others which I wished to examine, and while the slowly moving periscope brought different parts of the large room to the ground-glass plate before me I saw the figures of two women, and instantly I recognized them. One was Sanoma Tora and the other Phao, and upon the figure of the former hung the gorgeous trappings of a jeddara. The woman I had loved had achieved her goal, but it caused me no pang of jealousy. I searched the balance of the apartment, and finding no other occupant, I brought the deck of the Jhama close below the sill of the window. Then I raised a hatch and leaped into the room.

At sight of me Sanoma Tora arose from the divan upon which she had been sitting and shrank back in terror. I thought that she was about to scream for help, but I warned her to silence, and at the same instant Phao sprang forward and seizing Sanoma Tora's arm, clapped a palm over her mouth. A moment later I had gained her side.

"The fleet of Jahar has gone down to defeat before the ships of Helium," I told Sanoma Tora, "and I have come to take you back to your own country."

She was trembling so that she could not reply. I had never seen such a picture of abject terror, induced no doubt by her own guilty conscience.

"I am glad you have come, Hadron of Hastor," said Phao, "for I know that you will take me too."

"Of course," I said. "The Jhama lies just outside the window. Come! We shall soon be safe aboard the flagship of the Warlord."

While I had been talking I had become aware of a strange noise that seemed to come from a distance and which rose and fell in volume and now it appeared to be growing nearer and nearer. I could not explain it; perhaps I did not attempt to, for at best I could be only mildly interested. I had found two of those whom I sought. I would get them aboard the Jhama and then I would try to locate Tul Axtar.

At that instant the door burst open and a man rushed into the room. It was Tul Axtar. He was very pale and he was breathing hard. At sight of me he halted and shrank back and I thought that he was going to turn and run, but he only looked fearfully back through the open door and then he turned to me, trembling.

"They are coming!" he cried in a voice of terror. "They will tear me to pieces."

"Who is coming?" I demanded.

"The people," he said. "They have forced the gates and they are coming. Do you not hear them?"

So that was the noise that had attracted my attention—the hungry hordes of Jahar searching out the author of their misery.

"The Jhama is outside that window," I said. "If you will come aboard her as a prisoner of war, I will take you to the Warlord of Barsoom."

"He will kill me too," wailed Tul Axtar.

"He should," I assured him.

He stood looking at me for a moment and I could see in his eyes and the expression of his face the reflection of a dawning idea. His countenance lightened. He looked almost hopeful. "I will come," he said; "but first let me get one thing to take with me. It is in yonder cabinet."

"Hasten," I said.

He went quickly to the cabinet, which was a tall affair reaching from the floor almost to the ceiling, and when he opened the door it hid him from our view.

As I waited I could hear the crash of weapons upon levels below and the screams and shrieks and curses of men, and I judged that the palace guard was holding the mob, temporarily at least. Finally I became impatient. "Hasten, Tul Axtar," I called, but there was no reply. Again I called him, with the same result, and then I crossed the room to the cabinet, but Tul Axtar was not behind the door.

The cabinet contained many drawers of different sizes, but there was not one large enough to conceal a man, nor any through which he could have passed to another apartment. Hastily I searchd the room, but Tul Atar was nowhere to be found, and then I chanced to glance at Sanoma Tora. She was evidently trying to attract my attention, but she was so terrified that she could not speak. With trembling fingers she was pointing towards the window. I looked in that direction, but I could see nothing.

"What is it? What are you trying to say, Sanoma Tora?" I demanded as I rushed to her side.

"Gone!" she managed to say. "Gone!"

"Who is gone?" I demanded.

"Tul Axtar."

"Where? What do you mean?" I insisted.

"The hatch of the Jhama—I saw it open and close."

"But it cannot be possible. We have been standing here looking——" And then a thought struck me that left me almost dazed. I turned to Sanoma Tora. "The cloak of invisibility?" I whispered.

She nodded.

Almost in a single bound I crossed the room to the window and was feeling for the deck of the Jhama. It was not there. The ship had gone. Tul Axtar had taken it and Tavia was with him.

I turned back and crossed the room to Sanoma Tora. "Accursed woman!" I cried. "Your selfishness, your vanity, your treachery have jeopardized the safety of one whose footprints you are not fit to touch." I wanted to close my fingers upon that perfect throat, I yearned to see the agony of death upon that beautiful face; but I only turned away, my hands dropped at my sides, for I am a man—a noble of Helium—and the women of Helium are sacred, even such as Sanoma Tora.

From below came the sounds of renewed fighting. If the mob broke through I knew that we should all be lost. There was but one hope for even temporary safety and that was the slender tower above the women's quarters.

"Follow me," I said curtly. As we entered the main corridor I caught a glimpse of the interior of the great hall where Tul Axtar had held court. It was filled with terrified women. Well they know what the fate of the women of a Jeddak would be at the hands of an infuriated mob. My heart went out to them, but I could not save them. Lucky, indeed, should I be if I were able to save these two.

Crossing the corridor we ascended the spiral ramp to the storeroom, where, after entering, I took the precaution to bolt the door, then I ascended the ladder towards the trap-door at the summit of the tower, the two women following me. As I raised the trap and looked about me I could have cried aloud with joy, for circling low above the roof of the palace was the cruiser flying the flag of truce. I apprehended no danger of discovery by Jaharian warriors, since I knew that they were all well occupied below—those who were not fleeing for their lives—and so I sprang to the summit of the tower and hailed the cruiser in a voice that they might well hear above the howling of the mob. An answering hail came from the deck of the craft and a moment later she dropped to the level of the tower roof. With the help of the crew I assisted Phao and Sanoma Tora aboard.

The officer in command of the cruiser stepped to my side. "Our mission here is fruitless," he said. "Word has just been brought me that the palace has fallen before the onslaught of a mob of infuriated citizens. The nobles have commandeered every craft upon which they could lay hands and have fled. There is no one with whom we can negotiate a peace. No one knows what has become of Tul Axtar."

"I know," I told him, and then I narrated what had happened in the apartment of the Jeddara.

We must pursue him," he said. "We must overtake him and carry him back to the Warlord."

"Where shall we look?" I asked. "The Jhama may lie within a dozen sofads of us and even so we could not see her. I shall search for him, never fear, and some day I shall find him, but it is useless now to try to find the Jhama. Let us return to the flagship of the Warlord."

I do not know that John Carter fully realized the loss that I had sustained, but I suspect that he did, for he offered me all the resources of Helium in my search for Tavia.

I thanked him, but asked only for a fast ship; one in which I might devote the remainder of my life to what I truly believed would prove a futile search for Tavia, for how could I know where in all wide Barsoom Tul Axtar would elect to hide? Doubtless there were known to him many remote spots in his own empire where he could live in safety for the balance of his allotted time on Barsoom. To such a place he would go and because of the Jhama no man would see him pass; there would be no clue by which to follow him and he would take Tavia with him and she would be his slave. I shuddered and my nails sank into my palms at the thought.

The Warlord ordered one of the newest and swiftest fliers of Helium to be brought alongside the flagship. It was a trim craft of the semi-cabin type that would easily accommodate four or five in comfort. From his own stores he had provisions and water transferred to it and he added wine from Ptarth and jars of the famous honey of Dusar.

Sanoma Tora and Phao had been sent at once to a cabin by the Warlord, for the deck of a man-of-war on duty is no place for women. I was about to depart when a messenger came saying that Sanoma Tora wished to see me.

"I do not wish to see her," I replied.

"Her companion also begged that you would come," replied the messenger.

That was different. I had almost forgotten Phao, but if she wished to see me I would go, and so I went at once to the cabin where the two girls were. As I entered Sanoma Tora came forward and threw herself upon her knees before me.

"Have pity on me, Hadron of Hastor," she cried. "I have been wicked, but it was my vanity and not my heart that sinned. Do not go away. Come back to Helium and I will devote my life to your happiness. Tor Hatan, my father, is rich. The mate of his only child may live for ever in luxury."

I am afraid that my lips curled to the sneer that was in my heart. What a petty soul was hers! Even in her humiliation and her penitence she could see no beauty and no happiness greater than wealth and power. She thought that she was changed, but I knew that Sanoma Tora never could change.

"Forgive me, Tan Hadron," she cried. "Come back to me, for I love you. Now I know that I love you."

"Your love has come too late, Sanoma Tora," I said.

"You love another?" she asked.

"Yes," I replied.

"The Jeddara of some of the strange countries you have been through?" she asked.

"A slave girl," I replied.

Her eyes went wide in incredulity. She could not conceive that one might prefer a slave girl to the daughter of Tor Hatan. "Impossible," she said.

"It is true, though," I assured her; "a little slave

girl is more desirable to Tan Hadron of Hastor than is Sanoma Tora, the daughter of Tor Hatan," and with that I turned my back upon her and faced Phao. "Good-bye, dear friend," I said. "Doubtless we shall never meet again, but I shall see to it that you have a good home in Hastor. I shall speak to the Warlord before I leave and have him send you directly to my mother."

She laid her hand upon my shoulder. "Let me go with you, Tan Hadron," she said, "for perhaps while you are searching for Tavia you will pass near Jhama."

I understood instantly what she meant, and I reproached myself for having even temporarily forgotten Nur An. "You shall come with me, Phao," I said, "and my first duty shall be to return to Jhama and rescue Nur An from poor old Phor Tak."

Without another glance at Sanoma Tora I led Phao from the cabin, and after a few parting words with the Warlord we boarded my new ship and with friendly farewells in our ears headed west toward Jhama.

Being no longer protected by the invisibility compound of Phor Tak, or the disintegrating ray-resisting paint of Jahar, we were forced to keep a sharp lookout for enemy ships, of which I had little fear if we sighted them in time, for I knew that I could outdistance any of them.

I set the destination control compass upon Jhama and opened the throttle wide; the swift Barsoomian night had fallen; the only sound was the rush of thin air along our sides which drowned out the quiet purring of our motor.

For the first time since I had found her again in the quarters of the Jeddara at Jahar, I had an opportunity to talk with Phao, and the first thing I asked her was for an explanation of the abandonment of the Jhama after Tul Axtar had grounded Tavia and me in U-Gor.

"It was an accident," she said, "that threw Tul Axtar into a great fit of rage. We were headed for Jahar when he sighted one of his own ships, which took us aboard as soon as they discovered the identity of the Jeddak. It was night, and in the confusion of boarding the Jaharian warship Tul Axtar momentarily forgot the Jhama, which must have drifted away from the larger craft the moment that we left her. They cruised about searching for her for awhile, but at last they had to give it up and the ship proceeded toward Jahar."

The miracle of the presence of the Jhama at the top of the peak, where we had so providentially found it in time to escape from the hunting men of U-Gor, was now no longer a miracle. The prevailing winds in this part of Barsoom are from the north-west at this time of year. The Jhama had merely drifted with the wind and chanced to lodge upon the highest peak of the range.

Phao also told me why Tul Axtar had originally abducted Sanoma Tora from Helium. He had had his secret agents at Helium for some time previous and they had reported to him that the best way to lure the fleet of Helium to Jahar was to abduct a woman of some noble family. He had instructed them to select a beautiful one, and so they had decided upon the daughter of Tor Hatan.

"But how did they expect to lure the fleet of Helium to Jahar if they left no clue as to the identity of the abductors of Sanoma Tora?" I asked.

"They left no clue at the time because Tul Axtar was not ready to receive the attack of Helium," explained Phao; "but he had already sent his agents word to drop a hint as to the whereabouts of Sanoma Tora when John Carter learned through other sources the identity of her abductors."

"So it all worked out the way Tul Axtar had planned," I said, "except the finish."

We passed the hours with brief snatches of conversation and long silences, each occupied with our own thoughts—Phao's doubtless a mixture of hope and fear, but there was little room for hope in mine. The only pleasant prospects that lay before me lay in rescuing Nur An and reuniting him and Phao. After that I would take them to any country to which they wished to go and then return to the vicinity of Jahar and prosecute my hopeless search.

"I heard what you said to Sanoma Tora in the cabin of the flagship," said Phao after a long silence, "and I was glad."

"I said a number of things," I reminded her; "to which do you refer?"

"You said that you loved Tavia," she replied.

"I said nothing of the kind," I rejoined rather shortly, for I almost loathed that word.

"But you did," she insisted. "You said that you loved a little slave girl and I know that you love Tavia. I have seen it in your eyes."

"You have seen nothing of the kind. Because you are in love, you think that everyone must be."

She laughed. "You love her and she loves you."

"We are only friends—very good friends," I insisted, "and furthermore I know that Tavia does not love me."

"How do you know?"

"Let us not speak of it any more," I said, but though I did not speak of it, I thought about it. I recalled that I had told Sanoma Tora that I loved a little slave girl and I knew that I had had Tavia in my mind at the time, but I thought that I had said it more to wound Sanoma Tora than for any other purpose. I tried to analyse my own feelings, but at last I gave it up as a foolish thing to do. Of course I did not love Tavia; I loved no one; love was not for me— Sanoma Tora had killed it within my breast, and I was equally sure that Tavia did not love me; if she had, she would have shown it, and I was quite sure that she had never demonstrated any other feeling for me than the finest of comradeship. We were just what she had said we were—comrades in arms, and nothing else.

It was still dark when I saw the gleaming white palace of Phor Tak shining softly in the moonlight far below us. Late as it was, there were lights in some of the rooms. I had hoped that all would be asleep, for my plans depended upon my ability to enter the palace secretly. I knew that Phor Tak never kept any watch at night, feeling that none was needed in such an isolated spot.

Silently I dropped the flier until it rested upon the roof of the building where Nur An and I had first landed, for I knew that there I would find a passage to the palace below.

"Wait here at the controls, Phao," I whispered. "Nur An and I may have to come away in a hurry and you must be ready."

She nodded her head understandingly, and a moment later I had slipped quietly to the roof and was approaching the opening that led down into the interior.

As I paused at the top of the spiral ramp I felt quickly for my weapons to see that each was in its place. John Carter had fitted me out anew. Once more I stood in the leather and metal of Helium, with a full complement of weapons such as belong to a fighting man of Barsoom. My long sword was of the best steel, for it was one of John Carter's own. Besides this, I carried a short sword and a dagger, and once again a heavy radium pistol hung at my hip. I loosened the latter in its holster as I started down the spiral ramp.

As I approached the bottom I heard a voice. It was coming from the direction of Phor Tak's laboratory, the door of which opened upon the corridor at the bottom of the ramp. I crept slowly downward. The door leading to the laboratory was closed. Two men were conversing. I could recognize the thin, high voice of Phor Tak; the other voice was not that of Nur An; yet it was strangely familiar.

"—riches beyond your dream," I heard the second man say.

"I do not need riches," crackled Phor Tak. "Heighoo! Presently I shall own all the riches in the world."

"You will need help," I could hear the other man

say in a pleading tone. "I can give you help; you shall have every ship of my great fleet."

That remark brought me upstanding—"every ship of my great fleet!" It could not be possible, and yet——

Gently I tried the door. To my surprise it swung open, revealing the interior of the room. Beneath a bright light stood Tul Axtar. Fifty feet from him Phor Tak was standing behind a bench upon which was mounted a disintegrating rifle, aimed full at Tul Axtar.

Where was Tavia? Where was Nur An? Perhaps this man alone knew where Tavia was, and Phor Tak was about to destroy him. With a cry of warning I leaped into the room. Tul Axtar and Phor Tak looked at me quickly, surprise large upon their countenances.

"Heigh-oo!" screamed the old inventor. "So you have come back! Knave! Ingrate! Traitor! But you have come back only to die."

"Wait," I cried, raising my hand. "Let me speak."

"Silence!" screamed Phor Tak. "You shall see Tul Axtar die. I hated to kill him without someone to see—someone to witness his death agony. I shall have my revenge on him first and then on you."

"Stop!" I cried. His finger was already hovering over the button that would snatch Tul Axtar into oblivion, perhaps with the secret of the whereabouts of Tavia.

I drew my pistol. Phor Tak made a sudden motion with his hands and disappeared. He vanished as though turned to thin air by his own disintegrating rays, but I knew what had happened. I knew that he had thrown a mantle of invisibility around himself and I fired at the spot where he had last been visible.

At the same instant the floor opened beneath me I shot into utter darkness.

I felt myself hurtling along a smooth surface which gradually became horizontal, and an instant later I shot into a dimly lighted apartment, which I knew must be located in the pits beneath the palace.

I had clung to my pistol as I fell, and now, as I

arose to my feet, I thrust it back into its holster; at least I was not unarmed.

The dim light in the apartment, which was little better than no light at all, I discovered, came from a ventilator in the ceiling, and that except for the shaft that had conducted me to the cell, there was no other opening in the wall or ceiling or floor. The ventilator was about two feet in diameter and led straight up from the centre of the ceiling to the roof of the building, several levels above. The lower end of the shaft was about two feet above my finger-tips when I extended them high above my head. This avenue of escape, then, was useless, but, alas, how tantalizing. It was maddening to see daylight and an open avenue to the outer world just above me and be unable to reach it. I was glad that the sun had risen, throwing its quick light over the scene, for had I fallen here in utter darkness my plight would have seemed infinitely worse than now, and my first ancestor knew that it was bad enough. I turned my attention now to the chute through which I had descended and found that I could ascend it quite a little distance, but presently it turned steeply upward and its smoothly polished walls were unscalable.

I returned to the pits. I must escape; but now, as my eyes became accustomed to the dim light, I saw strewn about the floor that which snatched away my last hope and filled me with horror. Everywhere upon the stone flagging were heaps and mounds of human bones picked clean by gnawing rats. I shuddered as I contemplated the coming of night. How long before my bones, too, would be numbered among the rest?

The thought made me frantic, not for myself but for Tavia. I could not die. I must not die. I must live until I had found her.

Hastily I circled the room, searching for some clue to hope, but I found only rough-hewn stone set in soft mortar.

Soft mortar! With the realization, hope dawned anew. If I could remove a few of these blocks and pile them one on top of the other, I might easily reach the shaft that terminated in the ceiling above my head. Drawing my dagger I fell to work, scraping and scratching at the mortar about one of the stones in the nearest wall. It seemed slow work, but in reality I had loosened the stone in an incredibly short time. The mortar was poor stuff and crumbled away easily. As I drew the block out my first plan faded in the light of what I saw in front of me. Beyond the opening, and from somewhere above, daylight was filtering down.

I know that if I could remove three more of those stones before I was detected I could worm my body through the opening into the corridor beyond, and you may well believe that I worked rapidly.

One by one the blocks were loosened and removed and it was with a feeling of exultation that I slipped through into the corridor. Above me rose a spiral ramp. Where it led I did not know, but at least it led out of the pits. Cautiously, and yet without any hesitation, I ascended. I must try to reach the laboratory before Phor Tak had slain Tul Axtar. This time I would make sure of the old inventor before I entered the room, and I prayed to all my ancestors that I should be in time.

Doors, leading from the ramp to various levels of the palace, were all locked and I was forced to ascend to the roof. As it chanced, the wing upon which I found myself was more or less detached, so that at first glance I could see no way whereby I could make my way from it to any of the adjoining roofs.

As I walked around the edge of the building hurriedly, looking for some means of descent to the roof below, I saw something one level below me that instantly charged my attention. It was a man's leg protruding from a window, as though he had thrown one limb across the sill. A moment later I saw an arm emerge, and the top of a man's head and his shoulders were visible as he leaned out. He reached down and up, and I saw something appear directly

beneath him that had not been there before, and at
the same instant I caught a glimpse of a girl, lying a
few feet further down, and then I saw the man slide
over the sill quickly and drop down and disappear,
and all that lay below me was the flagging of a courtyard.

But in that brief instant I knew what I had seen.
I had seen Tul Axtar raise the hatch of the Jhama.
I had seen Tavia lying bound upon the floor of the
ship beneath the hatch. I had seen Tul Axtar enter
the interior of the craft and close the hatch above his
head.

It takes a long while to tell it when compared with
the time in which it actually transpired; nor was I so
long in acting as I have been in telling.

As the hatch closed, I leaped.

CHAPTER XVII

I FIND A PRINCESS

IT WOULD BE as unreasonable to aver that I fully
visualized the outcome of my act as I leaped out into
space with nothing visible between me and the flag-
stones of the courtyard forty feet below as it would
be to assume that I acted solely upon unreasoning
impulse. There are emergencies in which the mind
functions with inconceivable celerity. Perceptions are
received, judgments arrived at and reason operates to
a definite conclusion all so swiftly that three acts appear simultaneous. Thus must have been the process
in this instance.

I knew where the narrow walkway upon the upper
deck of the Jhama must lie in the seemingly empty
space below me, for I had jumped almost the instant

that the hatch had closed. Of course I know now, and I knew then, that it would have been a dangerous feat and difficult of achievement even had I been able to see the Jhama below me; yet as I look back upon it now there was nothing else that I could have done. It was my one, my last chance to save Tavia from a fate worse than death—it was perhaps my last opportunity ever to see her again. As I jumped then I should jump again under like conditions, even though I knew that I should miss the Jhama, for now as then I know that I should rather die than lose Tavia; although then I did not know why, while now I do.

But I did not miss. I landed squarely upon my feet upon the narrow walkway. The impact of my weight upon the upper deck of the craft must have been noticeable to Tul Axtar, for I could feel the Jhama drop a little beneath me. Doubtless he wondered what had happened, but I do not think that he guessed the truth. However, he did not raise the hatch as I hoped he would, but instead he must have leaped to the controls at once, for almost immediately the Jhama rose swiftly at an acute angle, which made it difficult for me to cling to her, since her upper deck was not equipped with harness rings. By grasping the forward edge of the turret, however, I managed to hold on.

As Tul Axtar gained sufficient altitude and straightened out upon his course he opened the throttle wide, so that the wind rushing by me at terrific velocity seemed momentarily upon the point of carrying me from my precarious hold and hurtling me to the ground far below. Fortunately I am a strong man—none other could have survived that ordeal—yet how utterly helpless I was.

Had Tul Axtar guessed the truth he could have raised the after hatch and had me at his mercy, for though my pistol hung at my side I could not have released either hand to use it, but doubtless Tul Axtar did not know, or if he did he hoped that the high speed of the ship would dislodge whoever or whatever it might have been that he had felt drop upon it.

I had hung there but a short time before I realized that eventually my hold must weaken and be torn loose. Something must be done to rectify my position. Tavia must be saved, and because I alone could save her, I must not die.

Straining every thew I dragged myself further forward until I lay with my chest upon the turret. Slowly, inch by inch, I wormed myself forward. The tubular sheeting of the periscope was just in front of me. If I could reach that with one hand I might hope to attain greater safety. The wind was buffeting me, seeking to tear me away. I sought a better hold with my left forearm about the turret, and then I reached quickly forward with my right hand and my fingers closed about the sheathing.

After that it was not difficult to stretch a part of my harness about the front of the turret. Now I found that I could have one hand free, but until the ship stopped I could not hope to accomplish anything more.

What was transpiring beneath me? Could Tavia be safe even for a brief time in the power of Tul Axtar? The thought drove me frantic. The Jhama must be stopped, and then an inspiration came to me.

With my free hand I unsnapped my pocket pouch from my harness, and drawing myself still further forward, I managed to place the open pouch over the eye of the periscope.

Immediately Tul Axtar was blind; he could see nothing, nor was it long before the reaction that I had expected and hoped for came—the Jhama slowed down and finally came to a stop.

I had been lying partially upon the forward hatch, and now I drew myself away from and in front of it. I hoped that it would be the forward hatch that he would open. It was the closer to him. I waited, and then glancing forward I saw that he was opening the ports. In this way he could see to navigate the ship and my plan was blocked.

I was disappointed, but I would not give up hope. Very quietly I tried the forward hatch, but it was locked upon the inside. Then I made my way swiftly and silently to the after hatch. If he should start the Jhama again at full speed now, doubtless I should be lost, but I felt that I was forced to risk the chance. Already the Jhama was in motion again as I had my hand upon the hatch cover. This time I was neither silent nor gentle. I heaved vigorously and the hatch opened. Not an instant did I hesitate, and as the Jhama leaped forward again at full speed, I dropped through the hatchway to the interior of the craft.

As I struck the deck Tul Axtar heard me, and wheeling from the controls to face me, he recognized me. I think I never before beheld such an expression of mingled astonishment, hatred and fear as convulsed his features. At his feet lay Tavia, so quietly still that I thought her dead, and then Tul Axtar reached for his pistol and I for mine, but I have lead a cleaner life than Tul Axtar had. My mind and muscles co-ordinate with greater celerity than can those of one who has wasted his fibre in dissipation.

Point-blank I fired at his putrid heart, and Tul Axtar, Jeddak and tyrant of Jahar, lunged forward upon the lower deck of the Jhama dead.

Instantly I sprang to Tavia's side and turned her over. She had been bound and gagged and, for some unaccountable reason, blindfolded as well, but she was not dead. I almost sobbed for joy when I realized that. How my fingers seemed to fumble in their haste to free her; yet it was only a matter of seconds ere it was done and I was crushing her in my arms.

I know that my tears fell upon her upturned face as our lips were pressed together, and I am not ashamed of that, and Tavia wept too and clung to me and I could feel her dear body tremble. How terrified she must have been, and yet I knew she had never shown it to Tul Axtar. It was the reaction—the mingling of relief and joy at the moment when the despair had been blackest.

In that instant, as our hearts beat together and she drew me closer to her, a great truth dawned upon me.

What a stupid fool I had been! How could I ever have thought that the sentiment that I entertained for Sanoma Tora was love? How could I ever believe that my love for Tavia had been such a weak thing as friendship? I drew her closer, if such were possible.

"My princess," I whispered.

Upon Barsoom those two words, spoken by man to maid, have a peculiar and unalterable significance, for no man speaks thus to any woman that he does not wish for wife.

"No, no," sobbed Tavia. "Take me, I am yours; but I am only a slave girl. Tan Hadron of Hastor cannot mate with such."

Even then she thought only of me and my happiness, and not of herself at all. How different she was from such as Sanoma Tora! I had risked my life to win a clod of dirt and I had found a priceless jewel.

I looked her in the eyes, those beautiful, fathomless wells of love and understanding. "I love you, Tavia," I said. "Tell me that I may have the right to call you my princess."

"Even though I be a slave?" she asked.

"Even though you were a thousand times less than a slave," I told her.

She sighed and snuggled closer to me. "My chieftain," she whispered in a low, low voice.

That, as far as I, Tan Hadron of Hastor, am concerned, is the end of the story. That instant marked the highest pinnacle to me which I may ever hope to achieve, but there is more that may interest those who have come thus far with me upon adventures that have carried me half-way around the southern hemisphere of Barsoom.

When Tavia and I could tear ourselves apart, which was not soon, I opened the lower hatch and let the corpse of Tul Axtar find its last resting-place upon the barren ground below. Then we turned back towards Jhama, where we discovered that earlier in the morning Nur An had come to one of the roofs of the palace and been discovered by Phao.

When Nur An had learned that I had entered the palace just before dawn, he had become apprehensive and instituted a search for me. He had not known of the coming of Tul Axtar, and believed that the Jeddak must have arrived after he had retired for the night; nor had he known how close Tavia had been, lying bound in the Jhama close beside the palace wall.

His search of the palace, however, had revealed the fact that Phor Tak was missing. He had summoned the slaves and a careful search had been made, but no sign of Phor Tak was visible.

It occurred to me then that I might solve the question as to the whereabouts of the old scientist. "Come with me," I said to Nur An; "perhaps I can find Phor Tak for you."

I led him to the laboratory. "There is no use searching there," he said, "we have looked in a hundred times to-day. A glance will reveal the fact that the laboratory is deserted."

"Wait," I said. "Let us not be in too much of a hurry. Come with me; perhaps yet I may disclose the whereabouts of Phor Tak."

With a shrug he followed me as I entered the vast laboratory and walked towards the bench upon which a disintegrating rifle was mounted. Just back of the bench my foot struck something that I could not see, but that I had expected to find there, and stooping I felt a huddled form beneath a covering of soft cloth.

My fingers closed upon the invisible fabric and I drew it aside. There, before us on the floor, lay the dead body of Phor Tak, a bullet-hole in the centre of his breast.

"Name of Issus!" cried Nur An. "Who did this?"

"I," I replied, and then I told him what had happened in the laboratory as the last night waned.

He looked around hurriedly. "Cover it up quickly," he said. "The slaves must not know. They would destroy us. Let us get out of here quickly."

I drew the cloak of invisibility over the body of

Phor Tak again. "I have work here before I leave," I said.

"What?" he demanded.

"Help me gather all of the disintegrating-ray shells and rifles into one end of the room."

"What are you going to do?" he demanded.

"I am going to save a world, Nur An," I said.

Then he fell to and helped me, and when they were all collected in a pile at the far end of the laboratory, I selected a single shell, and returning to the rifle mounted upon the bench I inserted it in the chamber, closed the block and turned the muzzle of the weapon upon that frightful aggregation of death and disaster.

As I pressed the button all that remained in Jhama of Phor Tak's dangerous invention disappeared in thin air, with the exception of the single rifle, for which there remained no ammunition. With it had gone his model of the Flying Death and with him the secret had been lost.

Nur An told me that the slaves were becoming suspicious of us, and as there was no necessity to risk ourselves further, we embarked upon the flier that John Carter had given me, and, taking the Jhama in tow, set our course towards Helium.

We overtook the fleet shortly before it reached the Twin Cities of Greater Helium and Lesser Helium, and upon the deck of John Carter's flag-ship we received a welcome and a great ovation, and shortly thereafter there occurred one of the most remarkable and dramatic incidents that I have ever beheld. We were holding something of an informal reception upon the forward deck of the great battleship. Officers and nobles were pressing forward to be presented, and numerous were the appreciative eyes that admired Tavia.

It was the turn of the Dwar, Kal Tavan, who had been a slave in the palace of Tor Hatan. As he came face to face with Tavia I saw a look of surprise in his eyes.

"Your name is Tavia?" he repeated.

"Yes," she said, "and yours is Tavan. They are similar."

"I do not need to ask from what country you are," he said "You are Tavia of Tjanath."

"How do you know?" she asked.

"Because you are my daughter," he replied. "Tavia is the name your mother gave you. You look like her. By that alone I should have known my daughter anywhere."

Very gently he took her in his arms, and I saw tears in his eyes, and hers too, as he pressed his lips against her forehead, and then he turned to me.

"They told me that the brave Tan Hadron of Hastor had chosen to mate with a slave girl," he said; "but that is not true. Your princess is in truth a princess—the granddaughter of a jed. She might have been the daughter of a jed had I remained in Tjanath."

How devious are the paths of fate! How strange and unexpected the destinations to which they lead! I had set out upon one of these paths with the intention of marrying Sanoma Tora at the end. Sanoma Tora had set out upon another in the hope of marrying a jeddak. At the end of her path she had found only ignominy and disgrace. At the end of mine I had found a princess.

SCIENCE FICTION CLASSICS FROM BALLANTINE BOOKS